MY FAVORITE APOCALYPSE

MY FAVORITE APOCALYPSE

A COLLECTION OF STORIES

EDITED BY JENNIFER TOP

A TULIPTREE ANTHOLOGY

Library of Congress Control Number: 2015909371
TulipTree Publishing, LLC
Fort Collins, Colorado

ISBN-13: 978-0692464458
ISBN-10: 069246445X

Cover design by TulipTree Publishing, LLC

Designed and typeset by TulipTree Publishing, LLC

www.tuliptreepub.com

CONTENTS

Hell is empty and all the devils are here.

—William Shakespeare,
The Tempest

INTRODUCTION: A LOVE STORY

JENNIFER TOP

They say to pray most effectively you should thank your higher power for the outcome you want, as though you already have it, with clear and unwavering intention. And furthermore, that wherever two or more get together and focus on holding the same intention, the power granted to that request is exponentially greater. My intention was to cast open the gates of hell so My One could walk out. I called for visions of life after the apocalypse, to focus this energy and intention on making it happen. Thank you all for your cooperation.

You might also have a loved one who's trapped in some hell, metaphorical or otherwise. If so, you know how it feels when your heart bleeds, when hopelessness is easier than frustration but infinitely more painful; when you know there is no other answer except to destroy the chains.

And why did I think it would take an apocalypse to break him free? Because what I needed was a no-going-back kind of shift. A new paradigm. An earth-shattering (literally) cataclysm, enemy invasion, government plot—I hate to be picky. I guess I should also mention, the older I get the more I gravitate toward the truth that this beautiful planet desperately needs to purge herself of the human virus. There is poetry in her warnings, you know: the way cancer or parasites multiply, for example, feeding off the host only to kill it, to show people exactly what we're doing to her. But nobody listens. Oh, fine, some people listen. But more people succumb to bickering among themselves about the inane, all heated and violent and yet, impotent. And so I wanted My One, but I also wanted the planet to win a little something like relief for herself, too.

I pictured myself as Psyche, from the myth. She undertook an almost impossible mission to reunite with her Cupid, including going to hell and back—tasks given to her by Cupid's frankly unreasonable goddess-mother, Aphrodite. Just when Psyche faced her greatest difficulties and was ready to give up, someone would take pity and help her. I prepared to walk through hell for him, with or without help, open gates or not.

I surrendered to the task, and started on my way through every account of the apocalypse. A commonality I encountered over and over in all of the offerings for this book was the elusive and dangerous Others. Here's what you need to know about them: They run in small bands. They are purely vicious. They will get you. Rape you. Eat you.

Really, what are the odds that even those idiots would survive very long without knowing how to plant a potato, or without considering the sustainability of their lifestyle? How exactly are they going to survive a winter? It's almost as if we create these monsters just so we can fear them.

It turns out there's plenty to fear without them. For starters our worshipping of and connectivity to the electronic gods seem to have won over our connectivity to each other, although, to be fair, I think this may be a more deliberate tendency than most would like to admit, rather than an accidental side effect. Nevertheless, I find myself in a cold hallway and immediately know My One isn't here by the feel of the place. Or I should say, by the lack of feel to it. The people I encounter as I try to find my way out appear to have forgotten how to speak to me. Not that I get the impression they want to. They stare out of eyes that might be afraid if they could muster it. Even fear would be something to work with.

They gaze at me curiously as I push open the door and step out into the sunlight. In the neighborhood outside I can see evidence that some soul at least used to be at work here: graffiti, made by a human hand—is that hand still attached to a living, breathing human? But that's the only encouraging thing I see. I consider the logistics of burning down the entire neighborhood, but it won't get me any closer to My One, so I decide to move on.

The air here feels thick, like it has to squirm its way down my throat for me to breathe it. I want to run, but the strange electric hum has me in a trance, like the subtle but persistent vibration is drawing my limbs into the concrete, binding them as they sink. The heaviness begins to shake loose the more I struggle to move, until I'm trotting, in slow motion, which is like walking, only harder.

Finally my legs become lighter and I'm really running. I run until the sidewalk ends and then I run in the street until the pavement gives way to gravel. It's a dusty gravel road like the one I grew up on in the hills of the Ozarks. The trees are lush and green and something makes me want to abide here. Something that used to be familiar. I think I'll sit for a while and regroup but as soon as I find an old stump at the edge of the woods and begin to relax, I'm overcome with an urgency to keep moving, like something is trying to tell me not to linger. The woods suddenly feel unfriendly. I remember I'm not actually in the Ozarks. I can't be. So I keep walking. West. Except I know My One is in the south and that's the direction I want to go so I can meet him. I'm afraid he won't know where to go when he walks out of the Underworld.

When the trees give way to open pasture, I duck through a barbed wire fence and keep the setting sun to my right. Someone is screaming, others are yelling, off in the distance. It doesn't sound like they're adapting very well to the new paradigm. Or maybe they ran into some Others.

I have to step higher to walk through the tall grass. This too reminds me of Missouri grass, and out of habit as I move forward I grasp a handful of stalks to slide a handful of seeds off of them. I used to collect the seeds in my palm, then let them rain back down to the ground, like I was helping plant more. But as if to remind me again that I'm not in the nostalgic meadows of my youth, the grass slices viciously into my hand rather than yielding its seeds. I let go instantly but there are already gashes across my palm and fingers, and the blood drips within seconds. Like a shiver of sharks, the grass around my feet comes alive when my blood hits the ground. Soon my feet are tangled and sharp blades reach under my pant legs at the ankles, slicing and gripping. The flesh above my socks is slashed and bleeding on both legs, but I'm rather determined to keep my feet attached, so I tear them out of the tangles one at a time, over and over again until I can gain enough momentum to run.

The terrain is long, rolling hills and I can see mountains to the west. I top a hill, out of breath, and find a large pond down in the valley below it. Several deer are by the water's edge, which I can see is blissfully free of grass. They lift their heads to stare at me as I run toward them. The one closest to me is a buck with the biggest rack I've ever seen. The fact they're not running away from me is, somewhere in the back of my mind, disturbing, but I'm more worried about being swallowed by a sea of murderous fescue than I am about a few deer.

I swing wide around the animals until I get to the

other side of the pond and sink down on a bank of gravel and sand. A drink is a good idea. I just saw the deer drinking so I decide it's probably safe. The water is clear and cool and after I rinse the blood off my hand, I drink as much as I can. I don't know when I'll find good water again. I sit and rest by the edge of the water and then decide to lie back, just for a couple minutes. I'm suddenly not in any hurry.

I didn't intend to sleep, but when I open my eyes again it's dark. I can see more stars than usual. I stare at them for a long time, until the moon rises. When she does, I pull my socks up as high as they'll go to cover the cuts and start walking again, thinking maybe the grass is sleeping. My hand throbs and it doesn't want to open all the way because of the new blood drying sticky. I keep it curled and try to think about something other than the pulsating ache.

Once I'm into the grass for a few minutes I start walking faster. I didn't want to get too far from the pond in case I needed to retreat, but I think my suspicion that it sleeps in the dark is correct. So far. I keep my bloody hand drawn up to my chest, so it can't get a whiff of it, just in case.

I remember the deer and relief washes over me as I realize they could've been dangerous, but obviously spared me. That's when I hear the snort. And a low, guttural moan that turns into a growl. Then a chorus of howls overpowers the growl and my steps slow to a stop. Perhaps the deer were something else's dinner.

The way forward is a black hole of forest and behind me is bloodthirsty pasture. I can't sit here, don't want to go back, and really, *really* don't want to go into the trees with whatever's making that noise.

Fuck.

Sometimes I think I hear my intuition speaking, and sometimes I'm pretty sure it's just a dark and self-destructive impulse masquerading as intuition. I'm not sure which one whispers, "Keep walking." I don't have much choice anyway. My steps are slow and cautious. Individual forms of trees begin to emerge from the solid mass of black that I'd seen from a distance. I realize I've been hearing tree frogs the whole time, but now they're almost deafening the closer I get to the woods. Tree frogs and crickets. Maybe I am back in Missouri. I don't really care where I am as long as I can get back to some pavement soon.

The moaning starts up again and I stop to listen. I think it's coming from my right, so I veer left. Every few minutes I stop and listen again. There's more than one . . . thing . . . that's making that noise. The howling has stopped. I'm finding it harder and harder to make myself move forward each time I stop. I feel a writhing mass of fear trying to force its way up my throat, like a rat up a drain pipe, both constricting it and inspiring the dry heaves all at once. Pin pricks of sweat line up on my forehead. I'm not moving. Unlike the electric hum that seemed to paralyze me earlier, this immobility comes from within. My legs refuse to take another step. Possibly because they're trembling, or I could be in quicksand, I honestly can't tell the difference right now.

I don't know what a banshee even is, but I think *that* must be what they sound like. The screeching gets louder and I can tell it's homing in on me, and if my legs hadn't given out completely it probably would've taken my head with it as it roared and whooshed past me. Half a second later the menace turns to horror as bodies crash together with a sickening crunch only a few feet behind me. Bodies of what, I still don't know. The shrieks of agony and terror infuse my legs with newfound purpose and I am sprinting away from the sound of struggle—the cracking of bones and rending of flesh. Tears stream down the sides of my face as I run, but I don't get far before I trip over something and faceplant into some thorny bushes. Each limb I attempt to extricate is held in place with sharp and insistent stabs. I take a couple of deep breaths and go from frantic to merely terrified. I can get my feet under me and just yank my arms out, like ripping off a bandage, I think. Damn, these thorns are wicked, though. Tugging my arms back slowly is excruciating but maybe that way I can keep them from going in too deep.

The shrieks have stopped coming from whatever it was that swooped past me. I imagine that whatever killed it is coming for me next. I'm still delicately twisting and pulling my arms, trying to maneuver in the least painful way to get out of this sadistic bush, when a blinding light explodes in front of me and the bush is ripped away from me, taking a fair amount of my flesh with it. I let out a scream that's part pain and part rage as I realize I've actually been thrown backwards by the force of the lightning. The initial blaze dissipates but several small fires are burning now. It's like new versions of this fucking apocalypse keep happening (despite the fact I specifically requested stories from *after* said event).

At least I can see better, and I'm out of the thorns, even if my forearms are shredded and singed. I am ready to be done with the woods, but then I see movement up ahead. I know the thing, one thing, is still behind me, whatever it was that attacked . . . whatever that other thing was.

I close my eyes and take the deepest breath I can manage, and when I open my eyes again I know I have to get moving. The fires, naturally, are spreading. I pick my way around the crater left by the lightning strike and hurry, carefully this time, farther into the woods. As I move away from the fires I start to think that maybe the moaning and growling thing actually saved my life by killing the flying banshee thing that almost took my head off. Maybe that thing I saw moving up ahead *won't* kill me straight away.

That is only barely a smidgen in the direction of "comforting" and only for a moment or two because I finally come face to face with the low growl, the wiry black hair covering its entire body—a wolf and a bear and a tarantula all in one. Then another banshee screech sears through the night behind me.

Perfect.

The beast moves toward me and I'm about to duck like I did last time, but I'm a second too late. Talons grip each of my shoulders and the breath is sucked right out of me as I'm lifted airborne. The black hairy tarantulabearwolf looks like he's as surprised as I am and so he's also a second too late with his futile grab at my feet. I struggle for air while my fingers clutch and pry at the iron-strong talons that dig ever deeper into my shoulders. I feel my flesh giving way. When I catch my breath I scream again, and as if to outdo me this winged thing screeches its piercing, godawful cry. It's the last thing I hear before I black out.

🦇 🦇 🦇

Pain wakes me up; the slices in my palms, the bloody gorges that trail down my arms, and the punctures in my shoulder all vie for attention. Then, happily, I realize I haven't been eaten. I'm propped up against a tree—a lone tree—by the side of a road. A paved road! I'm stiff, but I struggle slowly to my feet. The sun is just above the horizon and it's a new day. I'm not sticking around to find my screeching savior so I can thank it. I don't see any woods and I have no idea how far or what direction I came from the night before, but as long as this is still the sun I used to know, I can point myself south and keep walking.

🦇 🦇 🦇

I walk for days through this menagerie of destruction. I am sure by now that the gates are standing wide open, because hell is here. I encounter groups of children now and then, apparently left to rely on only what their parents taught them before the shit hit the fan. They might be more terrifying than the beasts in the dark woods, but then, I've never trusted children. As a safety measure, I cover my face with my own fresh blood—my hands and arms are still oozing—just so they don't think I look like an easy target. I stare them down and hiss at them when they get too close. Sometimes if they don't see me first, I just hide until they pass by.

The other people I've seen have kept their distance from me too. I guess I've looked more presentable, on better days, when I wasn't caked in blood and no doubt looking as deranged as I feel. That's fine with me though. A couple of people who are sitting by the edge of the road run away when they see me and leave all their stuff. I don't want their stuff, but the canteen catches my eye, and I help myself to a long drink.

Shortly after that I get to what's left of a town and I'm feeling almost cocky. That is until a burly fellow, I assume it's a fellow, grabs me from behind while I'm busy hissing at some children who ventured too close. Little freaks were probably in on it. He manages to clamp both of my arms to my sides, and then he lifts me. Pain burns up both arms, fueling my sudden rage as I mule kick his shins over and over. He doesn't seem to notice. He lugs me up the steps of a nearby porch where a well-armed man in camo is politely holding the screen door open for us. He flings me inside and I land hard on the floor. It takes a moment for my eyes to adjust to the unlit interior. The stench is sickly sweet and putrid and I gag on it. Both men laugh.

"What'sa matter? Rotting flesh don't suit ya?" Burly Man says.

I glance over at the couch and notice the source is sitting there. I think it's a corpse, until it moves and turns to face me. I can see its teeth through the holes in its cheek.

I should have expected this.

I look up at the burly man just before he punches me. My neck snaps backward and things go black once again.

In a haze, in a dream, I can see a bridge. It's spanning a bottomless gorge and I know, somehow, that the gorge holds the vastness of despair between fear and purpose. It's funny how you know things in dreams.

I'm in the desert walking south, toward the bridge. Around me there's smoke, like the gates of hell did open and the fires are pouring out. Other people pass me on the road. Some seem to know their help is coming; others seem to know it isn't. I get the sense there's freedom in their hopelessness, and I feel drawn to relax into that freedom. To stop. To rest. To lie down and sleep. Suddenly I'm freezing despite the flames all around me. *Never take a nap in a snow bank.* I shake my head and refocus my eyes to the south, through the fires. I hear the voice again, saying, "Keep walking."

I wish My One were here to walk with me. Where is he, anyway? The gates are open; I think he needs to cross the bridge. Maybe I should cross the bridge.

Someone is calling my name. Her voice is familiar and I know instinctively she belongs here. Is it Persephone? But she also sounds like me. Can I be both Psyche *and* Persephone? I am vaguely and sluggishly irritated by the feeling that now is not the time for an identity crisis. My thoughts dream-swim back to my task.

"What's so scary about walking through hell if you already live here?" the disembodied voice asks.

"Where is he?" I reply.

"Don't you know?"

If I knew . . .

"Remember that you did this. You called in the beasts. You asked for the flames. You cut loose every repressed human desire."

I can see her point. And judging by the enthusiastic response to my call, lots of people are in favor of the idea, although, it's pretty clear that as a race we need a better plan for it.

The voice responded without my uttering a reply, like she was already in my head. "You thought the whole purpose of the apocalypse was to weed out the unworthy, but you had your own agenda."

"I just wanted it to set My One free."

"Freedom's just another word for—"

"Don't—"

". . . nothing left to lose."

". . . say it. We both have something to lose now."

My gaze returns to the bridge, and I realize I've crossed it before. Probably a few times. I look around at the destruction—this *is* exactly what I asked for. I did create it, with the help of my friends. I'm not just traipsing through hell on a mission. I pretty much *own* the place! Why make it harder than it has to be?

"That's my girl," the voice says. "Now wake up. He's here."

🐦 🐦 🐦

I open my eyes and see that I'm still in the house, on the floor in front of the couch. I must be used to the stench because I'm not gagging on it anymore, although Mr. Undead is still here. I'm on my side and my hands are tied behind my back. My ankles are tied together too. Though my shoulders are still stiff and they ache as relentlessly as they have for days, I struggle until I'm able to slide my arms around my ass and get my hands in front of me again. Nobody else is around that I can see. The voice said he's here. I study the zombie on the couch skeptically as I untie my feet. "Josh?" I say, just to be sure. He doesn't respond. What's left of his hair is brown—too dark—so I hope, I'm pretty sure, it's not him. I'm puzzling how to get my hands free when I hear footsteps on the front porch. I remember suddenly that the voice didn't clarify *who's* here. I glance around frantically and grab the first thing I see, an iron fireplace poker, and crouch behind an armchair. Burly Man steps into the room.

"What the—"

I swing the poker as hard as I can from my position and whack him across the shins. This he seems to notice; he cries out as he crumbles. On his way down I swing again and catch the spike on the end of the poker in the top of his skull. I watch him fall to the floor. Mr. Undead is on him in an instant and begins to tear into his flesh like a rabid vulture.

I step back to give him some room, then get up and go to the kitchen. There's a huge assortment of boning and butcher knives out on the counter, some of them still bloody. I pick a smaller boning knife that I can maneuver to cut the ropes around my wrists and finish freeing myself. Once the ropes are off I head for the door, then stop, pick the knife back up, and walk out onto the porch.

I let the knife clatter to the wooden planks when I see Josh standing at the bottom step, smiling up at me.

"What's up, baby?" He raises an eyebrow as he looks me over and his smile starts to fade.

Before he can ask if I'm okay, I step off the porch straight into his arms.

💀 💀 💀

We found an old hunting cabin in the mountains above the desert and claimed it as our home. Josh took care of all my cuts and bruises with the first-aid kit he found in our new place, and aside from listening to the occasional radio reports, we've been living our lives like we are the last two humans on earth.

Now I sit cross-legged on the floor in front of the fireplace and gaze into the flames, elbows on my thighs, and twirl a strand of long brown hair around two fingers, twirling and twirling until it's wrapped around my fist like a boxing glove. I lean my cheek against it petulantly. "You have more faith in humanity than I do, Josh."

He laughs and looks up from the book he's reading. "Did you really expect humanity to get wiped out completely? We're more resilient than that."

"Hm. Like cockroaches."

No, the long-anticipated apocalypse was not *all* I had hoped for. It seems more than a fourth of the world's population actually survived. Hardly even worthy of the name apocalypse, in my opinion. Some assholes even got the electric grids back up and running. What was the point? What was the planet thinking, leaving so many behind just to do the same horrific things to her that tipped the scales in the first place? It didn't make sense.

"Maybe this is still only the first wave," I said.

"Babe."

I turn to look at him, and once again I remember that it doesn't really matter. "Why are you *still* so far away from me?" I ask.

He grins and sets the book on the end table, then moves from the arm chair to his knees and crawls the short distance to reach me. "It's gonna be okay." He kisses the side of my neck and growls.

I smile. "I guess it's not all bad." I close my eyes and follow the euphoric sensation singing through my flesh from my neck to my toes. "Actually, I think everybody got the exact version of the apocalypse they wanted."

"I know I did." Josh rocks back on his heels into a squat and then stands and reaches out a hand to help me up. "Come on, let's go to bed. We can read some more stories—the ones where everybody's fending for themselves and tearing each other apart."

I roll my eyes, but then smile as I let him pull me to my feet.

PART I

CYBER FUTURE

THE GARAGE

TERRY SANVILLE

Tony Matteson and Fox Slade hustled down Main Street, past the boarded-up courthouse and the torched movie theater, heading toward home. On a side street, a police crawler rattled toward them, its knobby tires rolling over decades of debris, its blue and white roof lights flashing. Tony slung the half-full can of paint into a gaping storefront and took off running. Fox matched his speed, her flyaway red hair complementing the indigo latex spattered across her coveralls.

The 'Forcers turned onto Main. "Hold it right there, you two," blasted from their crawler's speaker.

The pair ran faster, dodged around junker cars, piles of refuse pulled from long-abandoned shops, around mounds of books outside a place called The Phoenix, the volumes turning into mush from years of sun and rain. The crawler gained on them. They cut through an overgrown park near the creek, past the ruins of Mission de Tolosa. Tony glanced at Fox and grinned. They'd been sixteen when the 'Forcers had last put up a good chase. Now, a couple years later, they still could outrun them.

Another crawler pulled from a driveway and skidded to a stop directly in their path. Winged doors shot upward from its beetle-shaped fuselage and two officers jumped out. The 'Forcers made a grab for them but missed. Tony and Fox angled through a parking lot, and clawed their way over a rotting fence into a back alley. A skip loader rusted where it had last worked on some kind of construction job. They slid past it and reached the edge of the town's old commercial district.

A warm September wind blew eastward along the boulevard, pushing them toward the Garage, a half block down. More flashing lights. The Police closed in. The couple bobbed and weaved around grasping hands, past hastily aimed stun guns. Something slammed into Tony's shoulder. He tucked his compact body into a ball, rolled once, and came up running. Reaching the entrance to the five-level parking structure, the pair sprinted inside. The Police didn't follow, wouldn't follow. Tony and Fox climbed the stairs two at a time, passing dark floors full of the Touchable Clan's campsites. At the top level open to the sky, they rushed to the parapet and stared down at the Police. Fox flashed her burning blue eyes at Tony and grinned, her chest heaving. The officers stood with hands on hips in the littered street, calling through their megaphones for the teenagers to surrender.

A few of the new arrivals that lived on the roof joined the pair, shouted insults at the 'Forcers, and waved antique rifles and handguns in the air. An old guy with dreadlocks and his son emptied their waste buckets over the side and the patrolmen scattered. The Roofies laughed.

"They almost got us," Fox said. "Are you all right?"

Tony grinned. "Yeah, I'm fine. But I told you one of those Untouchables would call the Police. You have to paint quicker."

Fox glared at him. "You're the one that wants details. You can't rush details. You can't force art."

"Yeah, yeah, I know. We'll let things cool for a few

days then go back and finish it. How's our paint supply holding out?"

"We'll have plenty," Fox said, "unless they find our stash."

They descended the stairs to the second level and moved to their campsites, shoved side by side against the Garage's east wall where the morning sun warmed them and the thick concrete walls blocked the Pacific winds. Tony stood on his toes and kissed Fox, a soft one on the mouth that lingered, then ducked inside his tent. His mother looked up from her reading and scowled.

"Where the blazes have you been? You missed your afternoon session. We were going to talk about Descartes and the other philosophers."

"Sorry, Mom, I was out helping Fox—"

"Yes, I'll bet you were."

"We're just having fun, Mom."

"Uh huh. That girl's a fine artist. But if the Police catch you kids painting those hillside homes, your old mother's gonna be lonely for a long time."

"It's just a game, Mom. Gives the 'Forcers something to do. Besides they'll never catch us. You should see the big houses above the hospital. The murals really tell a story."

"Do they show two teenagers behind bars?"

Tony laughed. "No, but we can work that in somehow if you want. We're mostly painting landscapes, you know, camouflage, so that the buildings disappear against the hill."

"Well, enough art for one day. Come on, it's suppertime and you know how quick the line forms when they serve meat."

Tony retrieved his mother's cane and helped her to her feet. They joined Fox and her parents and climbed the stairs to the roof where the communal kitchens stood beneath an open-sided shed. That day, the cooking crew had plucked and roasted chickens taken from their coops south of town. The meat smelled wonderful and at least half of the Touchable Clan's three hundred members had already lined up, plates in hand, awaiting their ration of chicken, green beans, salad, and beer brewed on the third level by a half dozen enthusiastic families. Every adult contributed something to the clan's life. Tony's mom taught school, from the smallest tykes to the most advanced adults. Fox's dad helped take care of the community garden. Her mother worked in the rooftop food prep area, tending the drying trays filled with apples, almonds, and cabernet grapes scavenged from abandoned orchards and vineyards.

The families sat at long tables and ate their meals. The head of the clan climbed onto a packing crate and yelled for their attention.

"Listen up, clansmen. Just a reminder, tomorrow is autumn cleaning day. Public Works will be here bright and early to charge the sprinklers with disinfectant. For you new folks who just joined the Roofies, they'll be pumping cleaning fluid through the standpipes and flooding the top deck. So everyone needs to clear out by 0800."

"Why'd they ever start doing that?" a new Roofie asked Tony's mother.

"Back in 2080 there was a cholera outbreak in the Garage. Ever since then, it's been drenched with Pine-Sol on each solstice and equinox day. It's a real pain, but after more than thirty years we've had few health problems."

"You kids better leave early tomorrow morning," Fox's mother told the teenagers. "You really pissed off the Police with that cat-and-mouse act of yours. They'll be waiting for you."

Tony nodded. "Fox and I can hole up at the library."

Fox smiled at him, her face smeared with chicken grease. "While we're there, we can grab some more books for you, Mrs. Matteson."

"Thank you, Fox. Some of my students need reference materials. I'll give you a list."

The two families chatted about the day's events and

complained about having to spend half the night packing everything onto rickety carts to haul from the Garage the following morning, only to drag it back near sundown.

After dinner, the teenagers carried their families' waste buckets south through the deserted industrial district to the sewer farm, an expanse of downwind pastureland managed by the Roofies and Romero, their leader. Tony remembered when he and his mom had turned up at the Garage a decade before and joined the clan. All new members had to live on the roof and work at the sewer farm—afternoons spent pouring caustic lye into the waste ditches and covering it with fresh soil, all under the watchful eye of King Dave. They had camped on the roof in a leaky tent for three years before a space opened up on the second level next to Fox.

After dropping off their buckets and picking up clean ones, Fox and Tony moved north to the creek and their favorite pool hidden beneath a bridge and a tangle of willows. They stripped naked and slid into the black water, scrubbing hard at their bodies to remove the grime and the paint stains. Afterwards, Fox laid her slender body on the long grass under the trees. Tony slid his muscled arms around her and they spooned. In the warm Indian summer evening, night herons squawked and egrets and great blues beat the air above them. The couple made slow love, slept, then woke and hurried back to the Garage to prepare for the morning move and their next scrape with the Police.

"Wake up, Tony. We're late."

He opened his eyes and looked up at Fox. "What time is it?"

"0530. We should've been outta here an hour ago."

Tony glanced at his mother, slumped on a cushion and snoring. "Just let me roust Mom and I'll come get you."

In a few minutes he joined Fox outside her family's tent. They snugged their backpacks tight around their shoulders, pulled on black knit caps, and descended the stairs to the Garage's main entrance. Three crawlers with lights flashing waited outside. At the rear and side exits, they found more 'Forcers with stun guns drawn.

"We're screwed," Tony muttered.

"Not yet, come on." Fox led him to the roof. A few of the families had started edging their overloaded carts toward the first ramp and the precarious descent to ground level. The couple moved to the south wall and peeked over its edge at the Police.

"What are we supposed to do, fly?" Tony asked.

"No, stupid. See that old utility line?" She pointed to a thick black cable attached to a metal stanchion on top of the parapet. It angled downward into the gray dawn.

"You're kidding me," Tony said.

"No, it's our way out. When I was a kid, I hooked myself up to that thing and slid down the block. It passes through some trees and ends at a pole maybe a hundred meters away."

"But you were smaller then and—"

"You calling me fat?" Fox said, smirking.

"God, no. But I'm not sure that line will hold."

"Quit worrying. We'll go one at a time. I'll meet up with you at the Library, at our normal spot."

Before he could say anything more, Fox removed her belt and tied it in a loop around the utility line. "Now listen. When you hit the tree branches, grab hold."

"You're not gonna get stuck out there dangling, are you?"

Fox grinned. "Relax. This line drops quickly and you'll be going fast enough to reach the trees."

"Be careful," Tony said and kissed her.

She pushed off from her perch on top of the parapet. The line sagged and she disappeared. Tony listened but heard nothing. He laid a hand on the wet cable. It jounced a few times then stilled.

The sky continued to brighten. He hurried to hook his belt around the line and stuff his jacket down his pants.

He slipped one arm through the loop. Sucking in a deep breath, he dropped off the parapet and slid through grayness, passing over the crawlers' flashing white and blue lights. An ocean fog had pushed inland and hung at treetop level. It wet his face. He continued to slide, his arms numbed from clutching the belt loop. Something brushed his side. He smashed into a mat of small twigs, reached out and grabbed hold with one hand, stopping his forward motion. He couldn't see the ground. But he released his other arm and pulled himself up the slender branches to a large limb, across the limb to the trunk, then down, the tree's bark digging into his flesh. Dropping onto the sidewalk, he backed against a church with shattered stained-glass windows, his chest heaving. Something touched his arm, and he jerked, struggling to hold back a yelp.

"You made it without breaking your stupid neck," Fox said.

"What are you doing here? You're supposed to—"

"Yeah, well I couldn't leave you behind if you crash-landed."

He hugged her, could feel her body tremble, or maybe it was his own, he couldn't tell. He also felt his pants slipping down his thighs, yielding to gravity since he had abandoned his belt on the overhead line.

"Not now, Romeo," Fox said and backed away from him. He yanked up his trousers and tucked in his shirt and jacket.

They walked along quiet streets, cutting a zigzag route to the brick library, across the square from the boarded-up City Hall. The pair found the hole cut in the chain link fence at the rear loading dock. Fox struggled to slide her long body through it while Tony easily slipped between its jagged edges. His mother liked to call him her wire terrier because of his curly brown hair and compact features. But so long as Fox loved him, he didn't care what others called him.

Tony kicked at the metal service door then yanked it

open. The inside smelled of dust. Moving along a carpeted corridor, they emerged into what must have been the main lobby, with reading rooms opening off it.

"Where do you want to start?" Fox asked.

Tony pulled a scrap of paper from his pocket and they stared at his mother's clear handwriting. "Most of what she wants is medical reference, geology, with a few bug books. Let's start upstairs then move to special collections if we need to."

They climbed to the second floor. Sunlight poured through wire-glass windows, allowing them to move easily between the stacks. Thick dust covered the volumes. The pair pulled on painting masks before dislodging anything from the shelves. Tony always enjoyed this part; it felt like a treasure hunt. It wasn't long before he and Fox had stashed the desired books in their backpacks and had returned the ones his mom had finished with to their rightful places. His mother felt adamant about taking back what she'd borrowed. "Someday, libraries will be important again," she'd said.

They moved to an open balcony off the third floor, sat on rusting chairs, and watched the sun move across the valley, chasing the retreating fog toward the Pacific coast.

"So do you want to go paint?" Fox asked.

"Naw. We should wait until they're done cleaning the Garage and ditch these backpacks. Besides, the 'Forcers will be looking for us. They know we've been painting on that house, so we need to take a break."

"Then, what do you want to do all day?" Fox grinned at him and he grinned back.

"You could try reading something. You can read, can't you?"

She stuck out her tongue at him. "You know I'm more of a visual and tactile person."

"Great. Let's go look at the special collections."

Tony took her hand and they pushed through a series of doors into a musty room with a bank of tinted windows across one wall. He opened a wide drawer and removed a stack of large pages, black ink on fragile paper. On the first page, a colored photograph showed a mob of smiling people, standing elbow to elbow. The caption read, "Farmers market draws thousands."

"What's that all about?" Fox asked.

"My mom says the farmers used to bring their goods to Main Street one night a week. They'd close it off and sell all sorts of stuff."

"It looks like they're having fun. Are they from a clan or are they Untouchables?"

"Look," Tony said, pointing to the top of the sheet, "it's from 1995, the beginning of the Gadget Age."

Fox nodded. "Yeah, now I understand. Your mom taught me about the Change, when people began to shift from face-to-face contact to remote contact, for just about everything."

"It must have been wild before the Change, when everybody moved all over the place, met each other, went to schools, gathered to listen to music or poetry."

Fox stared absently out the windows. "The Internet replaced all of that. And people got lazy, then scared after the Nouveau-Polio and Indonesian Plague outbreaks killed millions. They figured they could live out their lives without contact."

"Yeah. All those gadgets that connected everyone eventually left them . . . alone."

Fox paged through the stack of sheets and paused to stare at photographs of streets clogged with cars, and people speaking in groups. She clapped a hand over her mouth. Full-sheet pictures showed masses of people lying on cots in football stadiums, in parking lots, in auditoriums, with masked medical staff wandering between the rows.

Fox slid the drawer shut and shuddered. "Have you ever met an Untouchable?"

"Only once, near the airport runway where the supply drones land. The guy scared the hell out of me. Actually, he looked more upset than I was."

Fox grinned. "Well, with that wild hair of yours, who could blame 'im."

They ate their lunch of soda bread, carrot sticks, dried apple slices, and beer on a shaded balcony overlooking the downtown. A red-tailed hawk had built its nest at the top of a building's vent pipe. The bird's hoarse cries echoed down the corridors between decaying facades, bounced off plaster walls of dull gray and ochre that hadn't felt fresh paint in almost a century. Tony sat and read an illustrated book about the Chumash Tribe of Native Americans and their slow and peaceful demise. He was always reading something, but especially liked history. Fox covered page after page in her sketchbook with detailed pencil portraits of crumbling parapets, cracked walls, shattered windows, sidewalks with weeds sprouting from fissures caused by the roots of monstrous trees and their seedlings left unpruned for decades.

"Someday, I'll make a book about all of this," she said.

"That would be great. But you'd need to find a way to get it digitized before anybody would see it. You can't exactly sell them door to door to the Untouchables."

"Hey, quit stomping on my dream. At least I have one."

Tony knew she was right and shut up. In addition to painting, he liked playing his homemade guitar and performing with a group of other guys at the clan's weekly beer fests on the roof. The band hung out on the fourth level under the stairs, practiced tight harmonies for songs that they'd taught each other, and whaled on their homemade guitars, banjos, tambourines, and on Jimmy's bass fiddle. But Tony would turn eighteen in a few days and would have to join a work detail to help the clan. Fox had a few more weeks of freedom. Both had talked about running away, but to where, and to what?

As the sun set, they worked their way across the downtown and approached the Garage. Crawlers parked on the surrounding streets with officers watching the entrances. Midnight passed before they finally cleared out and the teenagers rejoined their parents. The camps smelled of disinfectant and full waste buckets. Tony couldn't wait until they painted once again in the clean air of the upper highlands.

Four days later after breakfast, they climbed the foothills that formed one side of the town's valley. Traffic in the Untouchable neighborhood was mostly remote-controlled vans and trucks serving each home, depositing groceries, medical supplies, clothing, or whatever had been ordered on the web. The vans moved fast, their cameras normally ignoring wayward pedestrians. But Fox and Tony took no chances and ducked behind shrubbery or abandoned cars whenever they heard the high whine of an electric vehicle.

They each carried four big cans of paint with brushes shoved into the pockets of their coveralls. The house they sought stood high in the foothills near the edge of town. Its wide glass windows had been replaced long ago with solid plaster, its sloping yard overgrown with chaparral plants covering the concrete walkway and steps that had once led from the street to the front door. But the solar panels on the roof looked new, along with four wind turbine units. Their mural covered half of the house facing the valley, a hillside scene that spread over walls, old window openings, and part of the front door. After trudging up the steep hill carrying their paint, Tony and Fox collapsed in the shade of a manzanita, sucked in deep breaths, and wiped the sweat from their faces. Fox had forgotten to bring her water bottle. They took turns sipping from his canteen and watched the heat shimmer above the asphalt.

With the street clear, they hurried up the driveway and slid along the house's wall to the front door.

"Be quiet," Tony whispered. "Whoever's inside is probably real twitchy."

"It's worth it. Will you look at the definition I'm getting?" Fox pointed to the mural.

"Yeah, it's some of your best work. But just be quiet.

We can finish up and be outta here by lunch. You did bring the lunch, didn't you?"

Fox grinned and patted her backpack. They set to work, opening paint cans, mixing the colors in cups, and rising to dab blotches of green, blue, yellow, and ochre onto the smooth plaster. They worked fast, with Tony laying down big blocks of color with his four-inch brush. The latex paint dried quickly, allowing Fox to come through and create images out of the seemingly random pattern of colors. They worked steadily, not talking, the sun burning their backs.

Fox worked on the fine points of a rock outcropping that covered the front door, concentrating, a small paint brush clenched between her teeth. She rose from her squatting position and swayed, her face flushed. Tony grabbed hold of her just as she collapsed. He stretched her body out on the concrete pad, her long red hair forming a blazing corona around her head. Fox's arms and legs twitched and her eyes rolled back in her head. He grabbed his canteen and placed it to her lips. But she pushed it away, moaning. He splashed water on her face. Her whole body shook.

Tony stood and stared at the vacant street with not a van or even a garbage truck in sight. In the distance, the Garage rose above the town's skyline. He thought about running for help, but didn't want to leave her. He turned and pounded on the front door. Silence. He continued pounding.

"My girlfriend is sick. We need help."

Tony repeated his plea over and over. Finally, the metal slab cracked open. From the looks of it, the door hadn't moved in years. A green eye peered at him.

"Please, help us. We won't hurt you."

"How do I know that?" a man asked in a raspy voice.

"We're artists, not criminals. Please help."

"So you're the ones that have been messing with my house."

"Yes, yes. Just let me bring her inside. We won't hurt

you."

The green eye looked down at the redheaded girl shuddering on the concrete. The man chanted under his breath, "to do good or do no harm, to do good or do no harm, to do good or do no harm." Tony recognized the phrase but couldn't remember where it came from.

The door scraped open and a towering blond guy, with muscular arms and wearing a headset, motioned him inside. Tony bent and grabbed Fox underneath her arms and dragged her through the opening onto clean carpet. The Untouchable slammed the door behind them.

"Bring her in here," he directed.

Tony followed him into a large room with banks of video screens streaming a dozen or more different images. The room felt like the Garage did in wintertime after a rain. His sweat turned cold and he shivered.

"Lay her on the sofa." The man pointed to a long cushioned chair and Tony did as directed.

"Wait here."

The Untouchable moved to another room and returned with plastic bags filled with clear cubes. Tony touched them and drew his hand back.

The guy frowned. "What's wrong? You've never seen ice cubes?"

"Ah, no," Tony muttered.

The man took three small bags of cubes and placed one under each of Fox's armpits and one down her shorts. She moaned but continued to tremble.

"What's wrong with her?" Tony asked.

"Heatstroke. You're crazy to . . . to be outside in that sun."

He left the couple but returned shortly with a thick cut-glass pitcher of water. He poured some into a cup and handed it to Tony. "You'd better drink some yourself. You don't look so good. But then I haven't seen anyone face to face in . . . years."

Tony gulped the water, then held a full cup to Fox's mouth. "Come on," he murmured, "you gotta drink."

She opened her blue eyes, grabbed the cup, and emptied it. After a while her flushed face returned to its normal color and she sat up, casting off the ice bags. "What happened? One minute I'm painting and the next I've got freezing water between my legs."

The Untouchable's hoarse laughter echoed throughout the house. Tony had noticed that the guy talked too loud, as if he wasn't used to speaking with people in the same space.

"Excuse me for laughing. I believe what you . . . you had was a heatstroke."

"How would you know about heat?" Tony said, glowering. "You probably never go outside this, this refrigerated bunker."

"Quite right, Mr. Painter. I moved to the CenCal Coast eight years ago from the Northeast. I haven't been outside since."

"So what do you do?" Fox asked. "Do you have, ya know, a wife? Girlfriend?" She massaged her cramping arms and legs, stood and moved unsteadily around the room, leaning against countertops for support while staring at the flickering vid screens.

The man watched her nervously. "I'm CEO of a physicians' consulting service, and a licensed doctor. This hillside spot gives me good satellite access, great for data and video uplinks and downloads."

The couple stared at each other. Tony had read the terms in books. But no one at the Garage had a computer or web access. It was all part of the weird stuff that the Untouchables did.

Tony asked, "But don't you have to meet your . . . your patients?"

"Good God no," he said. "We can do all our work in cyberspace, and leave the rest to the regional hospitals and labs. Hell, I haven't talked to another body in months. The drone vans unload supplies directly into my storage unit. If I need something repaired or serviced inside this house, I go to my safe room while the work's being done."

"But why?" Fox asked. "Why not go outside? There's lots of cool stuff to see and do. Aren't you lonely?"

"To answer your previous question, no, I don't have a wife, and no, I'm not lonely. I can get everything I need from the web."

"Everything?" Tony asked, and gave Fox a quick squeeze.

"Yes, even sex," the man shot back. "Today's pornography involves all five senses, and I can direct the action and have my choice of thousands of partners."

"But, don't you want . . . friends?" Fox stammered.

"I have thousands of friends. I write or speak to dozens of them every day. And I can choose when to be alone and when to link up."

"Sounds frightening," Tony said and frowned.

"On the contrary. Your world is the scary one, where nothing is certain or controlled, where people do cruel things to each other. As a consulting physician, I've viewed what your kind is capable of."

"But what about love?" Fox asked. "Do you love any of your cyber friends?"

He looked away. "I'm afraid that emotion is pretty much useless. Some of my fellow physicians are married. From what I can tell, love is a temporary condition, not worth the long-term investment."

Tony grunted and poured himself another glass of water. "So, thanks a lot for helping us, mister. We'll get out of here and leave you and your house alone."

"I don't think so," the man said, a faint smile spreading his lips for the first time. "You've been trespassing, defacing my house and lowering its resale value. I can't let that go unpunished."

"But why?" Tony asked. "You don't go outside, don't even know what we've painted."

"I know. I can see everything." He muttered something into his headset and a bank of vid screens clicked on, showing images of the outside of his house from various angles. One screen showed Fox and Tony dabbing away with their paint brushes.

"So you've known all along," Fox muttered.

"Yes. And now I have you."

Tony and Fox glanced at each other then bolted for the door. But it wouldn't open. They ran throughout the house but didn't discover any other opening to the outside. Returning to the video room, they found the Untouchable standing with his bulging arms folded across his chest, waiting.

"Why don't you have some more water, kiddies, while I contact the Police? They should be here momentarily."

"Wait, wait," Tony pleaded. "What if we repainted your house so it looked like it did before?"

"Nice try. But once outside in that savage world of yours, who knows what you'll do. I'm afraid that you don't have anything to bargain with. Except maybe . . ."

"Except what?" Tony asked.

"Except maybe the affections of your girlfriend. The porn vids are good, but there's still room for improvement."

"You want to . . . ?" Fox clenched her fists and stepped forward.

"Easy, girl. I can break you and your pipsqueak boyfriend like twigs."

"Who's being savage now?" Tony muttered and moved next to Fox.

The man lunged at her, grabbed the front of her coveralls at the neckline and yanked downward, ripping the material away, exposing tanned flesh. She screamed and lashed out with a leg. But the guy twisted sideways and the blow glanced off his hip. Tony threw himself at the attacker, his fists swinging. The Untouchable held him off with one massive arm. A huge fist shot toward Tony's face, a burst of light as if a star went nova, then blackness.

He came to, sprawled on the floor across the room with a throbbing jaw, loose teeth, and a mouth full of blood from a mangled lip. Fox lay naked on the sofa, screaming. The attacker pinned her down with a knee and roughly fingered her groin. She flailed at him with clawed hands, trying to reach his eyes, her body bucking and heaving. He raised an arm and backhanded her hard across the face. He hit her again, and again. She lay still and moaned. He stepped back, removed his headset, and stripped naked, a hulking white and hairy man. He stretched out next to her. She remained motionless. The guy rolled on top of her and propped himself up, one massive paw around her throat and the other caressing her breasts.

On hands and knees, Tony crawled across the carpet and pulled himself up on a table leg. He grabbed the near-empty water pitcher, crept to where Fox and the Untouchable lay, and slammed it against the back of the man's head. It struck with a dull thud. Sucking in a deep breath, he drew it back and swung again with all his might. This time the pitcher came away smeared with blood. The attacker collapsed onto Fox. She pushed him off. He rolled onto the floor and stared up at them, his eyes fixed. A large crimson puddle stained the carpet.

Fox staggered to her feet and fell into Tony's arms. They stood trembling. Finally, when they had calmed, Fox tied what remained of her clothes onto her body, her chest bloodied from where the man had scratched her with his fingernails. A red mark covered most of one cheek. Tony bent and checked the Untouchable for a pulse. He couldn't find one.

"Are you all right?" he asked Fox.

"God, I can still smell that creep," she said and shuddered. "We gotta get outta here."

"I know, I know. We'll figure it out."

They stared at the bank of video screens that flashed printed information, graphs and charts, photographs and written messages from around the world. Tony put on the man's headset and tried various voice commands, pressed several buttons. But nothing he did unlocked the front door.

"Wait here, I got an idea." He disappeared down a hallway and returned with an old-fashioned fire ax. "I think I can cut through the wall where the windows used to be. Stand back."

A short time later he stood with his hands on his knees, panting. They both stared out the hole that he'd slashed in the wall, then squeezed through it into the sizzling afternoon. After being trapped inside the cold house, the air felt like fire. Tony grabbed his canteen and splashed both of their faces. The high whine of a police crawler moving in their direction sounded in the distance. They raced downhill into the old commercial district. At a shady spot next to the creek, they talked about how much to tell their parents, and afterward, where to run.

Tony dipped his head in the stream then ran his fingers through his tangled curls. "When the 'Forcers drive by that house, they'll know something's up. Besides, we left our paints behind. They'll know it was us."

"Maybe if we go to the Police and tell them our story—" Fox began, but stopped when Tony scowled.

"Who's gonna believe that an Untouchable invited two clansmen inside? That sounds crazy."

"Yeah, and there's no evidence that he tried to . . . to rape me."

"But there's plenty of our cells and prints around that place. We're pretty much screwed." Tony covered his face with his hands. "And when somebody who pays the 'Forcers' salaries gets killed, the Police will never let up."

They ran back to the Garage. Tony dreaded telling his mom and the Slades about what had happened. But once he started, he recounted the full story, leaving out nothing. His mom sat stunned while Mrs. Slade hugged her daughter and cried. Mr. Slade disappeared and returned with the clan leader. The adults huddled and grumbled to themselves. Finally, they broke apart and scattered, except for Tony's mom.

"You two come with me," she ordered. They followed

her hobbling form across the second level to the barber's camp. Inside the tent, the teenagers sat side by side, while Mr. Bochum clipped Tony's curls, shaved off his mustache, and bleached what was left of his hair blonde. He cut Fox's scarlet hair short then dyed it black, along with her eyebrows. As they finished up, three other couples that Tony and Fox didn't know well entered the tent.

"So these are the fugitives," one of the boys cracked. "It's about time us small guys get some recognition."

Mr. Bochum ordered the couples into hastily arranged chairs. The guys had their dark locks curled into bouncy mops, while the girls had their hair dyed crimson.

"What's this all about?" Fox asked.

"Does the word 'decoy' mean anything to you?" one of the new redheads answered.

"Don't worry, kids," Tony's mom said, "I'll explain it all when we get back to camp."

Once inside their tent, she poured the teenagers herbal tea and laid out the plan. The couple sat in stunned silence as shadows lengthened and sunset approached.

Outside, a fleet of police crawlers encircled the Garage. They'd been parked there since shortly after the fugitives had returned, barking out orders for Tony and Fox to surrender. Vans full of reserve officers had pulled up behind the crawlers and formed a gapless perimeter, their stun guns held at the ready. The blue and white flashing lights lit up the entire block and half the Garage's interior. An armored truck with blacked-out windows parked behind the vans and waited silently.

Inside the Garage, the clan members huddled in groups at the exits. Each group included one couple with a red-haired girl and a curly-headed boy. On the roof, the snickering Roofies knelt behind the parapet, fingered their full waste buckets, and waited for the signal.

Tony and Fox stood silently with one of the groups and listened to his mom's final instructions.

"Your packs are stuffed with food and the canteens are full. Head south into the foothills. Stay away from the roads. You'll be too easy to spot if you use them. Keep moving and don't stop until you run out of food."

Tony hugged his trembling mother, her tears wetting his neck. Fox's father folded his daughter into his arms, his face gray and set. Her mother sobbed.

Tears streaked Fox's cheeks but she tried to smile through it. "Don't worry. We're gonna have a grand adventure, aren't we, Tony?"

Tony's mother brushed away her tears and lowered her head. "And one more thing, Anthony," she murmured. "Don't ever come back."

Outside, a new voice blared through a loudspeaker. "Listen up, Touchables. This is Lieutenant Statler speaking. We don't want any trouble with your clan. Just send Tony and Fox out and we'll leave you alone. They'll be treated fairly. But if you don't cooperate, we're coming in to get them. You have five minutes to decide."

The rumble of voices within the clansmen groups grew then died. Tony grasped Fox's hand and squeezed. She kissed him. The minutes dragged by. Then, it started with a whistle blast.

The Police advanced on the Garage.

"Who are the savages now?" Tony muttered.

As the 'Forcers neared the building, the Roofies stood and emptied their waste buckets over the parapet. The line of Police fell back, the officers using every swear word Tony had ever heard. But they regrouped and advanced again, yelling, their stun guns raised, face masks lowered, shields up. From inside the Garage someone struck the old school bell. The clansmen charged from the exits and ran in all directions, rushing the police lines, darting between them. The officers broke ranks and chased after the red-haired girls and their curly-headed companions. Some of them knelt and emptied their stun guns into the crowd. Dozens of people lay in the street, moaning.

"I got 'em, I got 'em," an officer bellowed and other

Police joined him and hustled one of the decoy couples into a van. When the bell had sounded, Tony and Fox had held back and watched the mêlée develop. Now, they sprinted from the rear exit and cut a serpentine path down the boulevard until coming to a side street. A beanbag round hit Fox in the back of her thigh and she went down hard. Tony grabbed her and they hobbled away. Fox moaned, her face streaked with tears. But they kept moving. At the south edge of the city, they followed a drainage swale across open fields and climbed into the coastal hills, not stopping until they reached the ridgeline. Staring into the valley, they could pick out the cluster of crawlers, their lights still flashing. But another orange light poured from the Garage's openings. A haze of smoke hung over the building as the campsites burned.

The couple watched the flames for a long time. The crawlers retreated. A loud explosion shook the valley. A dust cloud engulfed the Garage. When it cleared, there was a new gap in the skyline, one less building for Fox to draw. The crawlers disappeared and the town once again became a black abyss in the center of a valley where only security lights twinkled from the hillside homes of the Untouchables.

"There'll be more of us heading south," Tony said.

Fox shook her head. "No, they'll take over the Library or find a school with a good roof. They're not leaving. It's their town too."

"We're losing a lot, ya know," Tony muttered and dropped his head.

"Yes, I know."

She encircled him in her arms and squeezed, his head pressed against her shoulder. He kissed her and they swayed together, their hearts pounding steadily, resolutely. Tony shuddered. Stepping back, he ordered Fox to drop her trousers. He lightly touched the angry-looking red welt on the back of her left thigh. She jerked away from him.

"If we just keep moving, it'll feel better in a while. But

you'll have a fist-sized bruise there in a day or so."

They slid down steep canyon slopes, heading south and west toward the half-submerged and abandoned beach towns, toward the rumored communes on the Channel Islands just off the Pacific Coast, where Chumash Indians had long ago worshiped their gods, painted strange images on rocks, and enjoyed their face-to-face lives.

PUTTiNG OFF THE END

RUSS BiCKERSTAFF

I'd gotten the notices in the mail. I'd gotten the phone calls. They'd left messages on my voicemail. There had been text messages. There had been requests on social media. There had been emails. There had been numerous opportunities to respond to the messages. I think I'd started getting the notices something like a year before the final notices came up.

At first I genuinely didn't see the early notices. Somewhere around the second or third attempt to contact me, I guess I felt kind of embarrassed that I hadn't responded to the first notices. By the time the third and fourth notices popped up, I was actively avoiding them. Eventually the final notices started to pop up. They looked big and ugly the way final notices always do. When I had finally taken notice of what it was that was trying to contact me, I guess I was kind of confused. Thankfully, I wasn't the only one who hadn't been paying attention to the notices. Everyone seemed to put off paying attention to the notices until they started getting ugly. No one seemed to take notice until they saw the big, angry letters plastered all over the mailings and the flashing lights on the online notices and such.

They were extremely harsh and threatening and everything, but the notices in question were all so aggressively *vague.* They didn't really explain to me (or anyone else) exactly what it was that we hadn't been doing other than actually responding to any of the prior notices. They issued some of the most serious consequences imaginable, mentioning that it would be highly unlikely that we would be able to escape our fate without any consequences of any kind, but if we acted now we might be able to avoid the worst fate imaginable if we were to contact them and open the dialogue they'd been trying to establish this whole time.

I tried calling the customer service number, but I got put on hold. After the first hour of listening to hold music, I put my headset on and went out of the apartment. I continued to listen to hold music as I took a half-hour drive out to the office that was listed on the form. I figured that as long as I had the time, I might as well head out to try to fix things face to face in case I wasn't able to get ahold of anyone over the phone.

It took me a few minutes to find parking. I walked in through the front door of a large office tower in the business district. Listening to hold music in one ear, I asked the man at the front desk how to go about making it to Suite B on the 23rd floor. With the music filtering through one ear, I thanked him and went off to the elevator. The elevator nearly gave out a couple of times on my way up to 23. For some reason I guess I was okay with that. My feeling of self-satisfaction at finally dealing with the notices evidently made me completely impervious to fear.

When I got to the office suite in question, I was asked to take a number. I did so and went to sit down in a vast, empty waiting room. Just about everyone on the planet may have been getting these notices, but it wasn't surprising that I was the only one to actually swing by the offices to try to say something to these people. I imagine that there was probably no one else who would actually bother to come down here and try to straighten things. The threats were so vague that most people probably casually discarded them as some strange joke or misfiling of records in an office somewhere. Honestly the only reason I was taking it seriously was because I didn't have anything better to do at that moment.

I sat there in an empty waiting room listening to hold music and making occasional eye contact with the attractive woman at the counter who handed me my number. Looking closer at it, I couldn't help but notice that I couldn't quite identify what the number was. Every time I looked at it to confirm what it was, I instantly forgot what it was and had to look at it again only to find that it was something other than what I had thought it was. I felt like I must be going mad or having some sort of a stroke until I looked up at the number currently being served and experienced the exact same phenomenon.

I walked over to the desk to ask the woman sitting there for help, but was stopped dead in my tracks when I saw that she was trying to get my attention from around the corner of the waiting room. I looked over to see her sitting there at the desk. Then I looked over to see her trying to get my attention. She put a finger to her lips to let me know to keep quiet for some reason and led me into a hallway that was lit with crackling fluorescents and smelled of musty, old paper. I'd followed her far enough in to see that she wasn't actually there. Looking around I saw row after row of boxes filled with paper forms of various kinds. I turned around to try to approach the desk only to find that the waiting room was nowhere to be seen.

I've been wandering the files ever since. Row after row after row of tall racks filled with box after box of paper forms filed away detailing various things about nearly everyone who had ever been in the world. The music never lets up. It's the same hold music in my headset constantly. My phone never seems to lack reception and for some reason it never actually runs out of battery power. It's been a very, very long call that's been going on for months now. I've been on hold for months. I never seem to get tired either. If this is to be the end of the world, it's not quite how I would have expected it to be.

THE EDIFICE

LORRAINE SCHEIN

THE APPROACH

To those coming upon it from the outside, the Edifice is said to loom up abruptly after the last bend in the road, like an insect buzzing into your face from nowhere. It has the forbidding air of every yellowing mental hospital with its high concrete wall, barred windows, and rotting vines. Some see a prison camp with small guard houses posted high in four corners, each with trained watch-apes. Its wide, laser-eyed gates are patrolled by our teacher-clergy, ever vigilant in their caps and gowns, swinging their taser-bludgeons.

Yet others say the building looks like a giant castle, because of the deep water circling it like a moat and the corporate creed flags flying high above the crenellated ramparts, bearing the symbol of the Edifice—a pointed gold cross thrust into a bleeding brain.

Each night the banging, sizzling green coils of the snake aurora caused by our dim failing sun look ready to strike us. But they cannot harm us because we are within the Edifice.

I have been here so long I have forgotten how I got here and if I had a name, but it does not matter for I know I am one of the lucky interned conscripted students. I remember the first day I arrived—how they took my clothes away, burned them, and stamped my head with a blue radiating light that seared lines onto my forehead, cut and covered my hair with an electrified wimple like a nun's, and gave me a white hospital gown to wear.

THE CHAPEL

Then I was told because it was Monday, I was to go to service in the chapel, which was also the school. After I was registered by having blood and fecal samples taken, I was evaluated by our Dr. Father Reverend Holy Imam, psychologist-priest of the Human Relations Dept. and CEO.

"Do you know why you are here?"

Father's voice came from above me, as he sat on the spindly, gilt-encrusted papal throne towering over the leather sofa I was fastened to. The straps around my arms and ankles were tied securely, but not so tight as to hurt.

"No. Why?"

"Good. Don't let that worry you—none of us do, me included." He made a check in a box with a stylus on his screen device.

"Do you know who you are?"

"I don't know my name, but I know I am a Remnant like the others here."

"Yes, that's right." He nodded. "How do you feel about crucifixion and algebra?"

"I'm not sure—I guess it depends on the circumstances. I never was good at math, but with an incentive like that, I'm sure I can change . . ."

"And how do you feel about history and insanity?"

"History is insanity. Insanity is the only sanity," I chanted. "Rules keep us sane."

He looked at me intently, checked another box on his screen, then pointed to a bright red fractal shape on a screen.

"What do you see?"

"I see the destruction of civilization by the sun's blood. I see chaos, and the new rules of society that have arisen from it. I see Recombinant civilization—reason freed from memory."

He looked satisfied, then released me and ordered me to kneel and recite my prayers to His Greenness in the chapel. We pray to Green Od, who is new in the sky. His echoing jade coils in the sky call to us every night to repent on these last Earth days.

THE SCHOOLROOM

I must have passed the tests, because I was taken to my first class on hospital religion. Here we learned how to pray to the doctor-teacher-priests (DTPs) of the Edifice, and were graded according to our piety, fervor, and rote memory.

My brain was jabbed with a large gleaming Algebra inoculation, followed by a large pious one to increase my religious observance. After the pain subsided, I was able to recite the square roots of the twenty numbers the teacher asked for in rapid succession. We were caned in front of the board of directors if we did not recite the psalms and memorize the daily no-futures market prices correctly.

ASSIGNED TEXTS

Our assigned books are the Bible, the Diagnostic and Statistical Manual of Mental Disorders (DSM), *Malleus Maleficarum*, our Corporate Governance and Identity handbook, an Astrological Ephemeris from when there were years, Dow Jones Stock Index, *The Complete Guide* to *DOS 6.22*, *Robert's Rules of Order*, *Dictionary of Occupational Titles and Acroynyms*, and some ancient *Farmer's Almanacs*.

We must memorize, then kneel and recite from these while mock-crucified to an ancient ATM.

THE DORMITORY

This is where the mutated after the post-Conflagration live, sleeping in segregated dormitories—men, women, the undetermined, and the diseased. Sometime in the very early morning before dawn, the teachers wake us for the ceremony of the Saint Lucia. We hear their heavy steps as they come in procession down the hallway.

Each wears a white robe and a crown of laser pointers on his head. They check to see if we are in our proper beds and clean by lifting our nightshirts and smelling us. If so, one of the teacher-nurse-priests (TNPs) will reward the worthy students with coitus or cookies. The lucky ones get both.

These nightly events are recorded on film by the overhead Eyes in our dormitories. The resulting films are used as instructional videos to inform new students about the ceremony and to allow us all to learn the sexual techniques that most please the TNPs.

ASSIGNED SEATS

We are assigned seats according to our blood type, stigmata, and how well we do on the STDs—standardized tests of comprehension and dogma. If we have pleased our teacher with an orgasm the night before, we are allowed to sit up front, so we can gaze at their holiness, and learn from proximity to their business savvy. Sometimes they let us help them cane the inattentive students.

Everyone has their proper place. If we stay in our place, and follow the rules, we will be safe and happy.

I think I have forgotten the difference.

THE CAFETERIA

Twice a day, we file into the cafeteria. After the bitter fibrous holy wafer is blessed by the corporate-teacher-priest (CTP) and put between our teeth, we must swallow it—if we spit it out, we are punished, and not allowed to eat. We genuflect to the nun-cooks, then pick up our trays and head toward the steam tables, behind which stand CTP women in starched caps and black heels ready to dole out food to the good and productive. Those who have not been good, get gruel that tastes like the wafers.

THE WATER CLOSET

We must raise our hands to get a pass from the CTP to go to the water closet. It has a lovely pictogram of Christ using a urinal. A picture of a bleeding saint hangs over the toilet.

There are small knives placed on the shelves next to the sink for those who want to cut themselves, so it can be done easily, precisely, and then the dark riveleting mess can be washed away with cold tap water run in the sink. Evidence of stigmata is rewarded with extra scones at tea time or colon cleanses.

THE CORRECTION CHAMBER

Those who don't follow the rules get straitjacketed and put in isolation rooms, expelled, or excommunicated. The unruliest have a small piece of their brain removed by the DTPs to help them obey. Every other day, some are dunk-drowned like witches in the deep moat around the Edifice.

My gown has become my skin. We are bled with leeches regularly. They slurp at my flesh as I lie in my bed-desk in class, or kneel in the corporate church, looking up at Our Green Lady of the Two Tails, who holds a hamburger in each one.

I hear the bell for first period Electroshock—I must

punch my timecard and go. I must not be late. Lateness is a venial sin, punishable by fecal immersion.

THE EXIT DOOR

We've been taught that the only way out is to become fired, expelled, or excommunicated. Or to become so diseased you are contagious, and then banished for the protection of all.

But I have heard rumors that there is an exit door. There must be, because I know that some of us Remnants are no longer here. It is said to be a bolted wooden door that was built long before the Conflagration, at the end of a secret underground passage that leads to the sea. There is a gold key hanging from a pointed cross thrust into it.

Some say the exit door only exists in our minds, and that we Remnants can only see it by closing our eyes and believing. Believe in what is not Religion or Science or Economics.

Yet how would I live on the outside? Only the Edifice can keep us safe.

I try to visualize the deadly sun rays outside, and close my eyes . . .

TiN MAN

MAGGiE DENTON

Benjamin prepared himself for getting up off the park bench. First he slid his body to the edge of it and got his knees at just the right angle. Then he leaned forward and pressed down hard on the handle of his cane, using it as leverage to push his body up off the seat.

He now set his cane aside and turned to his wife Louise so he could help her get up too. Even with her own cane, she couldn't rise up off a low seat without assistance. They had this down to a well-practiced drill. He placed his hands beneath her armpits and looked at her to make sure she was ready. She nodded and gave him a brave smile. He then bent his own knees, and as he straightened them, pulled her gently to her feet as he rose. It wasn't hard. His hands were still steady and strong, and at ninety-four, she was a frail, slight woman.

She let out a gasp of pain as she usually did when getting up from a sitting position, but the discomfort didn't last long. She raised up one palsied hand to his face and caressed it gently, then brushed back a lock of white hair from his forehead. She made a mental note to herself that he needed a haircut. Benjamin took her hand and kissed it, picked up his cane again, and looped his other arm firmly through hers. They started walking back toward their house, just across the street from the park.

Even after seventy-two years of marriage, she still felt a warm glow when he touched her and was aware of his arm and the comforting, gentle pressure of his side against hers as they walked. Benjamin, of course, couldn't feel her touch at all, or her warmth, or any pain of his own when he stood up, because as an android, he didn't have that capacity.

❧ ❧ ❧

While there were many such federally funded institutes worldwide, Grow-With-Me Cybertronics, on the forefront of advanced robotics since the beginning, was still considered the premier, showcase facility of its kind.

A mere fifteen years after the techno-flu of 2115 had reduced earth's population by half and destroyed the genetic reproduction capacity of most of those who remained, G-W-M had their patents in and their prototypes dancing around on the assembly-room floor.

After the pandemic, only one in every three hundred humans was born with the ability to procreate. Mankind would not multiply at a rate needed for the race to get on with the business of modern living over the next decades; the world had to be reenvisioned and recreated to accommodate the current state of affairs.

By 2152, there were mechanical husbands, wives, farm workers, mechanics, nannies, secretaries, bakers, valets, prison guards, and anything else that was needed to keep the society moving forward and progressing in an orderly fashion.

The only humans allowed to marry other humans were those gene-scanned and verified as able to have children so that the race could be repopulated, but with the advent of advanced robotics, no one need ever go through life alone, or even do without vital services, conveniences, or friends. The march of life went on.

The androids all looked and acted human in every respect. The spouse-drones were engineered to externally change and age in the time stream, along with their human counterparts, and through this, the world came to a new, established norm. In any given society, in any country, the population consisted of roughly 65 percent mechanicals, 35 percent humans, living and working side by side.

This is what the world was in 2210, when Louise, at the age of twenty-two, walked into Grow-With-Me Cybertronics and met Benjamin for the first time.

After sharing the initial social pleasantries, they went to a coffee shop. Louise avoided looking at him and was pushing a piece of chocolate cake back and forth with her fork.

"Is this your first date with a droid?" Benjamin smiled with a look of mild amusement in his eyes.

His question startled her and she looked up at him.

"Yes. I mean no. I mean—I don't know what I mean. There were plenty of mechanicals at the youth centers, skating rinks, places like that, and I think they unleashed around fifty of them at my senior prom. Those were all stock models though. This is my first time with a custom drone created specifically for me. They had me fill out a twelve-hundred-item questionnaire as part of the paper work. It took me a week to finish it."

Benjamin put down his own fork and laughed.

"Yes, I *do* know about that form, intimately."

"Of course you know about it. Didn't all my information get downloaded into your chip or disk, or something?"

"Sure did. That's why I'm so irresistibly attractive to you."

Louise stared at him for a moment, stunned.

"Oh my God! You even have human vanity."

"Not to mention my sense of humor."

"Well! In that case, I guess you're perfect."

Benjamin smiled and took another sip of coffee.

Louise shook her head, smiled back, and took a bite of cake. "Do you know what is kind of strange? There was a separate form I had to fill out about my physical preferences in a man. You hardly have any of them—not even the hair or eye color, but somehow, you look, well, right to me. I don't understand why that is."

"To tell you the truth, I don't either. I guess we can leave enigmas like that to the genius programmers that put together the custom jobs like me." He was no longer smiling.

Louise nodded and fell silent. Perplexed, she looked into his attentive blue eyes.

Behind their metallic glass, and with a speed beyond human comprehension, a billion components in inter-linked chips sparked, repositioned, and integrated in just the right way, so that when he smiled at her this time, his eyes contained the exact, appropriate amount of electronically fabricated sadness.

※ ※ ※

"Okay, my turn. What about her?" Louise pointed to a fat, jolly-looking woman with salt and pepper hair, manning a beverage and ice cream kiosk. A herd of antelope galloped gracefully behind her.

Benjamin studied her carefully for a few moments, as well as her interactions with the children gathered around her snack stand.

They were at the Barnum and Bailey Hologram Safari, and now, a colorful, tropical bird hovered around the woman's head, causing the children to scream with laughter.

Benjamin shook his head. "Nope. She's human."

"Are you sure?"

"Yep."

Louise got up and went over to speak to the vendor,

who nodded and laughed. With a mock-apologetic expression, the woman looked over at Benjamin and gave him a thumbs-down. He shook his head in mock disgust.

Louise returned with her hand held out to him. "Pay up! What does this make it, seven to two my favor?"

Benjamin pulled a dollar out of his shirt pocket and slapped it onto her palm.

"How is it that I'm one of the most advanced computerized entities built by man, am myself a mechanical, but you're able to tell an android from a human more than twice as many times as I can?"

"It's a gift, Ben. A true gift."

They often played this game on their dates—spotting whether someone was an android or not. Louise had an uncanny knack for nailing it, even from a distance.

"Seriously, how are you able to tell?"

"I don't know. I just can."

"Louise, with that in mind, maybe this isn't the best time to ask this, but what would you think of spending the next seventy years or so with a humble bucket of nuts and bolts like me?"

She frowned, wrinkled her brow, and looked down at the ground, lost in intense thought for a moment. She jerked backwards suddenly, because a holographic snake slithered by her foot. Benjamin lowered his eyes to what she was looking at, looked back up at her with alarm, and his expression caused her to burst out laughing.

"Okay, yes."

"Yes, you will?"

"Yes. I know it's part of the programming of every mechanical that's been engineered as a spouse-drone to bring things to this point, and that it's what non-procreators do if they want to be married. I paused because, even though it's been this way for decades, in growing up, I always thought I would not be interested in mating with a drone. I know it's our way of life, but I always viewed it as akin to marrying something nonsentient.

"I guess I don't really view you as a machine anymore. I mean I do, but I don't. I know you're not really alive, that there's a high-level façade in place that veils the truth of what you are, but in our current society, life can go on in a better state because of that façade than it can without it. Ice cream tastes as good from that nice vendor-drone as it does from anyone else. Because of your programming, you respond to me the same as a real person would. Knowing you has made me reevaluate everything I've believed while growing up about android culture."

"You know, Louise, there's a very good reason for us to get married."

"What's that?"

"We make a great pair—like Romeo and Juliet, Anthony and Cleopatra, Bonnie and Clyde. Louise, the cool, beautiful chick, and Benjamin, the hot, handsome circuit board. That's not the main reason we should do this though."

"Okay, I'll bite, what's the main reason, Ben?"

He was facing her, as he was programmed to do when they spoke, and through his optic sensors, as usual, saw streaming binary code against a white background.

"Because I love you."

❧ ❧ ❧

Louise sat up in bed and pulled the pillow up behind her to cushion her back.

"Ben, since they can make droids that externally change and age the way humans do, why haven't they been able to make a drone child that changes and grows into an adult?"

"The technology just hasn't advanced that far yet. It's one thing to build an exo-structure programmed to get thicker or thinner, weaken, or release chemicals that cause skin to wrinkle or hair to lose pigment gradually over a period of time. It's another entirely to have an outer shell that grows and develops over a short time span the way a child's would. It's just too many and too drastic as far as the changes that would need to happen. I'm sure they'll eventually be able to do it. What got you thinking about this all of a sudden?"

"I dunno. I guess lots of non-reproducers think about what it would be like to have children, or wish they could. From the time I was old enough to understand what it was all about, I carried a certain amount of bitterness and regret over the knowledge that I would never have children."

"I can't have them either."

"Yes, but you don't really, I mean, well, you know what I mean."

"Yes. Sorry, Louise. I guess that *was* a little too much of a preprogrammed, robot-cliché response."

"That's okay, Ben."

"Happy tenth anniversary!" Benjamin held out the package to her. It was a flat box wrapped in textured gold paper, tied with a black velvet bow.

"A present! Gimme!"

"Hey! Don't rip off the gift wrapping so fast. It took me half an hour to get the box to look that good."

"Ben, this is *amazing*!" She held up the necklace. "Wait, these stones can't be what I think they are."

"Yep, they're the real thing—star-tears mined from Venus. I've been monitoring the space-shuttle inventory lists for months and finally they showed up on one of the lists. Only fifty were brought back from that trip, and you, my dear, have three of them in that necklace. I figured a tenth anniversary called for something special. Turn around and let me fasten it."

He did, and she went to a mirror to look at it around her neck.

"Wow! It's beautiful. It's like something out of a dream."

The Venusian jewels, each of them one of a kind,

shivered and changed colors in response to her body heat. She threw her arms around him.

"Well, don't you want to see what I got you?"

"Sure."

"Stay here then. I'll be right back."

She returned holding a small object wrapped in a piece of soft cloth and handed it to Benjamin.

He unwrapped it and stared in silence at what was inside.

"Well, do you like it? It was my father's, actually my grandfather's originally. They were both procreators and had as many kids as possible, so I was really blown away when my dad gave it to me as a graduation gift, even though he knew I wouldn't have children to hand it down to. Anyway, do you like it?"

Benjamin continued to stare at the magnificent, antique pocket watch, which he had known about since her data-form was downloaded onto his chip years before. It was one of the things she listed on the "most prized possessions" question.

He opened the lovely, engraved case to look at the face, then gently wound it. With the case open, the tic-tic sound was audible in the quiet room. He closed and put the watch in his shirt pocket, the one directly over his heart, and pulled Louise to him. She laid her head sideways against the pocket and cried.

🐦 🐦 🐦

"Ben, I'm so glad we came to the islands for our twenty-fifth anniversary. I'm having the time of my life. Thank you for this wonderful surprise."

"Yes. I thought a twenty-fifth anniversary called for something special."

They walked along the beach hand in hand. Louise sometimes looked to the right at the thundering waves, sometimes to the left at the misty mountains in the distance, and sometimes up at the fluffy, white clouds rolling like lazy sheep across a powder-blue sky.

Benjamin turned his head whenever she did—not at the exact same moment, but maybe a second or two after, as would more naturally occur when peopled walked together and casually looked at things. Of course, no matter where he looked, all he saw were streaming digits and symbols, which, in nanoseconds, relayed the instructions and micro-messages he needed in order to interact with her properly.

By the time they arrived back at their house from the park, Louise's face was flushed, and she was breathing heavily with gasping, labored breaths. Benjamin knew it was her heart and that he needed to call for help. He momentarily let go of her arm so that he could quickly fish his cell phone and house keys from his pocket. When he did, she slowly bent forward from the waist like a wilting flower stalk. He dropped his own cane and grabbed her with both his hands.

She looked up at him. Her mouth was stretched like a rubber band in a grimace of pain, and by the time he had dragged her, moments later, over to their living room couch, she was already dead.

The funeral was held five days later. It was a warm spring day, the cemetery peaceful and beautiful. Louise had many friends, who, though also elderly, showed up for both the memorial service and the burial, taking advantage of the gentle weather.

By three in the afternoon, it was over, and the group had started to disperse. Upon leaving, each person, even the ones who did know that Benjamin was a mechanical, took his hand and gave their condolences. He nodded and thanked them, and remained at the cemetery long after everyone else was gone.

At 2:00 a.m., a security guard passing through did not in any way disturb the white-haired man he saw standing at the newly turned earth of a gravesite. He slowed his vehicle as he drove by, saw the back of the man in the dark with his head tilted slightly as he looked down at the grave, decided the man was not a vandal but a mourner, and drove off to check on other areas.

It was sunrise when Benjamin turned to leave. There must have been a momentary glitch in his programming, because before he turned, he touched his shirt pocket where he normally kept the antique pocket watch. He acted as though he'd forgotten he had placed it, open, in Louise's casket, after winding it one final time.

PROJECT BLESSING

RACHEL E. BAILEY

The mission was simple:

Go *Back—way* Back—to before The 'Phage . . . and kill Aaron Blessing.

*   *   *

The intel we had on Blessing's life was sketchy—but then, we really didn't need it to be detailed. We just needed to know where he was living a few years before the CDC finally informed the populace of the spread of The Nanophage. By which time it was, of course, too late. Blessing was long dead by that point, and only years of desperate reverse-engineering by the CDC and damned near every qualified scientist in the First World pointed at this heretofore unknown man as the creator of The 'Phage . . . and its patient zero.

No, not much was known about him beyond the bare facts. But then, we didn't need much, did we? All we needed was just enough to get one soldier in his vicinity to take him out.

I was that . . . *soldier.* That *assassin.*

The mission called for a sledgehammer, not a scalpel. Kill Aaron Blessing and destroy all his work on nanotechnology, if indeed, any had yet existed. Kill anyone that got in my way, or tried to continue or resurrect his work.

But the most important thing was Blessing. Everyone—everyone that was left on this emptied world—agreed that he had to die.

The night before they sent me Back, I spent wandering in the house Luka and I had shared for over ninety-seven years. That night was the first I'd been home in the years since the physical training and psychological conditioning that was supposed to make me a remorseless killer.

Everything was exactly as I'd left it, only dustier. The chandelier in the front hall—Luka's pride and joy . . . he'd loved that thing like it was a baby—had cobwebs, but still worked when I flipped the switch near the door. Every floor, with the exception of the kitchen and front hall, practically devoured sound because of the carpeting, which Luka had wanted. Whimsy or melancholy led me first to the library, which had been Luka's workspace. The huge dry-erase board was still littered with multicolored equations that might as well have been in Greek for all the sense I could make of them. Luka's notebooks still lay where they'd fallen or where he'd dropped them, crammed from margin to margin and front to back in his tiny, anal print.

I turned my back on the library almost as soon as I entered it, and made my way to the living room. More shades of Luka were to be seen there, from the interior design—Luka had loved masculine, baroque furniture and Oriental rugs, ornate fixtures and area lamps—to the few of his notebooks that had migrated from the library. Everything was the same and had been the same for nearly half a century. There was only one way in which I'd changed the house since he'd gone.

Pictures of Luka adorned every wall and any flat surface that wasn't meant for an ass or for feet. The whole house had been little more than a shrine to him since he passed, forty-three years ago. I used to spend days wandering the large old colonial, repairing what needed repairing on occasion, but mostly remembering and looking at the past. Looking at the time before Luka's madness began to outpace the nanites that kept us all so damnably sane and alive, before the chemicals those same nanites created to regulate our emotions and moods stopped being enough, as they had for so many of the few that remained.

Before Luka went and killed himself.

I spent my last night in my past *in my past*. Saying good-bye. I waited in the empty, cavernous abyss of a house for anything to happen. A breakdown. A catharsis. A *something*. But nothing came. Nothing happened. It wasn't home anymore. *Home* had died with Luka.

Nothing was all I felt anymore, and even the nanites couldn't change that. Since the conditioning had really gotten under way in earnest, I'd been hard put to feel anything other than grim satisfaction that I seemed to take to hand-to-hand combat and simula-kills like a fish to water.

At sun-up, I left the house that'd once been my home, mine and Luka's. The Institute wasn't a far walk. The house was even in their name, and though Luka, who had once been one of their preeminent experts on displacement theory, was dead, I, as his spouse, was allowed to stay on. Indeed, in a world with more homes than people to fill them, no one cared enough to bother about evicting one widower.

None of us, we immortal few, cared about anything, anymore, but The Project. Project Blessing.

I left that house with nothing but the clothes I'd arrived in and one perfect photograph of Luka. He's smiling in it, sitting in the sun, head tipped back and eyes half closed. I don't remember what he was laughing at, or even taking the picture. But it seemed like the best way to remember him, rather than as a silent, melancholy ghost haunting our house for a decade before finally going ghost all the way.

I locked the door against intruders, as I had three years ago. But I'd never be back. Even if I'd felt inclined to return to a shrine to a man I remembered but could no longer feel in my heart except as an everlasting sense of loss, ache, and betrayal. Even if I'd felt inclined to return to a place that had slowly been becoming my tomb. I couldn't. The trip Back was one-way.

This good-bye was for keeps.

And if all went as planned, then, well, Luka, who'd been born a year after The Nanophage made the first news reports, might cease to be. He'd been one of the last of the Final Generation: the last children born to a populace rendered sterile by the very nanites that made them nearly immortal. I would, in all likelihood, never meet him. Never *love* him.

I was certain it was for the best.

The needs of the many.

The Institute wasn't a far walk, at all.

$$\textbf{3 3 3}$$

I'd closed my eyes in a lab, surrounded by men and women whom I'd known for nearly a century but, at this point in my conditioning and at this point in humanity's final inning, could only call colleagues. There'd been a needle-prick in my arm, a cool wash of numbness, then darkness a thousand times deeper than the comparative noon-day of having simply shut one's eyes.

Then I was blinking and bolting upright from my prone position, like a man escaping the clutches of a nightmare.

I was in a garbage-littered basement of a house that I'd been reassured had stood empty for a number of years even before the 'Phage. I knew the day and the approximate time.

But I was groggy and disoriented. Thanks to the Institute, my nanites had been successfully—painfully, and over many months—flushed from my system, so I wouldn't contaminate Back with them. My mind and body didn't have miniature robots tirelessly tending to them and keeping them clear and operating at maximal readiness, as they had since I was nine years old.

So I lay there, staring at the shadows the sun made on the wall, and waited for my head to clear. I thought of Luka for a while, then of nothing at all.

When my mind had sufficiently rebooted, I stood up slowly, but easily, from the dirty, dusty floor, and brushed off my vintage mid-twenty-first-century clothing of khaki trousers, a cotton workshirt, tennis shoes, and a nylon windbreaker. Nearby was a *backpack*, an object I remembered from my own distant childhood, that contained a Velcro wallet in which were credit cards, one photo, and various forms of identification (but no cash), a street map, a baseball cap and sunglasses, and an old—or new, depending on how one chose to view it—cellular phone with some . . . modifications.

Early afternoon sunlight slanted into the small, high-set windows of the basement and exalted the trash and detritus that had greeted my landing. Dust motes that had been disturbed by my arrival swirled and eddied like golden specks in that light.

I shouldered my backpack and walked toward the rickety stairs.

❧ ❧ ❧

He wasn't hard to find.

Or he wouldn't have been if I hadn't been disoriented by all the *people*.

At first, it wasn't so bad, as I'd landed in the suburbs of the city, and at that time of day there weren't many people on the street. But as I walked on and got closer to the city center, more people and more cars began to appear and I began to get distinctly uncomfortable.

By the time I reached what the map identified as the city's commercial and cultural center, I was sweating—not from exertion—and breathing heavily. I felt jittery in my own skin and couldn't shake the feeling that everyone I passed—and there were *many*, so many hundreds—was watching me and somehow knew I was not of this When. That I was here to kill one of their own.

I couldn't remember the last time, aside from childhood, back before the world had emptied, that I'd seen more than twenty different people in the course of my day—even on the busiest, most travel-prone day. Where I'm from, the world population is closer to a few hundred million, rather than the seven billion that I could have sworn I *felt* surrounding me.

I also kept having the stunning realization that I *was truly* Back before the world had emptied and that I *was* a child, right now, in a different part of the country.

But it was that feeling of being stared at by so many that left me literally gasping by midafternoon. I was staggering down the street like a man having a heart attack—my recently nanite-free body was working overtime trying to regulate my breathing and heart rate but having little luck. My fight-or-flight was off the radar and I was about to bolt pell-mell through the streets of a strange city with no other thought than getting somewhere hidden and defensible, when I noticed—across a crowded, face-filled street—a sign: Java Cave.

It was a familiar name—*very* familiar—in this shifting morass of people and automobiles and buildings, and I ran for it, darting across the street amidst a chorus of horns. *Stop, look, and listen / Before you cross the street / Use your eyes, use your ears / And then you use your feet!* drifted out of my inconveniently whole memory. The little rhyme was from a childhood that was happening even as I pounded across macadam toward one of the places highlighted on the map in my zippered windbreaker pocket.

The large orange and green sign, with its irregular white letters, seemed to get farther away as I ran. Below the sign, there were two taken tables of patrons sitting to one side of a large picture window with an almost abstract rendering of a giant mug of steaming coffee.

Luka loved coffee, I remember thinking as I ran, dodging traffic, backpack joggling against my back. People really *were* staring at me, now. The passersby, the outside patrons of the café, a young guy serving one of the tables.

I was nearly clipped by something large and red and *fast*, and I faltered and almost fell before catching myself and, with a terrific lunge, leaping out of the road.

I had made it to the sidewalk and before me was the façade of the brightly lit café. I leaned heavily on a parking meter, huffing in breaths before just as quickly puffing them back out.

"Hey, buddy, are you okay?"

Startled, I looked up and into questioning dark gray eyes. *Familiar* eyes in a long, ascetic's face, and my heart skipped a beat. Or maybe ten. My problem with breathing—and breathing itself—was forgotten.

"'Cause you don't *look* okay, if you don't mind me saying," Aaron Blessing said to me, frowning solemnly and giving me a concerned once-over. "You *look* like you need to sit down. You wanna come inside and I'll get you some water?"

"I—" I started to reply automatically, before hiccupping and covering my mouth. *This is it! It's him! The man behind the extinction of humanity! Snap his neck! Kill him! Kill him* now!

My brain was screaming, my lungs were suddenly over-full, and my stomach was churning. I reached out weakly, and my hand hit his shoulder limply. His auburn eyebrows shot up in surprise but no fear, and then I was turning away from him, my stomach in full rebellion. I leaned over the curb to retch.

"Easy, there, buddy. Easy," Blessing soothed

worriedly, patting my back as I heaved up the little that'd been in my stomach into the gutter.

When I was done I wiped my mouth on the back of my hand then straightened up slowly. The world before me spun and dipped lazily, and I felt weak, dazed.

"Feel better now?" Blessing asked, his hand still light and comforting on my back, but no longer patting. I looked down at him—he was shorter than me, but then, I'd known that he would be from his dossier and photos: five-nine, 167 pounds soaking wet—and into his eyes. The eyes of the greatest mass murderer in human history.

"I—" I said once more. Then I was shoving his hand away as I turned and ran again.

🐦 🐦 🐦

I spent the next eight days locked in a cheap motel room on the outskirts of the city, fighting crippling panic attacks and unable to go farther than the motel's ice and vending machines for sustenance. Not that I needed more than the bare basics to survive off of. Thanks to my conditioning, I could've survived on air and sunlight, if necessary.

I watched television in between attacks, because it was comforting and reminded me of being a child. Which I was, somewhere in America.

When television began to grate on my nerves, I turned it off and instead stared at the peeling, beige walls of my room. The hideous orange drapes that I'd drawn to keep out sunlight. The saggy, mismatched, piebald furniture that creaked whenever I put weight on it. The sticky-tacky floor tiles in particularly vomitus shades of purple and green. The occasional lethargic cockroach.

I contemplated my palatial surroundings and tried not to think too much. Sometimes it worked. Most times it didn't.

And every time I thought about the Incident—about running so unexpectedly, so easily into Aaron Blessing, and about how I'd failed in my simple mission—I would become unable to catch my breath. Time would pass while I was locked in a Hell of my own making and I wouldn't be able to account for several hours at a time.

Had my inaction, my inability to be proactive, doomed humanity for a second time?

No, I'd tell myself. *They sent you Back years before The 'Phage happens. You have time. Time enough.*

But then I'd think of the look of concern in Blessing's dark eyes—they had seemed, for all that he'd been labeled *monster* and *world-killer,* to be *kind* eyes—and start retching and shaking and even, on occasion, weeping.

And for some reason, then I'd think of Luka, and when that happened, sometimes I'd have those spans when I'd go away, only to return to myself hours later, curled in a ball on the creaky motel bed or huddled in a corner of the room.

This was how it was for over a week.

But by the ninth afternoon, eleven pounds lighter and still vaguely disoriented, I went to the motel's office and among the many pamphlets and maps for sale, found a free bus map.

I had let the mission slip, true. But I felt ready, on that ninth day, to do what I hadn't—what I *should've*—days ago.

"I remember you from the other day," Blessing said when he came out to take my order.

I'd only been sitting for a minute or so before he ambled outside in his apron and with a notepad. The look of surprise in his eyes as he suddenly recognized me from the week prior struck a chord within me.

I tried on a smile that felt more like a dyspeptic grimace and wondered with detached fascination if I was going to throw up again. I'd become used to doing so over the past nine days, after not having done so for nearly two hundred years of my life prior.

Life without nanites was a bitch.

"Are you okay? I mean, I guess you must be. It's been over a week, but, *are* you okay?"

His concern, obvious and earnest, made my stomach clench and churn. "I'm fine. I just had a, panic attack, of sorts. Thank you for your concern, though. For trying to help." I paused, then added, "I didn't mean to take off on you like a purebred greyhound."

Blessing's worried smile became a wide, unreserved grin. I thought of Luka again—Luka when we'd *first met*—and tried not to let my dyspeptic smile slip back into my usual frown. I forced myself to notice details about Blessing that the few photos I'd seen hadn't managed to capture. The way his teeth were slightly crooked, but very white, as if not having been able to afford braces had made him take care of them all the more fiercely. The fact that his nose was also slightly crooked, as if it'd been broken once upon a time and not set properly. The way the stubbornness of his jaw was offset by the kindness of his gray eyes and thin but mobile mouth.

"Hey, not a problem. I know exactly how it feels when that instinct to run kicks in and—" Blessing snapped his fingers and I jumped, and stopped staring at his mouth. ". . . you just have to *run*. Believe me, I know."

My stomach churned and my heart beat faster. I tried to let my conditioning control what I thought at the time was another fight-or-flight response to the ultimate threat Aaron Blessing posed. But I couldn't quite calm myself.

In the meantime, silence fell between Blessing and me, in which he laughed and looked away, flushing just a little. But on his fair complexion, it was pretty visible. I found myself looking down at my table. At my hands thereon, large, calloused, and training-rough.

Kill him, a small—scarily small—part of me whispered. *Kill him, now.*

"So, I'm Aaron, I'll be your server today. What can I get for you?" When I looked up, Blessing was staring resolutely down at his pad, pen at the ready. His face was still flushed.

"Um," I said softly, once more wondering with that detached fascination what in the Hell I was doing letting Blessing talk at me instead of killing him with one fateful blow. I could look at him and catalogue all the vulnerable places on him, places where one swift, sharp strike would be enough to incapacitate and/or kill.

Catalogue, but apparently not make use of. Not yet.

Perhaps, not in public. I had to find some way to lure him to someplace hidden. Someplace I could commit a murder and get away with it. I had to lure him away from *his* safety zone and into *mine*. But how?

This had not been covered in my training. All that had been drummed into me had been ways to keep my mission simple. Now, here I was fighting that very conditioning and making everything complicated because of no better reason than the way he blushed.

I squarely met his as-yet-innocent dark eyes. Blessing's grin faltered and those eyes widened, as if he was experiencing his own fight-or-flight reflex. I felt my body coil in response, ready to leap should he try to make a run for it. I didn't know what had given me away and didn't care, but I was ready, now, public be damned, to end Blessing as expediently as possible.

But then, instead of backing away or simply turning to run, Blessing smiled at me, that flush spread across his face again, bright enough to read by on a dark night, and I suddenly understood. I added two and two together and got a number as perplexing as it was horrifying. "We've, uh, got some really great specials going on today. Are you in the mood for coffee, or tea—or maybe cocoa? It's definitely a hot cocoa kinda day." He laughed a bit, still looking down at his pad. When he snuck a glance up at me, his pupils were wide and dilated, and my suspicions were confirmed. "We've also got soup and sandwiches—"

"I have to go," I said and stood up.

"Well, have a nice day," Blessing called as I walked swiftly away.

⁂

Two days later found me back at the Java Cave.

I stood stiffly in front of the picture window, looking in till I caught Blessing's eye. When he saw me, he looked surprised, but then smiled and finished up with his customer and came outside.

"Hello again," he said, seeming amused, and I smiled uncomfortably.

"Hi."

He gestured at the tables. "Gonna have a seat and let me bring you a cuppa joe, or are you gonna dash off again?"

I let my body answer for me, and sat. And Blessing grinned.

⁂

"Um. I guess I'll have a coffee, black."

"Really? No cream or sugar?"

"No. Why?"

"I had you pegged for a cream-and-sugar man."

"A— why?"

"No reason. Small, medium, or large?"

⁂

"Say, do you like scones?"

"Uh. I don't know. I've never had one."

"What? *Never?*"

"Never."

"Well." Pause. "Well. Today might be the day to try one. Are you hungry?"

"I—"

"I'd say from the sound your stomach just made, you're *starving.* Lemme get you a pumpkin-spice scone to go with that cuppa joe. On the house."

"But—"

"I promise you'll *love* it."

"Chilly out today. Pretty soon, we're gonna probably bring the tables in for the winter."

"Really?"

"Yes, really. Don't look so blue! I promise the inside of the café's almost as nice as the outside. And definitely *warmer*."

"I dunno. I sorta like the chill."

"Hmm. Well, it certainly gives people a great excuse to find interesting ways to keep warm."

"Like coffee and pumpkin scones?"

"Among other things."

"Can I ask you a question?"

"I guess."

"What's your name? I mean, I've been wondering for the past few weeks. And I can't keep calling you *Mr. Coffee-Black-and-Pumpkin-Scone*, can I?"

"You can, if you like. It doesn't bother me."

"This is what I like about you, Mr. Coffee-Black-and-Pumpkin-Scone: my sarcasm rolls right off you."

"What would *you guess* my name is?"

"Hmm. I dunno. Maybe, *Rory*?"

"Uh, no."

"You *look* like a Rory."

"Looks can be deceiving."

"I dunno, something about you is giving me a fairly strong *Rory*-vibe."

"I assure you my name isn't *Rory*."

"Well, if it's not, then what *is* it?"

Long pause. "Andrew."

"Pleased tameetcha, Andrew."

Another long pause. "Likewise, Aaron."

"See ya later, Andrew."

"Ditto, Aaron."

"Say . . ."

"Yes?"

"Do you like slam poetry?"

"I don't know. Never heard any. Why?"

"Because there's a slam happening here, tonight around seven, and they're usually really cool. I was thinking if you're at loose ends tonight, you might, come check it out."

"Oh. I dunno. Poetry's not my thing."

"I mean, I'll be here with some friends after shift, so there'll be someone here you know."

"I'll think about it. See ya later."

"Later."

⁂

"Well, well, you made it!"

"Yeah. I don't really feel like I fit in, though."

"No one here does—that's what makes it so great!" A bright laugh. "C'mon, Andrew, my friends and I are sitting over there. They've been bugging me about whether you might show up."

"Really?"

"Yep."

"You told your friends about me?"

"Um, yeah." Another laugh, this one slightly nervous. "Just that another friend they don't know yet might be showing up. One I thought they'd like."

"Are we?"

"Huh?"

"Friends. Are we friends?"

An oblique glance. "Here's where I'd normally be tempted to flirt with you shamelessly. But I won't."

"You *won't?*"

"In the interest of not scaring you off." A brief pause. "*Have* I scared you off, Andrew?"

"You don't see me running away."

"No, I don't." A brilliant smile. "C'mon, before my

friends die of suspense."

"Thanks again for the lift."

Silence, as the engine was shut off. "Anytime, Andrew."

Silence. Then: "Look, I dunno if you—"

"Maybe I should—"

"I'm sorry—"

"No, *I'm* sorry. What were you gonna say?"

"I, uh, was gonna invite you in. I mean, it's not much. Just like any other motel room. But if you want, we could, I dunno. Talk."

Silence again. Then: "I'd love to come in, Andrew."

As soon as the door closed behind Blessing, The Plan—which had taken weeks of patience and grooming of Blessing—began to fall apart.

When the door closed, Blessing looked at me, blushing and smiling nervously, and in that moment, he became *Aaron* in my mind. Not just *Blessing* or *Project Blessing*. He became this guy I'd been courting—for lack of a better word—for the past eight weeks, and whose friends I'd met, whose taste in poetry I now knew well from having attended several slams with him—one in which he'd even read his own work.

And even though all of it—the poetry slams, letting him drive me back to my motel, the continued trips to the Java Cave, and only when I knew he'd be on shift—was just a means to an end, I suddenly couldn't look at him objectively anymore. Couldn't look at him and see the life I'd been sent to still. The mass murderer I'd been sent to stop.

I could only see *Aaron*.

See those dark gray eyes as they got closer to me, smell the pervasive scent of coffee on him, feel the clothing-muffled heat of his body as it pressed against mine and his cool hands as they cupped my face, taste the mint tea–sweetness of his lips when they pressed mine then coaxed them open, hear the way his breathing hitched as I wrapped my arms around him and kissed him hungrily . . .

I didn't know what I was doing.

I didn't care.

It was as if a yawning chasm had opened within me, a gaping maw of loneliness and need, and it was imperative that I fill it with everything I'd been missing since Luka—

I firmly pushed Luka away, not for the first time. It wasn't hard. I'd had nearly half a century of practice.

Aaron's hands settled on my hips and he pulled me closer, till I was flush against him. He was hard, and not shy about that fact. But then, neither was I.

"I want you more than anyone I've ever known," he admitted on my lips, one hand sliding tentatively around to my ass. Then he was sucking a hickey into my neck and I was moaning almost helplessly. A soft, stuttered, "*Fuck*," escaped my lips when Aaron squeezed my ass *hard.*

I began backing us toward the creaky motel bed.

🐛 🐛 🐛

The next morning I woke up suddenly, completely aware, as I have every day of my life since The 'Phage caught up to my corner of America. My mind was clear and for the first time in almost fifty years my heart was full.

Spooned up behind me, holding me and snoring, Aaron Blessing slept on, his breath warm on my nape.

I turned under his arm until I was facing him, and watched him sleep.

He looked so innocent—and he was—just a college student struggling to pay for his education and still make ends meet. His face wasn't a face I hated and feared any longer. He wasn't my nemesis. He wasn't *world-killer,* anymore. He was simply *Aaron.*

And I couldn't stop touching his face.

Whatever his reasons for releasing The 'Phage on mankind, I couldn't believe them to be evil ones. Misguided, perhaps, but not evil. The nanites had, after all, made those of us who'd survived the initial infection close to immortal and nearly invincible. As well as irreversibly sterile. But it's entirely *possible* that Aaron hadn't intended that last part. It was *entirely* possible he had only *intended* to make humanity better, stronger, and happier.

He had tried to plan for every conceivable outcome—don't we all?—and failed. And I knew how that song went.

Knowing what I now knew of him, I was certain his intentions were pure. He was an idealist and an optimist. He saw only the best in people and situations. Or tried to, anyway. He ignored the downsides he didn't like and clung desperately to his sunny skies and rainbows.

The way he was clinging to *me*, now.

Suddenly I was certain that with proper guidance, and, yes, manipulation, he could be steered away from any research into nanotech. I had gathered that at this point in his college career he was choosing from several different options. And even just a little *nudge* in a different direction—even one from a lover? Friend with benefits? Random guy he'd fucked?—might be enough to alter the course of human history. I didn't know what I was to him, or what, if anything, *last night* had meant to him, but I knew what it meant to *me*.

I knew I had to *try*.

I eased out from under his arm and out of bed, and got dressed quickly and quietly. I let myself out of the room just as my stomach began to growl, and stepped into the cold, overcast morning. Directly across from the motel parking lot was a twenty-four-hour diner that made waffles like I hadn't had since I was a kid.

I wasn't equipped to *make* Aaron breakfast, but I supposed he'd appreciate the gesture, nonetheless.

And while I waited for breakfast, I would think more on how to stop The 'Phage without killing Aaron. I was certain I could do it. I was certain that I could save the world and Aaron in one fell swoop if I could just figure it all out. Figure out what could've made such an unassuming young man set out to make humanity over into impervious, deathless freaks. And stop it.

And so I didn't notice the car speeding unsteadily toward me, until it was entirely too late to do anything but *understand*.

See, we'd never *understood* Aaron Blessing's motivations. Hadn't had anything so useful as a psychological profile to tell us what could prompt *him*, of all people, to kill the world while trying, ostensibly, to save it. We'd never understood, and thought we never would.

But as that car bore down on me, *I* understood. I knew not only Aaron's motivating factor, but that I'd let my mission slip not just a little, but disastrously. I knew, in one final, white-hot second, the true scope of my failure and the price mankind would pay for it. I knew that despite what the Institute had theorized, time was, indeed, a fixed phenomenon, and that one couldn't change it, only serve its ends.

I knew all that, and knew it was too late. Too late to tell Aaron that letting heartbreak rule you is a folly none can afford. That we can't let loss, even so catastrophic a loss as *love*, make us over into automatons. Or monsters.

Or gods.

We can't—

PART II

THE PLANTS

THE FiELD OF VENGEANCE

STANLEY B. WEBB

Pa awoke in the dark of the morning. Ma was already in the kitchen. He got out of bed, and found his overalls. As he was getting into them, his big toe caught in the torn knee. He swore.

"Is that you?" Ma called.

He opened the bedroom door, and squinted in the candlelight.

"It's me. I just tore these pants some more."

"I'm sorry; I've been out of thread."

Ma was already in her work clothes. With a cast iron skillet in one hand and a nubby wooden spoon in the other, she stood over the wood-fired cook stove. Steam from the teakettle wreathed her head.

"You shouldn't have let me sleep in," he said.

"You could use the rest."

Pa looked at the plank table. Four places were set. The chairs were empty.

"You let the boys sleep in, too?"

"It's going to be a hard morning."

"Life is hard."

He went across the kitchen, to the boys' room. The dog was curled up outside the door. Her eyes rolled up at Pa, and her tail thumped. Pa bent down and stroked her nose.

"Good Shepherd."

He opened the door with a bang.

"Time to get up!"

Hank began to cry.

"I don't want to," said Tom.

Pa snapped, "I don't want to either! Neither does Ma, and if Shep could talk, she'd say the same. Winter's coming, and we need to fill the pantry."

"Listen to your father," said Ma.

Pa said, "They will."

He took his place at the table. Ma filled his plate with fried potatoes and fish. The boys emerged as she served their places. They were dressed in old denim pants and cotton shirts. She poured tea for everyone, then seated herself.

They all bowed their heads and joined hands.

"Our Father who art in Heaven," prayed Pa. "We thank you for this meal, which you have provided for us. We ask forgiveness for all of our sins. We pray that you will watch over us today, and make this harvest bountiful. In Your Son's name we pray. Amen."

"You forgot to pray for Shep," said Hank.

Pa bowed his head.

"Please watch over Shep, as you will watch over us. Amen."

The family ate in silence. When they were done, a few pieces of potato remained on Tom's plate.

"Finish that," said Pa.

Tom complained, "It's burned."

Pa struck the table. Ma and the boys jumped.

"Wasting hard-won provender is the worst sin. Finish it!"

Tom obeyed.

Pa stood up, and pushed his chair in. His family rose with him.

"Let's get it over with," he said.

He led them outside. The dark morning air turned their breaths to steam. A gust of wind guttered Pa's candle and whirled a column of dust across the barren yard, to the property's south border. The creek that flowed there rippled under the fading moonlight.

Shep looked into the eastern darkness and growled.

They crossed the beaten yard. Pa tugged the barn door open and set the candle up on a shelf. The barn was nearly empty. Half a cord of firewood leaned in the rear. Empty metal bins were lined up along another wall.

The family helped each other into their armor suits, which were made of rusty stovepipe and faded motorcycle helmets with scratched Plexiglas face shields. Leather gloves served as gauntlets. Pa checked everyone's fit, ensuring that there were no chinks or loose straps that might be seized. Then he took a pair of razor-sharp hand scythes down from their shelf and gave one to Ma.

Hank and Tom took a pair of ten-foot-long aluminum torches from a corner. The end of each torch was encased in greasy charcoal. They knocked the charcoal loose and replaced it with lard-soaked rags. Pa lit the torches with the candle, which he then blew out.

They walked to the east. Hank and Tom held their torches high, and the wind stretched their flames into flags. Shep was close beside them, her back up, and her tail between her legs.

Suddenly, Shep charged ahead and barked at something in the naked dirt.

Pa squatted beside her. She was barking at a blade of young grass, which had sprung up in the hard-packed earth. He uprooted the blade. "Good girl."

Shep darted ahead again. Pa found a small dandelion, which he also uprooted. Shep barked again.

"Pa," said Ma. "You can get those little ones in the daytime. We have to harvest while it's still dark."

"You're right. Shep, heel!"

The dog came to his side. They passed several more

young plants, but Shep only growled.

A wall of intertwined crops towered from the darkness ahead. The varieties were traditional, but grew in excess of ten feet. The family halted on the beaten earth, twenty feet away from the barrier. Shep bristled all over.

"You boys stay back," whispered Pa. "Only use your torches if we have trouble; the flames will rouse the field, just the same as sunlight. Ma, we'll concentrate on beans, squash, and all the potatoes we can get. Then, we'll go for peas and carrots, and corn if you can reach it."

"Can we have some popcorn?" Tom asked.

"We'll try to grab a few ears," said Pa. "May God be with you, Ma."

"And you."

They advanced on the field. The boys stopped at a distance of ten feet, with their torches upright. Pa and Ma continued. He turned to the left, while she went right. Tom kept pace with Pa, and Hank followed Ma.

Pa first found a tangle of Hubbard squash vines. He pushed the quilled vines aside, scythed through the wrist-thick stem of a fruit, then bent in under the leaves. The vines' ivory pins scratched his back armor. He lifted the squash with both hands, turned, and rolled the fruit out onto the beaten earth.

Shep charged over to investigate.

Pa whispered, "Easy, girl."

He moved on quickly, harvesting three more big squash before reaching the end of the vines. He found some good pie pumpkins next. The veins of the leaves were armed with scarlet thorns. Pa harvested a clutch of pumpkins.

Next, there was a row of bean-infested cornstalks. Each heart-shaped bean leaf held a razor's edge. The corn leaves were serrated machetes. Pa cut the beans free in clusters, and tossed them out onto the dirt. When he had harvested all of the beans that were within reach, he jumped for a few ears of corn. Each ear was no less than a foot and a half long. He opened one of the husks to check its variety: sweet corn.

Pa looked over his shoulder. He could now see all the way across their earthen farm, to the hardwood forest on the western border. The sky had turned blue-gray, with a wisp of high cloud glowing pink in the light of the still-hidden sun.

"Not much time left," he whispered.

Pa moved on urgently and found a carrot patch. The giant roots bulged two inches from the earth, each topped with a cluster of spiked maces. He pulled five of the carrots, and tossed them out onto the bare yard.

The sixth plant stirred, its maces searching with languid motion. Some of the spiked balls tapped each other with a sound like a telegraph. Pa froze until the carrot went still. He bypassed the rest, moving on to a row of peas, where he scythed frantically. One pea plant reached out a thorny tendril. Pa held still as it drowsily searched for him. When the plant withdrew, he moved on to a cabbage patch.

The cabbages were larger than his helmet. The outer leaves were thick and muscular, and lay at rest. The leaves were jaws, edged with black teeth. Pa looked west at the forest. The upper branches were catching the sun's first rays, and the trees were beginning to move. Wooden clicks sounded across the barren field. He stepped away from the cabbages, and backed out to where Tom stood.

"I've found popcorn!" Ma cried joyously from a distant part of the field.

"It's too late, get back!"

The field erupted with hooked, toothed, and thorny vines. They whipped out at Pa and Tom, but fell short by inches. Tom struck at the vines with his torch.

"Stop it," said Pa. "They can't reach us."

Ma screamed.

Pa swore, and ran for her. Tom and Shep followed. They found Ma's legs sticking out of the field. She kicked as it swallowed her. Hank screamed and stepped forward, striking with his torch. The field reached for him.

Pa thundered, "Get back! Both of you stay back!"

Ma disappeared.

Pa charged into the field. The vines seized him. He laid about with his scythe. The severed ends constricted. The corn stalks stabbed their leaves at him, and their symbiotic beans slashed at his face, making new scratches on his visor. He slashed down, to either side, dropping the attacking crops. The plants vibrated in death, creating an eerie scream, as caustic fluid spurted from their cut stumps. Pa went forward, and slashed again. He saw Ma's feet ahead. She dragged her toes, pulling furrows through the soil. Pa bent to grab her ankle with his free hand.

"I've got you!"

He pulled her backward. The vines holding her contracted, resisting him. Screaming in terrified fury, Pa slashed all around Ma, making leaves and juice fly. The plants' strength faltered.

A vine reached in from the side, and pinioned his scythe hand. He had to release Ma to free himself. The field yanked her out of sight. He went after her. Beans on each side disengaged from their host cornstalks, and leaped on him. Their cutting leaves and thorny runners meshed as a constricting net. He lost his balance, and fell to one knee. The beans slid down his arm, and bound his armor's joints.

Pa cried, "Throw the torches at my voice!"

The flames speared into the field. The plants jerked aside. One torch stuck into the ground beside Pa, and the other struck his back. The beans recoiled. Pa surged to his feet, and scythed about himself. The beans and cornstalks fell to shreds. Then, he cut a path after Ma.

He found a huge bush of unknown species. Its overall shape was like a walnut shell, and its canopy hung to the ground. Ma's feet disappeared into the bush. Pa cut his way in after her. The canopy was hollow beneath. His boots sank in the earth, which stank of rotting meat.

Ma was pinned on her stomach beside the main trunk. Barbed roots emerged and embraced her. Pa attacked them. The roots were soft, but tough.

A root circled him from behind, and seized his arm. He realized that he could not save both Ma and himself. Pa screamed, took his scythe in his off hand, and continued the fight. Another root found him.

With a furious howl, Shep charged under the bush, and attacked the roots. The thorns tore her mouth, and the juices boiled her tongue, but Shep was berserk. The bush released Pa, and took Shep. Pa cut Ma free, and dragged her away.

"Come, Shep!"

The roots had Shep entwined. She whimpered, and turned pleading eyes to him.

"I'm sorry, Shep, I'm so sorry."

The root began to pull Shep down into the soil.

Pa wept as he dragged Ma out of the field, into the morning sunlight. The boys cheered, and ran to hug their parents.

"Stay back!"

They obeyed.

"Where's Shep?" Tom asked.

"She didn't make it."

"It's all my fault," said Ma, as she lay trembling.

"It's all right," said Pa.

Hank said, "It's not all right, I want Shep!"

"So do I," said Pa.

The field tapped out unknown messages. Squeaks and moans answered from the western forest. Pa looked to the towering hardwoods, which lashed the sky in anger. The trees grew to the north as far as he could see. To the south, the forest ended at the creek. Beyond the creek, there grew a jungle of unclassified species, where a century-old ruin stood. The building's masonry walls had long ago crumbled due to invading roots, but the steel framework remained, serving as a trellis for lethal vines.

Atop the ruin, a billboard remained legible:

Genetic Engineering: Feeding Tomorrow!

"Winter is coming," said Ma. "How can we face it?"

"We'll fill our bins with another good harvest," said Pa.

"That's not what I meant."

"I know."

He looked at the smoke drifting from their chimney, then again at the forest.

"We need firewood."

GAIA'S GIFT

CHANTAL BOUDREAU

It was a very cold day, but it was not likely to snow. The air was just as dry as ever, as it had been for far too long. As Rhys exhaled an anxious breath, the moisture from his mouth clouded the air before him. His brassy brown eyes scanned the gray horizon with an expression of futility.

Rhys rubbed and slapped his mitts together, trying to take some of the chill off of his fingers. He hated having to head out on scrounging trips, now more than ever. It was too dangerous to take Allie with him anymore, but it was almost as dangerous to leave her at home alone. Their situation was an inconvenient miracle, but he wasn't about to dismiss it because it didn't fit well with their harsh lifestyle. There were some people out there who would have traded their very souls to have what Rhys and Allie were now expecting. Despite that, it scared him to death.

Rhys brushed away some of the ash that adhered to his bristled cheeks with the back of his mitt. He prayed for more charity from the divine, preferably in the form of good fortune in his search. Seeing the concentration of ash in the air rising, Rhys pulled his face mask back down over his mouth. His expression was grim. He hated going outside on a day like this, but he had little choice. The scrounging wouldn't wait.

The reason for his scrounging trip was twofold. The first and more pressing issue was that they were running low on food—a worry now that Allie was clearly eating for two. It had been easier to ration their food when he wasn't concerned about the pair of them going hungry now and then, but Allie couldn't do that anymore. Rhys refused to allow anything that might put her at risk.

Fighting his discomfort, Rhys felt his mind wander back to the place it obsessively dwelled. He could still remember the day that he had felt movement in her rounded belly against the palm of his hand. Before that moment, they had thought she was sick and dying, the more likely explanation for her symptoms with the way things were. When her abdomen had begun to distend, accompanied by nausea, they had just assumed it was a tumor, or some type of bowel disease.

Until they were sure it was not something like a tumor, Rhys had suffered in silence. He had been devastated, but tried to hide it from Allie. She'd remained positive, always believing things happened for a reason. Meanwhile, Rhys had been convinced he was losing his only reason for living. When the truth came out, they were both astounded. No one had been able to conceive since the world had gone to pot—no one. Why the powers that be decided they should be the blessed couple who finally could, Rhys had no clue.

Even though he knew he should be grateful for such a blessing, Rhys was actually terrified. He had never pictured himself as a parent before, and the world they were living in was certainly not one that welcomed the arrival of a child, even less so than the one he had come from. Things would have been different more than a decade ago. If he had gotten a woman pregnant, surely by accident, Rhys would have accepted his lot. He would have shouldered the burden of the new responsibility begrudgingly.

Then again, ten years ago, Allie would have been only thirteen and thirty-year-old Rhys would have been considered a horribly dirty old man if he had been involved with her. There were still days he questioned the reasonableness of being involved with her now. It hadn't been much better when they met, that age difference. She was only seventeen, and he was twice that, but they had both been so desperate for love and companionship that the age gap hadn't really mattered. Honestly, there were days when Allie seemed like a much older soul than Rhys. They both had to mature abnormally fast.

Rhys cringed at the thought. The war had changed everything; in particular, the biological weapon, Cascade or Bio-agent 329, was at fault. Their own government had created the menace and set it free, loosing it upon its unprepared victims. The scientists behind Cascade thought they could control it and target only the enemy, but they had been catastrophically wrong. Once released outside the constraints of a controlled laboratory environment, Cascade got away from them, and then it continued to spread. It jumped countries, then continents, and it even spanned oceans—a vicious, soulless killing machine intent on devouring the entire planet. Nothing in its path had been safe and anything that did withstand its deadly dehydrating effects was left struggling to survive in a world bereft of food and water, devoid of civilization.

Rhys had been a statistician before the Cascade incident. He was no life scientist, so he had no idea why he and Allie had been spared. He wished he knew, especially with what was coming. Perhaps it was a matter of genetics, a hopeful idea since that much would be shared with their child. Or perhaps it was something particular to their specific individual environments, a not so pleasant thought since they were often on the move. Either way, something about them had repelled the Cascade and it let them be. He could only pray that the same thing would apply to their son or daughter, once he or she had left the sanctuary that was Allie.

Rhys preferred to lean toward the idea that it was something genetic. Salvation was a very rare phenomenon. He had taken inventory of all survivors in his hometown and two of the neighboring towns during the first year following the incident. Based on original populations prior to Cascade, only about three out of every thousand people had survived the outbreak. If that held true everywhere, it meant that the global population had shrunk from seven billion to approximately twenty-one million in a matter of weeks.

And the death hadn't stopped there. Some of the initial survivors had dropped from starvation or thirst after the event. Others had died from illness caused by malnutrition and compromised immune systems, or untreated injuries of varying types. There were also those who had fallen at the hands of other survivors, while fighting over scarce resources. As with the humans, all but a small percentage of plant and animal life had been wiped out and most bodies of water were poisoned by the death that floated within. With nothing fresh worth having, canned goods and bottled water were like gold in the new world order.

There were a few other deaths that Rhys tried not to think about anymore. The last share of the mortality rate caused by Cascade could be attributed to those who just couldn't take it anymore. Some Cascade survivors had succumbed to despair, just as Rhys would have if Allie hadn't come along when she had. He probably still would, if he were to lose her again. He couldn't bear to think what he might do if complications with the pregnancy or childbirth stole her from him. Just a hint of such thoughts made his stomach do somersaults.

That was where the second reason for this scrounging trip came into play. His thankfulness for having her in his life was his other reason for this particular outing. In addition to scrounging food and water, he was looking for a gift, an extra-special gift. Beyond just celebrating their love and the anticipated addition to their family, Rhys had another motive to find her a present. Unlike most survivors, he had insisted on keeping track of every day that passed. He was probably the only person left who still followed the calendar. It was one of his ways of clinging to the past, and of holding on to his sanity. He wanted to know what he would have been doing from day to day if things hadn't changed. Like today, a week before Christmas, he likely would have been out shopping for gifts. This was the closest substitute he could muster.

The wind picked up a little bit, dousing him full in the face with the bluish-gray ash, one of the side effects of Cascade. Rhys was forced to close his eyes and readjust his facemask. While Cascade had failed to kill him in its typical way, it had brought him to the brink of starvation on more than one occasion, and its "dust" would readily suffocate him if he didn't protect himself.

Rhys felt around blindly for a rock to sit on and then rummaged around in his bag until his fingers made contact with his goggles. He slid them over his head, blinking rapidly to dislodge the ash from his lashes. It took a few moments before his vision cleared. He sighed, his eyes teary and stinging.

Rhys was still amazed that he had managed to endure the new world for as long as he had. He had been a pasty-faced, limp-limbed cubicle rat whose idea of roughing it was leaving his window open overnight and drinking his soda right out of the can. He hadn't even been camping since he was twelve. When he realized that he was the only person he knew still alive, he wanted to crawl into a hole and wish his existence away. How was he supposed to survive when the world he had known had turned into some bizarre and barren wilderness?

While not outdoorsman smart, fortunately Rhys was at least book smart. For that reason, when he found himself alone and feeling ultimately lost, his first inclination had been to head for the library. He'd packed up as much as he could carry, which included all of the nonperishables from his dingy bachelor apartment, and made his way through the choking, skin-blistering ash clouds to his new refuge. Once at the library, he went on a twelve-day research bender, searching for what he deemed the most useful books he could find to address his situation—all nonfiction and reference books, all about things like wilderness survival skills, first-aid skills, and indigenous plants and animals, unaware that many of them were dead too.

Rhys knew now that the only reason he hadn't suffocated by that point was because Cascade had filled in for the oxygenating functions of the near extinct plant life. He had stumbled across that information through one of the rare "friendlies" he met before Allie. They hadn't stayed together, Rhys and this stranger. It was struggle enough to keep one person alive, let alone two, and the man hadn't offered the same incentives as Allie, but they had chatted and hung out together for a couple of days, before parting ways. Rhys still wondered how involved the person had been in the creation of the bio-agent, to have that kind of knowledge. It was probably best not to know.

During his initial stay at the library, Rhys tried to absorb everything that he could. When his supplies ran out, he picked his favorite three books from the huge pile that he had pulled from the shelves. They would be added weight, but they were his own personal indulgence. Then he had gone out on his very first scrounging trip.

Rhys attributed his successes so far, merely living one day to the next, to those books and some lucky scrounging. He had left those books back with Allie at their current home. They didn't have a permanent place of rest, living like nomads, but they took the now tattered and worn books with them wherever they went. The tomes made up for Rhys's real-world ineptness and Allie's youth and inexperience on multiple occasions.

Those books were Rhys's security blanket, and they would certainly need the thick volume filled with first-aid instructions soon. He shivered at the thought. He had never dreamed of playing midwife, but unless they had some non-hostile survivor stumble upon their chosen shelter, one who was willing to stick around until the baby was born, Rhys was their only option. He wished they had a book specific to childbirth but that would mean returning to a more urban area. After their last unpleasant venture into such a place, about three years ago, he had no intentions of going back to more "civilized" areas. While they were moving on from their prior temporary home, he and Allie had accidently strayed into the outskirts of a city and been forced to use violence to fend off the crazed territorial survivors dwelling there. The pair had not escaped unscathed. Allie ended up with two broken fingers and Rhys barely made it out alive, with a severe gash in his head that took a long time to heal, even with stitches.

After that Rhys vowed to avoid the places that had been more populated before Cascade. The majority of stores and shopping malls had long been looted of anything of real value. He and Allie instead focused on independent residences—houses in the country, or cottages and cabins a little outside of what had been civilization. It had worked for them so far, keeping them out of trouble, even if it meant little chance of encountering friendlier faces as well.

The stinging and tearing finally stopped. His eyesight a little blurred by the bits of ash that adhered to the goggle lenses, but otherwise clear, Rhys got to his feet again. He found an area close to a lake—a dead one like all of the others—and was on the hunt for lakeside cottages. Many of them did not offer much for the scavenging, since they were vacation spaces and not equipped for regular daily living, but every now and then he came across one that belonged to someone who had sought to be a recluse. Those cottages were a virtual treasure trove of goods. Since the folks who had been living there didn't get out much and had stocked the cottage for regular year-long habitation, those places usually had plenty of non-perishables in their cupboards. Considering how little he and Allie had left to keep themselves going, Rhys was praying to whoever was listening for exactly that kind of a find.

"Give us an early Christmas gift," he murmured as he shifted his pack back up over his shoulders. "You've given us life again. Now please give us hope."

As he continued to trudge his way through the blowing ash, Rhys let his mind drift back to the day he first met Allie. He thought it somewhat ironic that he had been in a junkyard of all places when he stumbled upon his most precious find ever. He had been looking for some means of ending his life at the time. The loneliness and the pointlessness of everyday toils had overwhelmed his sense of reason. He hadn't wanted to commit suicide by confronting hostile survivors, although that would probably have guaranteed his death. That method could have ended badly, with him taking a gut shot and being left to die over the course of agonizing hours or even days. Rhys had wanted something that would be guaranteed to be quick and mostly painless. He had never carried a gun himself until he started traveling with Allie. On that particular day, she had been the one who ended up aiming one straight at his face.

"Go ahead, shoot me," he'd told her, swallowing hard and trying to remain collected. "You'll be doing me a favor. Just please try to make it as quick as possible. I'll admit, I'm a bit of a pussy. I'm not big on pain."

Allie had had that stray cat look: covered in dirt, somewhat emaciated with unidentifiable refuse tangled in her ash-blond hair. But her eyes were unforgettable, bright and green and fierce, despite what the rest of her looked like.

She had actually scared him more than one of the lean, cutthroat brutes you would run into if you dared travel through one of the cities. Rhys had always been terrible with women; he panicked around them, and that customary knot of fear had twisted around in his gut the moment she sprung up in front of him. She laughed at him later, when she found out that he had been more afraid of her than her gun.

How quickly Rhys had learned to love that laugh, but Allie hadn't mocked him on that fateful day. She had looked at him, quivering before her, with pity. That made him feel even worse.

"Come on—do it!" he said more harshly, wondering what she was waiting for. He twitched a little, blinking rapidly, and not because of the ash. "Hurry up! I'm not going to change my mind." He wouldn't have, even though he had been so terrified that he almost peed himself. Instead of shooting him though, Allie lowered the gun.

"Why? Why do you want to die?" she demanded. She eyed him carefully, passing judgment on him as the seconds ticked by. "You're not like the rest of them. Are you? You wouldn't use me for kicks, or hurt me for your own pleasure. And yet, you ask me to kill you? I'd never kill you. What a waste that would be."

Rhys's knees had gone weak with a mixture of relief and despair. Death would have been so much easier. There was a bestial part of him, however, that had still really wanted to live—it had just been overpowered at that moment by the rest of his negative emotions. He had hated Allie then, and had loved her for not shooting him, both at the same time.

"What do you mean?" he asked, his voice quavering.

Rhys hadn't been able to fathom how one more death would make a difference in the wasteland they were living in.

"You and I are two of the very few who were spared. We were meant to live," she insisted. "It's Gaia's gift. Throwing it away? Now that would just be plain ungrateful. I'll kill in self-defense, but I won't take the life of some arrogant fool who refuses to accept her blessing." She passed him the gun. "Do your own dirty work."

First threats, then pity, and finally shame—Rhys

hadn't been sure what to make of her little diatribe. He figured she was either new age flaky or tin foil hat crazy, but he learned to appreciate her soulfulness later, whether he believed in the things that she did or not. The fact that he couldn't understand her ways of thinking made her mysterious and heart-achingly beautiful. As bizarre as they were, her tactics had worked. Rhys shut down any notions of killing himself, and they left the junkyard together. They had stayed together ever since.

The cold was still biting at his extremities and a shiver ran through him from the chill. Rhys could make out the outline of some sort of small building in the distance through trees and swirling ash. He had hated snow once, for its cold wetness, but never as much as he despised the dry powdery residue that Cascade left behind. It was a constant reminder of all the damage that man and his ways of playing god had done. He could understand why Allie would have wanted to turn to some benevolent earth spirit for solace. Rhys was too rational to follow that path, but he would never try to deny Allie the pleasure. Their differences were what kept things interesting.

Now that Rhys had established where the cottage was, he set out in hopes that he might have found something to make his scrounging trip worthwhile. If this discovery offered enough bounty, he would fetch Allie and bring her back here, rather than try to drag excessive amounts of food and drink back to her. Even if the journey would be difficult and awkward for her at this stage, it would be worth it. More food immediately available meant less time he would have to spend away from her. Thinking of her all alone and more defenseless than she should be made him tense up, and he tried to distract himself with happier thoughts. They returned to his usual obsession.

He remembered when Allie had used that term for the second time, Gaia's gift. He had been tossing and turning restlessly, wrestling with the near debilitating idea that Allie was being taken from him by illness, when she had leaned into him and murmured into his ear.

"I'm not dying."

Rhys heard the jubilant grin in her whisper and he wondered if she had ventured so far into denial that she had convinced herself that was true. When he hadn't offered her a response after several seconds, Allie grabbed his hand, uncurled his fingers, and pressed them against her belly. When he felt the faint flutter there, Rhys recoiled away from her, afraid to believe what the sensation had suggested.

"It's life, not death," she said, capturing his eyes with her own. She had been enraptured with the idea; he had recognized that much.

She reached for his hand a second time, gently but firmly pressing the flat of his palm against her belly and holding it there. The subtle nudges were sporadic, but clearly not just muscle spasms.

"Gaia's given us another gift," Allie had declared.

Rhys wiggled his fingers in his mitt as he walked, phantom touches making them tingle when he recalled that moment. He had waited until she was asleep before he allowed himself to weep, partially out of gratitude that it was not some life-stealing tumor, but also out of fear that he would never be able to live up to the new responsibility that she had suddenly presented to him. He was no Adam, she was no Eve, and this was no Garden of Eden.

He paused for a moment, rubbing the cold away from his arms and gazing up at the ash that was drifting past him in the gray sky—no, definitely not paradise.

Rhys was pleased to see that the cottage was in reasonably good shape, although abandoned. It had not been maintained in many years, no doubt, but it had been very sturdily built to begin with. The decor was rustic but inviting: all stained wood, natural fiber linen, and treated leather. This had not been the summer cottage of some touristy vacationer. Rhys held his breath when he noticed what lined the walls. Every available space along each side of the room he first stepped into was end-to-end books. With a restrained yelp, Rhys moved farther into the room, shut the door, and then quickly pulled off his mitts. He let them fall to the floor as he ran his fingers along the spines there. It was a miniature library, with fiction and nonfiction of various types, and several reference manuals on botany and gardening. One of them had a list scribbled on an old envelope serving as a bookmark. It was marked "winter garden," and listed Latin names: *Hamamelis, Pieris japonica, Helleborus, Jasminum nudiflorum,* and, lastly, *Chionodoxa lucillae.* He looked each one up in the book, scanning over their pictures with great nostalgia. Not that he recognized any of these plants, he had never been a gardener, but just seeing the sight of greenery and blossoms again brought a tightness to his chest and a tear to his eye.

Forcing himself away from the books—they weren't what he had come for—he made his way into the kitchen and began to open some of the cupboards. By the third door, Rhys's hands were trembling, and when he reached the last one he had to grab the nearest chair to prop himself up, his knees were that wobbly. He had found the motherlode—a fully stocked larder. He wouldn't be bringing all of this back to Allie. It would take an impossible number of trips. When he left here, it would be to collect Allie and bring her here instead.

"Merry Christmas, Allie." He sighed.

Rhys pulled his mask off for a moment, in order to breathe deeply and laugh out loud. The sound seemed alien to his ears; he hadn't heard sounds of his own mirth in ages. He laughed so long and hard that his voice grew hoarse and his eyes started to water. He eventually managed to catch his breath as the compulsion to continue laughing eased off. He wandered toward the back door of the cottage, brushing away blissful tears.

He braced his hand there for a second, working at restoring his composure, before turning to leave to make his way back to Allie. That was when a flash of color outside caught the corner of his eye. Color? Outside? That wasn't right. There hadn't been any significant color outside since Cascade, most things dead, rotting, and coated in the bluish-gray ash. Rhys slipped his mask and goggles back on, and then headed out back to investigate.

Three steps was all it took for Rhys to get a full view of where the color was coming from—three steps that would change his life forever. His eyes took in the wonder of a sturdy plant with lush verdant foliage and brilliant blossoms that had stretched their way up through accumulated ash. The bright, star-like flower was glorious in contrast to the bland dust surrounding it, just like its name suggested. The vision brought words from the book to his lips.

"*Chionodoxa lucillae*, glory of the snow."

He wondered if it was like him and Allie, a rare survivor that had withstood the worst that Cascade could offer. He dropped to his knees on the ash-littered ground beside it. It looked healthy and strong. That was when he realized there were other bulky forms, smidgens of green, white, pink, yellow, and red, peeking out in places from underneath the clustered dust. Hyperventilating slightly in his excitement, Rhys hastily brushed the ash away, revealing a selection of plants underneath, all pristinely formed and ruggedly healthy. He had found an entire garden immune to the effects of Cascade. He had found a little patch of paradise. Now he had even more reason to bring Allie back there, and a new cause for gratitude.

"Gaia's gift," Rhys said.

And this time, he believed it.

PART III

THE BEASTS

THERE IS A LIGHT

TOM WORTMAN

There is light.

*   *   *

There is light. There are eyes.

*   *   *

There is light. There are eyes. They are gray-blue like storm clouds rolling in.

*   *   *

There is light. There are eyes. They are gray-blue like storm clouds rolling in. It is a reflection. Those are my eyes. This is my face. The room is quiet. I don't remember how I came to this place. I don't remember a lot of things. I know my name is Christopher.

My family called me "Chris." We were four. I can't remember their faces or voices or names. I remember a house on a hill. I remember having my own room. I remember trips to the zoo. Our tiny hands pressed against thick bars. We were two. The other was a "she." She was older.

I remember a disease, a virus, a genetic flaw. She

found me on the couch. "Christopher's lips are blue," she said. She wasn't worried, only stating a fact. She was smart like that.

There were hospitals. There were tubes running from my arms and my chest and my mouth and my nose. I fought them—the doctors, nurses. I bit. I clawed. I cried. She calmed me. She whispered it would be okay. I believed her because she was my sister and she was brilliant. That was the word they used to describe her.

I made her promise to keep taking me to the zoo. She promised.

All this remembering makes me want the darkness.

There is light. The floor is cold. Brown halos stain the ceiling. Sometimes water drips from those stains. It is quiet outside. It is quiet in here, except for my thoughts. They are full of remembering. I dream of remembering.

We are older now. She wore a navy-blue gown and smiled to us and waved and hugged me. I couldn't stand up. It hurt to try. She sat in my lap and introduced me as her brother and the reason for all this. She let me hold her diploma. It looked so simple, embossed paper and swirling lettering. She assured me it meant a lot. The other two, the older ones, pushed me and I am seated. We followed her across grass. Many people smiled at her and shook her hand. They stared at me sometimes. They didn't meet my eyes, only scanned my legs.

One man looked me in the eye. He was much older. He limped and held a cane. She talked to him in hushed tones. Their eyes watched me. They nodded a lot. I was talked about in the third person. I heard them, but understood none of it.

They said she was brilliant and could do anything. She wanted to fix me. That I remember. I don't like thinking of her because it makes me want the darkness. In the darkness, I remember her.

There is light. It is morning. Curtains are drawn over the window. The window is across the room. I push against the floor. I am sitting. I watch my legs and am scared.

In my remembering, my legs don't work. They stopped working when I was young. I grew up in a wheelchair. My arms grew strong and my legs grew weak. Sometimes I refused to get out of bed and my parents fought and it was she who whispered in my ear and helped me dress and sat me in my wheelchair. She drove me to school, in a van that helped me get inside. Sometimes she kept driving. We wandered the zoo. We talked. We planned. We dreamed. I dreamed of legs. She dreamed of college.

They couldn't afford to send her to school. This is what my parents fought about. I cost money: money for her, money for them. So she worked hard. She won scholarships and worked part-time. She promised to fix me, like I was some broken doll.

I watch my legs and am scared. I think about bending my arms. I bend my arms. I think about wiggling my fingers. I wiggle my fingers. I grab loose hospital scrubs. I pull the knees up. My legs fold. My feet lay flat on the floor. I lean back into my arms and hands. It is time to try. I try to remember standing. I can't. It's been too long.

I push. There is weight. I am heavy because I am tired. My hips flex. My quads flex. I fall forward. My knees hit the ground. It hurts. Hurting is good. I push again. My toes curl under me. I stand. I am standing. Standing is good. I take a step. The world seems so high. I am taller than I imagined. I take another step. My feet drag on the floor. I tell them to walk. I walk to the curtains. They slide on runners.

Outside, there is light. Outside, buildings are skeletal and vacant like starving children. Cars are rusting and abandoned. Plants grow across windows and parking lots and streetlights and fire hydrants. I can't remember what happened.

🐦 🐦 🐦

There is light. It comes from the window. Today I want to leave this room. A bed is pushed against the wall. Blankets and sheets hang from one end, the end where I started. There are computer monitors and an IV bag. I was alone in this room. I am still alone in this room. I want to leave. I don't want to be alone.

The door is closed. Sometimes I hear footsteps beyond the door. This is at night. During the day, it is quiet. Right now it is quiet. I cross the room. I've been practicing. I've been trying to run, but I don't know if I'm doing it right. I'm scared of breaking again.

I walk to the door. The latch is cold. I pull. It clicks. The door doesn't open. I pull harder. It won't move. I remember movies and television shows and endless days in front of a flickering screen. I put one leg on the wall. My hands hold the handle. I push with my leg against the wall. I yank with my hands.

I fall. My ass hurts. The door is open. I walk a long hallway. I thought it would be a hospital. It is not. It is some laboratory. Large machines sit under layers of dust and cobwebs. Stools are upended. Laptops are smashed along the ground. I try to remember, but can't. I don't know if I ever saw this before.

I remember her disappearing. She accepted a job in Europe. Europe had looser laws. Her voice rings through my head. She promised to return and take me to the zoo. I lived with my parents. They grew old. I stayed in my room. I watched television and movies. Sometimes I got on the computer, but it all bored me. I wanted to be outside. I wanted to see animals beyond the crows and nuthatches and jays that perched on my window. I wanted to be on my own, like her. I wanted to see the places in her postcards or in the emails she sent.

Darkness comes. My room will be safe. Tomorrow I will try another floor.

There is light. It streams through windows and open doorways. I do not explore. I only walk. I don't run. I am not ready. There are elevators, but they don't light up. I take the stairs. In there it is dark, but nothing moves except me.

All the floors are the same. There are machines and offices and storage closets. There is broken glass and abandoned coffee mugs and sometimes a photograph in a frame. I do not recognize any of this. It doesn't cause remembering. Sometimes I hear something behind closed doors. I don't open them. Maybe they are like me and need to be left alone. Maybe they aren't like me and I need to leave them alone. Either way, the doors remain closed.

I pass the time by remembering. My parents grew old. They shouldn't have been driving. I couldn't drive for them. There was snow and ice and darkness. They did not survive. She did not attend the funeral. She called. Her voice was tired. Her words were regretful and worried. I assumed they had savings. I didn't know they had so much debt. I caused their debt.

We sold the house. We sold their belongings. Even then, I couldn't afford much. Not even a computer. Not even a phone. There was nothing to keep in contact with her. We lost touch.

There is light. Red letters break the darkness. They mark the exit. I hear footsteps in the hallway. They sound heavier than mine. They don't move like mine. Maybe they are more acquainted to walking.

I wait. I barely breathe. This is not my room. It is empty. I checked before the darkness came. I barricaded the door. I rolled a desk across the room. I upended it. I pushed it against the door. I grabbed a letter opener. This must've been an office. I pulled a filing cabinet across the room. It cut the linoleum in deep gashes. I tipped it over. I pushed it against the desk and waited for the darkness.

Now that it is here, I wait for the light to return. I wait for the footsteps to disappear. I lie on the floor. I count my breaths. Something claws at the door. It tries the handle. It tries to push. It isn't strong enough. I wait. The letter opener is cold in my hand. It has an ivory handle and a brass blade. One stab and it will probably bend. One stab and I can run. One stab is better than none.

The footsteps disappear. I wait. There is darkness.

There is light. Everywhere there is light. It is warm on my arms and on my face. My shoes are nearby. My bare feet are cold. The earth is cold. The long grass is cold. I don't mind because it feels good. I want to lie down and start the darkness, but I must keep moving. Moving is good. I move. I walk.

Clouds move above me. I sweat. I cover miles. High buildings give way to small buildings. There are houses. There are train tracks. There is a hill.

I climb the hill. In the distance the sun sets. The darkness will come. The sun falls below the horizon. The light is red and pink and orange and beautiful. I am too far from my room to return. I must find a place to hide before the darkness.

There is light. There are lights carried by men. I watch them. They don't talk. They move in silence. They wear clothes to blend with darkness. They are not darkness. They will not find me. I am ready if they do. The letter opener is in my hand. I tucked it in my waistband. If I need to stab, one should drop their flashlight. If I need to stab, I can grab the fallen flashlight. I can use it to hurt the other.

There is noise. The noise is not far away. It is not the men with flashlights. They turn off their lights. They are scared. There are footsteps. They are heavier than mine. They are slow. They are deliberate. They are near.

The men whisper. They are scared. They should hide. I don't want them to hide with me. I remain quiet.

The footsteps grow louder. It is close. The pavement shakes. The men crawl under a skeletal bus. Their eyes are wide. Their eyes see me. They are scared.

The ground shakes. The pavement buckles. It walks on hooves. The hooves are wide. The hooves are strong. The hooves are darkness. They crackle with energy, with fire, with electricity. The men are scared.

I remember. She liked horses. She wanted one for Christmas. She wanted one for a birthday. We couldn't afford one. This was my fault.

Darkness bathes it. Its coat is darkness. Its eyes are darkness. It is darkness. It is beautiful. It is larger, stronger, better than nature intended. It moves in a blur. It bucks the bus. The bus topples. The men are exposed. They are beyond scared. The horse moves fast. They can't move fast enough. There is no fight.

Hooves fall. Pavement buckles. The men are gone. They are there, but they are gone. Their blood glistens in the moonlight. The horse moves on. It runs through the night. It shimmers in the darkness. The darkness is its home.

🐴 🐴 🐴

There is light. I stop hiding. Something came during the darkness. Not the horse. Something dined on the dead men. Something left ribs and a skull picked clean and scraps of clothing and two flashlights. I grab one. I walk. I remember.

I sold their house. I moved to a home. These homes were full of people like me. Broken dolls. A broken doll house. I lived on a bottom floor. Rent was cheap. I had no money coming in. Money ran out. I lost my home. I was left to the streets. I slept on couches and under awnings. I found hiding spots. Places away from ones that would hurt me. I hid, from ones that would take my things and ones that would leave me thrashing on pavement.

I was forgetting her voice. I was forgetting their faces. I was forgetting who I was. I was failing.

I walk all day. It is quiet. I crest a hill. I see a long distance. A crow flies straight. I watch it. It passes a barrier. There is a tower there. The barrier wraps a halo around the tower. This is where I want to be. I feel it. I know it. This is a home.

Dusk comes. I watch the tower. Lights spark along its length. I must hide. Darkness is coming.

🦅 🦅 🦅

There is light. The light is mine. It is a mistake. I was tired. I forgot. Hands grab me. This is bad. They pull me from my hiding spot. The ground is rough. Their hands are rougher. Their faces are roughest. They are three.

They ask no questions. They seek no answers. They have words.

"Ugly son of a bitch."

"One of them."

"That's one of our flashlights."

They kick. They punch. It hurts. I try to stand. A heavy flashlight slaps my face. It hurts. I fall. I fail. I flail. Their boots are heavy. Something cracks. Something hurts. I stop breathing.

The ground shakes. They stop. I find my breath. I taste blood. I watch them. Their eyes are scared.

It is fast. They are not. It charges them. They fan out. One pulls out a bent stick. It is metal. It is iron. Another holds a long knife. It glistens. It is sharp. The third turns to the shadows.

I stay to the ground. I hurt.

It is the same from last night. It is beautiful. It is darkness. They lunge. It bucks. They slash. It kicks. It stamps. One falls. He is hurt. His chest is broken. He labors to breathe. He is done. His stick is close. It is a fire poker, hooked and hard and covered in ash. It is in my hand. It is cold. I am kneeling.

The other swipes. He swings. He attacks. He is desperate. He stabs. There is blood. It glows in the darkness. It is unnatural. It glows. It glows. It glows. The horse cries. It rears. It kicks. It is desperate. The third springs. He holds a chain. It rattles around the horse's neck. The man flexes. The horse gasps. I stand.

I swing. The second falls. I stab. The second is dead. The horse spins. It bucks. It is scared.

I watch. I time. I calculate. I swing. The hook bites the third's calf. I yank. The man falls. His flesh is torn. His eyes are scared. I stab. I stab. I stab. It is done.

The horse pants. I pant. Its nostrils flare. It smells me. I am hurt. It is hurt. It bleeds. I am broken. I hold the stick. It is covered in blood that does not glow. I drop it. The horse relaxes. I back away. It watches me.

I find my hiding spot. The horse leaves to the darkness. I turn to the darkness.

There is light. It is a dream. It is remembering. Red and blue and red and blue in a cycle never ending. They are uniformed. They are two. They grab me. They pull me to standing. I cannot stand. I try to tell them. They don't listen. I fall. They talk on radios. Scratchy voices reply. They pull me to my feet. I fall. They won't listen. They fold me into the backseat. My hands are cuffed. They drive. I sit.

They ask for identification. I have none. They ask my name. They ask for spelling. They smudge ink on my fingers. They roll my fingers on paper. One holds me while the other snaps my photo. They lay me on a bunk. There is no pillow. The bed is canvas. There are stains. They close the door. It is barred. It is locked.

She arrives. She smiles. She charms. They talk down to her. She talks above them. Their words patronize. Their eyes linger on her body, on her breasts, on her tight jeans. They are assholes. Those are her words. They become defensive. They threaten. She speaks on her phone. Her words are fast and educated and loud.

There is a delay. She sits in the lobby, on a plastic chair. There is silence. She smiles at me. I wave. She waves. She touches her eyes. Her eyeliner runs. I look away.

He is handsome. He is confident. He wears a suit. The tie is tightly knotted. He talks to the cops. The cops are deferential. He points to me. He talks about my legs. She pipes in. She adds medical terms. There are threats. Another cop arrives. He wears brass. He has a belly and gray hair. He yells at the younger ones. He unlocks the lock. He helps me up. He finds a wheelchair. He carries me to it.

I am in a hotel room. She is in a hotel room. The suit is in a hotel room. We talk. She hugs me. She introduces me to him. She introduces him to me. They are lovers. I can tell. She is glad she found me. She'd been looking. That's what the suit explains. She helps me take off my sweatpants. I wear boxer shorts. They are stained and frayed. My legs are thin. The suit sits on a bed. He asks questions. His eyes linger on my legs. He looks me in the eye. He looks at my legs. They are scarred and horrible and I apologize. He dismisses the apology. I should never apologize. Those are his words.

They talk in educated words. They talk in the now. They talk in the future. They talk like she can fix me. Not maybe, but tomorrow or next week. She explains it will hurt. She talks about clinical trials and Europe. She explains mice and survival rates and injections.

He talks money. Not his fees, but how much she could make. He talks grand schemes about monetization. They look at me and I am lost. I am tired. I am tired even in my dream. They ask me and I agree. I don't care about pain. I care about being fixed. Those are my words.

🐾 🐾 🐾

There is light. I should hurt. I don't. I touch my body. I probe. I prod. I pull off my scrub top. My skin is smooth and pale. I am not even bruised. My ribs are solid. Last night they weren't. They crackled and hurt. I couldn't sleep on my side.

I was a broken doll and now I am not. I want to find the horse. I want to know if it even carries a scab. I want to touch its flank and look for a scar. I want to know.

I sit. I stand. I walk on two legs. I breathe. I haven't eaten. I'm not hungry. I'm not thirsty. I just am. I know it was her. Maybe I don't know what she did, but I know she fixed me.

I find the iron stick. Blood cakes it. The bodies are picked clean. I contemplate the culprit. I wonder if I am the culprit. I don't think I am. I may be in denial. My mind is a mess.

I pick up the stick. It is in my hand. It is directed at my leg. I can't do it. I drop it. It rings against the pavement. I find their knife. It is big. It is heavy. It glistens in the sunlight. The horse's blood should be on it. It is not. It is clean.

I run it across my left hand. I am right handed. I bleed. It glows. It looks like fire, like lava, like the horse's blood. I taste it. It tastes like blood. I watch myself bleed. It drips to the ground. It drips again. It sizzles. It smokes. It disappears. My skin melts together. It is fast, like someone zipping a zipper. There is no scar. There is no scab. There is my unbroken skin.

My heart beats. It surges. I'm scared, but not in the way the men were. I'm scared because I don't know what I am. I'm scared because I don't know what she made me into. I stop thinking.

I grab the stick. It is heavy. It is cold. I don't think. I don't think. I don't think. I swing. It smashes. My ankle shatters. I fall. There is pain. Bones point from my skin. I can't stand. I bleed fire. I bleed lava. I bleed electricity. I want to scream. I don't.

My ankle throbs. It jerks. It folds together. It hurts.

The bones tuck back in the skin. The skin melts together. It tingles. It is healing. I am healing. All of it stops. All the sensations cease. I simply am. I stand on it. I walk on it. I run on it. I am healed. I am scared.

I am one of them. That's what the men said. I am one of them. That's what I realize. I am one of them and don't know what they are. I know there are more of them. They walk the darkness and own the night.

❧ ❧ ❧

There is light. Torches illuminate the barricade. Men pace the edges. They squint at the night. I watch them. I watch the darkness because it is my home.

Shadows move in the night. It is their home too. There are winged ones. They swoop and flutter. They are bathed in darkness. They are small, but many. One can't do damage, but maybe many can. They are crows. They are ravens. They are black birds of the night.

The horse returns. It glides through the streets on heavy hooves. I approach. Its nostrils flare. It smells me. It is not afraid. It lets me touch its flank. It lets my hands roam. I find no scar. I find no scab. I find no wound. It trots off to the night.

There are others. I hear them. I hear fur and feather sliding through darkness. There is a menagerie. I am but one and they are many. We are alike and we do not hunt each other. The shadows hunt something else.

They hunt the men with flashlights. They hunt the men with flickering torches. Some of the men live behind the barricade. Many still live in the broken streets. These I fear. These are ones that seek to hurt.

I wander. I watch. They live in hunger and terror and filth. They hide in abandoned buildings or skeletal busses or clustered tents. They fear the shadows. The shadows hide. The men burn fire in a wide ring around their encampments. They hope it helps.

I watch a group. They dress in black, but I can see their fear. They whisper and point and take their time.

They hunt a bird. This one is large. This one is alone. They throw a net over it. It can't fly. It tries. It squawks. They attack. There is a fight. There is blood. They stab. Its blood glows. The net burns. A beak strikes. There is torn flesh. There is a scream. There is blood. The wound drips and oozes and does not heal.

The men stab. They cut. They injure. It screams. On the roofs, on the lampposts, on the useless telephone lines, others watch. The men strangle. The men chop. The body is headless. The head is bodiless. The bird is dead. They toss the body in a canvas sack. One throws it over a shoulder. They walk away. One holds a bleeding arm. They whisper. They see the roofs and lampposts and useless telephone lines. They see the gleaming eyes of the darkness. They are scared. Fear smells sweet. It is sickly sweet like cotton candy or melted caramels. It is not to my taste.

The men disappear. A bird swoops down. It waddles to the bodiless head. It sniffs the eyes. It nudges the neck. It squawks. The others squawk. The one on the ground, it screams. The others scream.

I hurt. My heart hurts. I feel tears, but they don't fall. I walk to the bird on the ground. It stares at me. The others watch me. It nudges the head towards me. I kneel. It is small in my hand. The eyes are still open. It never blinked. A flap of man-flesh hangs from its beak. It always fought. It fought until the end.

I drop the head to the ground. The one on the ground hops near. It tears the man-flesh away. It gulps. It eats. It watches me. It turns to the barricade. I turn to the barricade. There is weight on my shoulder. I know it is the bird. It does not bite. It does not attack. It only grips. It is darkness. They are darkness. I am darkness.

There is light. I sleep through it. I am not afraid.

There is light. I turn over. I sleep in shadows.

* * *

There is light. I hide in darkness.

* * *

There is light. It fades. I wake. It is dusk. It is their time. It is my time.

I remember many things now. My name is Christopher. My family called me "Chris." My sister's name was Mary. If she is alive, she is still Mary. She was brilliant. This became obvious when she brought me to her laboratory.

A nurse, an orderly, a doctor helped me to a bed. They wrapped a blanket over me. They injected me with liquids. The said it would work. Only Mary's eyes were sure of this. The rest feared they were wrong. They feared she was wrong. They feared of ethics and regulations and a million excuses Mary didn't care about. She cared about me. She cared about her broken doll.

The day before the injections and the laboratory and tubes running from my arms and my chest and my mouth and my nose, Mary wheeled me across the city. It wasn't my city. It was just a city—anonymous in its chain restaurants and its numbered streets and too many coffee shops. People yielded to us, to my wheelchair, to her looks, to my broken limbs. She talked fast. She always talked fast. She talked about our childhood.

"Remember how we wanted pets." It was not a question. It was a thesis statement. "I wanted a horse," she said. "Do you remember what you wanted?"

I did. I wanted a tiger. It seemed as realistic as her horse. It seemed as realistic as walking again.

She laughed when I remembered. She laughed when I told her my logic. She laughed when there was nothing more to say.

Before I went to sleep, with the injections and the laboratory and the tubes, she reminded me again. "As realistic as you walking again?" This was a question intended to jog my memory.

I nodded. I couldn't talk. Fear strangled my voice.

She touched my legs and told me to count backwards from ten. She had gray-blue eyes like me. I had gray-blue eyes like hers. They reminded me of storm clouds. I closed my eyes while looking at hers.

There is light. It is flame. It flickers across their faces as they squint at the darkness. I hide in the darkness. They patrol the border. I patrol the perimeter. They look out. I look in.

The birds are near. They sit on darkened lampposts and useless telephone lines. They watch me. They watch the men. They wait. They wait for me to learn, to adapt, to act.

Up in the tower there is a light. There are many lights. There are glass windows and electricity and the hum of life. Way up top, there is another light. It shines like a beacon. Someone special lives there. That light never goes out.

The border is wood. It is made of lumber hastily nailed together. It is made of pine or mahogany or oak. It is made from reclaimed doors and smashed furniture and splintering pallets. It is kindling. It will burn.

In my hand is a knife. In my hand is paper. I cut myself. I bleed. It glows. It falls to the paper. The paper burns. I am made of fire. Fire burns kindling. I stamp out the fire. There is darkness. I hear something in it. Something watches me. I am not afraid. It is one of us.

There is light. There is heavy breathing. The horse runs. I try to keep up. The men chase. They hold flaming sticks. They hold flashlights. They hold large sticks. I hold a knife. I run in hospital slip-ons. They run in shoes and boots. The horse runs in fear. There are too many: too many for me, too many for the horse, too many for us.

The horse cuts right. This is a dead end. This is a mistake. I keep running. I take the next street. I hope to draw the men. It doesn't work. They follow the horse. It was always the horse they wanted. I could feed one or two. The horse could feed legions.

I take a right. I take another right. Time is wasting. The horse will kill a few. Their numbers will win. I cut through a building. I jump furniture and desks and stairs and doorways and through a window. The wall is high. The wall is brick. I clamor up. I clamor over.

The horse is gone. They are gone. The fight is gone. There is blood. It still glows and smokes. There are a half dozen of them. Their bodies are broken. They are dead. The black birds come. I knew they would. They feed. I cry. The tears are hot. It smokes like my blood. It smokes like the horse's blood. It smokes like our blood.

The biggest black bird stops eating. It turns to me. It watches me. It cocks its head. It asks questions.

I walk to the street. The biggest bird lands on my shoulder. The tower is visible. Its lights are on.

"Tomorrow," I say.

The crow nods. Maybe it's a spasm. I don't know. I know we need more than us. I say as much. The crow takes wing. The crow seeks darkness.

🐦 🐦 🐦

There is light. Sunlight dances across dust motes. We are two. She is small. I am smaller. She curls on the couch like a cat we never had. I lie on shag carpeting. She reads. I watch. Her lips move across complex words. I am bored, but I know she is finishing a chapter. Then we will play. This is before I am a broken doll.

She reads anything. She reads Greek mythology borrowed from the library. She reads old paperback classics bought at yard sales. She reads miscellaneous poetry found in our mother's room. I read the same books. I read a lot when trapped in a wheelchair.

One book was worn. One book had a creased spine. One book was dog-eared and highlighted.

Before the darkness, before I was fixed, before I counted down from ten, she whispered in my ear.

"Be fearless. Be powerful."

I whisper this to myself. I stare at the barricade. Something watches me. It is darkness. I am darkness. We are darkness.

❧ ❧ ❧

There is light. It follows the crows. The crows swirl. The crows gather. The crows swoop. They distract. They divert eyeballs from the barricade. They give me time. My breath is hurried. I run from the shadows. I cross the gap between barricade and buildings. Light surrounds me. I stab my hand. There is blood. It glows. I wipe it on the barricade. Splinters bite me. There is more blood. There is more fire. It burns. It burns. It burns.

I run. I slash myself. I wipe. It burns. It is burning. It is burnt.

They notice. They leave the crows. They bring buckets of water. They use hoses. They douse the flames. I keep cutting. I keep burning. I keep attacking. They throw things. The things hurt. They are heavy. They are jagged. One hits my head. I fall. There is darkness.

I hear feet. I hear boots on pavement. I must rise. I must run and I must burn. They are close. I must rise. I must rise. I must rise. There is a hail of stones. There is a hail of heavy things. There is metal. There is fear. It is mine. I hear the crows. They scream. I scream. They swoop. They find flesh. They distract. It is not enough. The men circle. They hold sticks and knives and imminent death.

There is a growl. There is something in the darkness. It is darkness. It is big. It is fast. It rips through the circle. The circle breaks. The men scatter. The darkness chases. The darkness kills. It claws. It shreds. It is mine. It is what Mary made for me. I understand that now.

I cut my wrist. I slice a vein. I bleed. It glows. I wipe the barricade. It burns. I wait. The darkness surrounds me. It waits. The men gather. They wait. We are ready. They are ready. We shall see who wins.

There is light. There is flame. There is blood. It is not mine. It is not the darkness. Some of it is crow. Most of it is man. They scatter. They run. The barricade smolders. A ring of fire surrounds us. Smoke rises up the tower. Faces peer from windows. They stare with wide eyes. They are scared. I don't need to smell them. I can see it. I would be too.

The crows multiply. They fill the sky. They block the moon. They complete the darkness. My darkness paces in the shadows. It watches with fiery eyes and dark stripes.

I open the door. The door leads through the tower. There is light. There is electricity. There is life inside. It is not my life. It is not mine to take. I want none of it. I am covered in blood. I am covered in gore. I am covered in their friends, their family, their lovers, and their enemies. I know what I am. I see it in their eyes.

They don't attack. They stare. They scuttle to corners and huddle together. They fear me. I don't fear them. I cross the lobby. There is an elevator. I press the button. It lights up. I wait. There is silence. I want to talk. I want to speak. I don't know what to say. I am aware. They are aware. There are many sins to be assigned.

The elevator chimes. I press the top button. It lights up. I wait. The doors open. It is the top floor. There is a long hallway. Windows line the walls. The crows roost. The crows watch. I walk forward. I walk to the door on the far end. I know what will be there. I don't know what will be there. My mind is undecided.

There is light. The room is bright. There are windows all around. They watch over the city. The city surrounds us.

My feet are silent. There is shag carpeting. There are books. There is thick leather furniture. There is a chair on the far end. I know the kind. A huddled figure sits. They gaze outside.

They are gray-haired. They are small. They are fading. I clear my throat. I don't know what to say. They turn around. She is a she. She is old and withered and dying. Her hair is thin and tied back. A blanket lies on her lap. I cannot see her legs. I know this trick.

She smiles. She lacks teeth. I know this smile. Her eyes watch me. I know those eyes. Hers are mine and mine are hers. She does not need to speak.

I know now what I've become. I know what I've always been to her. I am the fruition of her brilliance. I am her brother. I am her broken doll. I am her Prometheus. She is my sister. She is my Frankenstein. She is my fire.

My hand cups her cheek. I kneel. Smoking tears drip down my face. Her hand rests on my arm. She whispers many words I don't want to hear. She explains many things I don't want to understand.

"How long," I ask.

"Many years. It was a success, but was too strong. Your body couldn't handle it. You went into a coma. I knew how to fix it, but it was too late for you. I knew you wouldn't die. That much I could guarantee. The world fought for it. They wanted this fire for themselves. There were wars. All you see now, that's all that remains. We have this city. There might be more like it somewhere out there. I dumped the serum in stronger animals. They proliferated. They took over the world, or what remains of it. I stayed here, waiting for you. I put faith in my serum and you. You didn't fail. You needed time to synthesize it. It took you so long. You are the lone human like you. The rest are animals. You are special."

Her hands are cold. Her words are warm. I stand. The night makes mirrors of the window. I see myself. I see her. I see what I am, covered in blood and gore and death.

I remember the smell of aging paper, of smeared ink,

of all the forgotten pages. I remember a quote.

"Did I request thee, Maker, from my clay to mould me man? Did I solicit thee from darkness to promote me?"

I fear speaking. I turn from her. A tear falls from her cheek. It disappears in a crease.

I find her desk. Pen and paper sit unused. I take the pen. I scrawl in big black letters. I leave it for her. I leave the tower. I leave the barricade. I enter the darkness and walk north.

Darkness follows me with soft feet and swooshing tail. The crows follow in their way. Behind me is light, a light that never goes out. It is her light and now the darkness is mine.

THiS iS HOW THE WORLD ENDS

WESTON BROWNLEE

You never really believe you'll wake one morning and find the world you knew is gone. Maybe you half wonder, "Is this it?" when you read about the latest act of nature worse than any before recorded, another rogue nation's uranium enrichment, or the latest plunge of an economy. A passing thought is all the more you shed, because the sun always rises the next morning and you always wake, even from the worst nightmares. You still fill your car up with gasoline, because it's never actually dried up. If the price of food is higher what's a few cents? You always tell yourself things keep spinning; even if they stop it will be long after you're gone. If anything, the fleeting thoughts you humor are the ones that tell you we'll cure diseases like Alzheimer's, never really see the ice caps melt, and put a man on Mars.

No one watched when it started. "Orange Goo Washing Ashore Near Remote Alaskan Village," made a headline no better than laughable—too outlandish to be important. Sure enough though it was real, pictures and all and I noticed. By three that afternoon, the story spread just like the vibrant sheen in the water. The buzz wasn't enough to garner much more than some jokes and the label of "strange news," but that was how it all began: a newspaper headline from a town even most Alaskans had never heard of spelled out the whole gruesome tailspin. After everything really went to hell, I tried to find everything I could—tried to piece it all back together. I read over it now. Mostly it kept my mind busy—keeps my mind busy; keeps me from thinking about what's waiting outside—keeps me from thinking about the choice I try and put off a little longer.

Taken from a local paper the first day: *April 12. Last night a bizarre orange material washed ashore along the Arctic coast of Kivalina, Alaska. The all-but-unknown Inupiat village is saturated with the material. Photographs by residents show an orange sheen spanning the harbor and beaches of the village. Kivalina sits about 625 miles northwest of Anchorage. Nothing like this has ever been seen before in Kivalina and village elders do not recall any stories passed down from previous generations detailing orange goo coming from the sea. . . . City employees examined a pump house two miles away, bounding the Wulik River. The material is there as well. The Red Dog zinc mine is located about 40 miles from Kivalina, leading some to suspect a link, but mine personnel have confirmed the substance is totally un-related to their operations. . . . The sun appears to have dried the goo in areas farther from water and high winds have scattered it in the form of thin orange dust. Investigators suspect it may be some form of pollen.*

I found this one online about a month later before the Internet went down: *April 13. Yesterday evening high tide dispersed the "orange goo." This follows a revelation that the substance might be toxic as dead fish have been spotted throughout the harbor . . . after an early rainstorm the next day revealed the goo was found floating in rain buckets, which the residents use to collect drinking water. The goo also was found on rooftops. Whatever it is, fear is growing that it is airborne.*

Even though the world took no notice, those of us working a gold mine called Shear Ridge talked about the goo all day the first two days. Down in the deep the right kind of news sunk low enough, but it was never the kind you'd think. Most of the time we were in our own world down there. Everything was too far away. Kivalina wasn't. All of us knew no matter what it is, if it ends up in the water, everybody's in trouble. The jokes and inevitable dismissal settled fast, but we were all a little nervous. Nobody imagined the truth; we all were set on thoughts of pollen or fungus. By the end those few paragraphs had spelled it out: the dead fish, the speed at which the goo was spreading, and the drinking water. If I knew then what I know now, maybe I would have tried to run. Maybe now it's just because I'm holed up inside a gold mine in the bowels of a mountain, but I can't help but wonder if I'd have run if I could have been safe. All it took to convince us we were safe was a couple beers. The hangovers got fainter. The news didn't.

An Anchorage paper. Same basic story, but the details kept growing: *April 14. Stacy Edgrin's husband was the first to see it. A call over the marine radio alerted the rest of Kivalina, the remote Alaskan village, of a bizarre orange goo floating in the harbor. . . . Among the dead fish were larger species, including an oarfish, which is unheard of at these latitudes. . . .*

Heavy rain the next day had deposited the goo in rain buckets Kivalina uses to collect drinking water. Residents are very concerned the substance is harmful. With winter coming, the state of the harbor is a top priority. "What if the fish that are still alive are unsafe to eat?" said one anonymous resident. "What will we do if we can't stock up for winter? We have seen the goo on leaves and berries. What about the caribou being hunted that are eating these berries?"

The material coagulated in the harbor in 10-foot-by-100-foot strands. . . . Kivalina was not the only location with reports of the strange goo. . . . Wendy Garmond was on a boat on the Buckland River, which is nearly 150 miles to the southeast. "The whole river was orange looking," she said.

It kept spreading. A local paper: April 15. Talk of orange tinged rivers and creeks continues. Residents are avoiding berries they usually gather as many were covered with the orange goo along with almost all the vegetation near the water. . . . Kivalina's residents are largely off the grid, relying upon the land for their food. Concern is now full-blown fear at the effect this goo will have on wildlife and plants; however, caribou in the region seem unaffected and reports from residents indicate they are feeding as normal, leading many to believe the substance, while odd, poses no real health risks. Nonetheless, samples are being collected for testing.

❧ ❧ ❧

We had lots of theories. The whole thing had turned into a big enough joke with some of the guys they had a $300 pot for the one that got it right. Guesses went everywhere from chemical agents courtesy of terrorists to all kinds of dirty jokes. I was running a drill that afternoon when the answer came over the radio, and nobody won the money.

Tests conducted on the substance found in Kivalina have conclusively revealed that the goo is in fact small invertebrate eggs, although we cannot tell which species. Additional tests are still being run and the results will be made public as soon as possible.

Another week passed. The orange goo disappeared from the water. Then it disappeared from the news. The guys at the mine laughed about it some more, and made as many dirty jokes about invertebrates as they could before someone threatened to report them for sexual harassment. I didn't think about the goo much more. I slipped back into getting through my shifts measuring the hours by the songs I listened to passing the daily grind.

It's not so different now, but I hit the repeat button more. I lie and listen to music, unable to sleep but not wanting to do anything else. I sit and I listen as every word brings me one step closer to a choice I want to keep avoiding. The generator should run at least another week before it will need more diesel. My iPod should last a day after. It won't get cold until two days after that, which means there'll be plenty of time to decide if biting a bullet or going to the surface is a worse way to go. "All Along the Watchtower" can probably play a few hundred more times before then. "MK Ultra" a dozen or so less.

* * *

A local paper: *April 19. "Evidence clearly shows these are some type of crustacean egg or embryo," said a press release from the lead scientist at the Juneau lab tasked with identifying the goo. . . . No answer as to why the sudden emergence of these eggs occurred has been found. Villagers in Kivalina have never experienced anything similar and have noticed no observable reason this bizarre phenomenon happened now.*

In masses, the eggs create a gooey slick and release a foul odor. The widest measured dispersal of the eggs came from the Wulik River and the lagoon—half a mile wide and 6 miles long. New reports place the eggs south of Buckland, which is 150 miles south of Kivalina.

That was the last writing about the goo I could find. The radio didn't say any more either. One of the guys saw four Chinook helicopters flying north, but everyone said it was just coincidence. A few days later it really started—T. S. Eliot had been right when he wrote, "not with a bang but with a whimper." It crept in the stillness of the night, quietly snuffing out everything.

⁂

An Anchorage paper: *April 24. Two grizzly hunters from Idaho reported what they called a disturbing kill, fueling local Inuit legends of a werewolf-like creature called the Adlet. . . . The find came when the two men stumbled upon what they believed was a bear kill. "We knew it was a caribou, but it didn't look like one. I've been hunting since I was fifteen and I've never seen an animal do something like this to another."*

The caribou was found literally ripped into pieces. Parts of the carcass had been picked clean to the bone. Portions of the skeleton were missing as well as internal organs. The department of wildlife has examined the carcass and announced that the wounds are consistent with a bear mauling. The carcass has been moved to Anchorage in order to determine if the bear is rabid, in which case it will have to be hunted and euthanized.

I knew it wasn't a bear and I knew those hunters knew it wasn't also. I thought about trying to find them —call them up. Then I realized there wouldn't be any point. What would I have asked them? They didn't know what killed the caribou. Maybe it was just the idea of talking to other people who knew something was very wrong. I never called. Just kept on with my job, mulling through the grind; looking forward to having a beer and listening to wolves howl somewhere far off in the night while I sat next to a warm fire.

I wonder that a lot now: What if I had found them? They'd have said, "We don't know what the hell that was." I'd have told them about the eggs and maybe they'd have thought what I did—what I know now. It's surreal I was right. I knew when I saw that story. All the articles I'd read and radio updates I'd heard, everyone kept crying out the stuff was on the berries the caribou ate and in everyone's drinking water. I still feel sick when I think about it—anything that ate the berries or drank the water.

Another week passed in quiet, but that Friday things hit hard. There wasn't any horrific reveal, no blasts or aircraft falling out of the sky. It was quiet, slow, and inevitable. Power in the mining camp was the first thing to go, then the people. It wasn't everyone at once, not even in numbers that stood out right away. No one noticed until everyone got back into the bunkhouses or their own cabin if they had a family. Five people were missing the first night. Search parties looked everywhere, but nobody found any sign of anyone. No one remembered seeing them go.

I was terrified, the same way I get now lying on my back, eyes gaping. There's lots of lights down here in the mine—down where it's deep enough I don't think they can get to us. It doesn't make any difference though—I still can't sleep.

It got worse after that first night. Emergency generators put the power back online, but more people vanished. Everyone knew something was wrong. Nobody was going anywhere alone. A few real skeptics, die-hards, and guys with nothing to lose still stayed in the bar late. On the third night, a lot of us already locked indoors saw two of them walking and then heard screaming just when they passed out of sight. We weren't looking for the people who went missing anymore. Gone was gone. Water pipes in the camp clogged later that night. The orange goo was everywhere in the pump house, not just in the water. It was on the walls, the ceiling, the floor, and everything else. I ran and didn't wait on anyone.

Thirty more people were gone by the end of that week. All I could think about was how long it would take: if someone drank water and, I hated to think it, the eggs had been inside. I'd told everyone I saw not to drink the water, afraid it was already too late. Some of us already had plans to get into the mine. There weren't any natural tunnels, and just two ways in and out.

The guilt is what weighs heaviest on me. I still haven't said more than a few words to the others down here. We did save a few women and children. That should make me feel better, right? That has to count for something. We saved everyone we could. There are no heroes in times like this—those guys go down first. Nobody would have done any differently than we did if they had seen what we saw.

One of the mining engineers got the first look. We were inside one of the garages, siphoning gas to move down to the mine. It wasn't dark, but just dark enough everything was muddled and blurry. The mining engineer and a few guys were over tinkering with the bigger machines, while the rest of us were draining the trucks. All of us heard the noise: a clunky chittering that buzzed for just a second, then silence. Nobody moved. Each of us looked at each other's wide eyes hoping someone would say it was nothing. The mining engineer shot toward the door, alone. We heard the sound again and in the dim light I saw a flash of what was coming. It was low to the ground, but long and wide. If it wasn't black it was almost, and had a dull sheen. There were no eyes, but I knew I saw lance-like spikes rimming a wide mouth.

There were no more preparations. The guys grabbed whomever they could and hollered for whoever could hear. We booked it for the mine. I'm not sure how many of us made it. The elevator going down can hold thirty people at once. There were more supplies on it than there were people. An argument broke out. It ended with a gunshot and the decision to seal the entrances. The first few days were a blur. I kept busy any way I could—mostly that meant drilling like I was at work. Got a good distance deeper. Kept trying to convince myself everything was fine, that things would keep spinning like they always did. Laughed and told myself they were going to owe me overtime when all this was done. Then I came to.

Everything is not fine. We are alive now, but soon we won't be. We are not safe. We are trapped at the bottom of a pit while everything we knew and loved is being destroyed. If anyone is coming to help they aren't coming here. If somewhere in the world they're fighting for survival, their battle won't bring them here. If they don't get us it will be exposure. If it's not exposure it will be starvation and dehydration. If it's not that, eventually those of us trapped down here will turn on each other.

I still can't decide. Maybe it will be faster that way. Maybe if I go to the surface and try to run or to get food or gas and I fail, maybe it's just the blink of an eye. If I stay down here I know exactly how long I'll wait. I can count the minutes, then the hours, and the days. There won't be many left, but when you measure time by the lyrics of a song, it's still an eternity. I hit repeat as the intro plays again and wonder what four minutes and thirty-two seconds will bring me closer to.

PLAGUE

ROSELYN PEREZ

As usual we got it wrong. The apocalyptic-like threat to humanity didn't come from global warming, disgruntled robots with artificial intelligence, or hordes of the undead clamoring for our brains. We stood at the pinnacle of the evolutionary ladder for so long that while the cynics in us could envision the end of our kind, our narcissistic nature could only imagine the death blow for such a dominant race would happen solely at its own hand. The truth, however, is vastly more humbling than that.

History has a way of repeating itself. In the fourteenth century the black plague swept through Europe, killing one-third of the population. Later, it was theorized that the plague was caused by the fleas on black rats that carried and spread the disease. Before the governments and media died along with the people that made them up, a similar scenario was hypothesized as the cause of the pandemic. Some kind of virus was passed from flea to rat, but instead of turning the rodent into an unwitting host, the virus flipped a switch in the rat's brain that changed their feeding and social behavior. They no longer scurried in dumpsters and gutters under cover of night. They poured from the shadows in even greater numbers than we could have imagined and in a matter of days devoured hundreds of thousands. In one horrifying instant our false sense of security was shattered and our civilization crumbled under the teeth of billions of gnawing rodents.

Wherever there are people, there are rats. There were some initial attempts to eradicate the creatures. Exterminators, scientists, and the military all tried their hand at fumigating, burning, and poisoning the things, but they ended up killing as many people as rats and it made no significant difference in the rodent population. It wasn't long before the supernaturally clever creatures learned to avoid even touching the arsenic-laced food people liberally surrounded their homes with. Most began sleeping curled up as tight as they could get in the center of a circle of elaborate rat traps and sticky paper. The rats stepped daintily over the ineffectual bait with the utmost confidence, turning up their noses at everything but the soft meat of the creatures who once thought they ruled the earth.

I've seen dozens of attacks firsthand. I've seen a person swarmed and killed in a matter of seconds, buried under a furry wave of ravenous teeth. And, then there were the survivors: men and women with missing fingers and ears, and the children, dragging their legless bodies across the hard ground, faces scarred by what they've had to endure. Still, I wonder if they aren't the lucky ones. I can hardly recall the sound of my own name. In this new world I'm only referred to as Rat girl, Rat freak, or my personal favorite, Rat bitch.

Not all humans are attacked by rats; a very small percentage could walk right into a nest of them and not receive so much as a nibble. It's as if we're invisible. The other survivors saw us, however, dubbed us rat people, and blamed us for bringing about the plague. As if we are a race of reverse pied pipers, calling forth rabid beasties and bringing them into the camps of survivors. And so we were cast out, hated, and hunted by our former neighbors.

I say *we* because humans are a social creature by nature, and although I haven't seen another rat person in over a year I like to think we are a community bonded by our rejected status from humans and rats alike. But really there is no we, there is only I.

Usually, I sleep in a tree, which is as comfortable as it sounds, but you'd be surprised at how few people ever bother to look up. It's a good system, or at least it was. Winter is coming on fast, most of the leaves have fallen from the trees, stripping me of their cover, but it doesn't much matter since it is getting dangerously cold anyway. I find myself dreaming more and more of the southern California sun; I can sometimes still feel it soaking into my skin just before I wake up shivering. In the days after the outbreak I fled the infested city of Los Angeles, thinking that my only chance at survival would be to head to an isolated place. Now, I know that my best recourse is to return.

The one upside to the coming winter is that the days are considerably shorter. And, as soon as the pale sun passes out behind the mountains I break from my cover and head south. I doubt I'll be able to make it back to my home city, but any major city will do.

I've become quite adept at traveling in darkness. Old habits die hard: as changed as the rats are they still are more active at night, and people have therefore reverted to viewing the night with a kind of wary Dread. It works out for me at any rate; if I'm spotted I'll probably still be shot at, but I'm much less likely to be hit or pursued.

My preference is to give any camps along the way as wide a berth as possible, but there is a charged expectancy in the atmosphere that I've learned to interpret as a sign of an incoming storm. The ground is still muddy from the last storm that passed through and I don't think I can survive another night of tramping through unfamiliar hillsides in the middle of a downpour.

So, when a survivors' camp comes into view I decide to

skirt around its borders instead of detouring through the hilly forest that surrounds it. If I die at least I'll do it relatively dry and rested. They've got a big bonfire going. I'm close enough to hear, but not feel it roar. I try not to curse the people that must be sitting around it, warm and surrounded by familiar faces. The notes of a guitar float in the air and stop me dead. It draws me in and I creep in closer, against my better judgment.

There's a man and a woman sitting by the fire. He is the one playing; he's not all that great, but when the woman starts singing along with the music it moves something within me. I'm not even aware of taking a step toward them until a twig snaps under my foot, and the music abruptly stops.

When the outbreak first began it was easy to pass myself off as a normal survivor. As time went on and attacks became more and more inevitable it was impossible to explain away my unscarred face and full set of fingers and toes. Most damning now, however, is the fact that I carry no fire, which seems to be the only thing the rats fear.

"Who's there?" the man shouts, starting to rise. I begin to back away slowly, hoping the shadows will swallow me back up before they see me.

"It's a rat freak," the woman shrieks as she clutches the man's arm. "Kill it, Jimmy! Jimmy, kill it!" With my cover now blown I turn and run before Jimmy has a chance to obey the woman's orders. The night comes alive with the sounds of semi-coherent promises of violence hurled at my back as I flee for my life.

My feet suddenly hit gravel, and I nearly pitch head long when I trip on what I assume is a cracked curb. I catch myself from falling face first onto the broken pavement. But, just as quickly I leap backwards, almost losing my hard-won balance when a white shape shoots from the darkness to stand before me. It is an albino rat, complete with red eyes. The shouts of the approaching people don't seem to affect it in the least. Calmly, it regards me, sitting on its plump haunches and tilting its head as if trying to place me.

It starts off again but pauses to look back at me. Lacking any better ideas I head after it. I'm afraid I'll lose sight of it as I stumble around the unfamiliar streets, but it seems to understand my predicament, waiting patiently when I fall behind, and even squeaking once when I turn in the wrong direction. It stops atop a manhole cover and looks up expectantly at me. No one, no matter how bloodthirsty, would follow me into the sewers seeing as they were flooded with rats even before the outbreak. On the other hand there's been no one to maintain them since then either and I wonder if it might not be better to just let the survivors tear me limb from limb.

The albino rat chatters at me impatiently as the sound of my pursuers intensifies. I drag off the cover as silently as possible and climb down before I can think better of it. The smell is obscene, and as I step down into the swirling shin-high water I nearly swoon at the fumes that rise from the disturbed sludge. I force myself to move forward, keeping my back against the wall and trying not to think about the things winding around my legs.

The survivors reach the manhole and shine a light down. I'm pretty sure I'm too far for them to see me, but I press myself flat against the wall and hold my breath just in case. They toss down a few insults and rocks before retreating. Some of the tension leaves my body, until I hear the manhole cover being eased back into place and the sound of an approaching engine. I feel the panic setting in as I realize what they're planning to do. The car is rolled on top of the cover, and the engine is cut. I hear them walking away, whooping with delight at their clever bit of deadly poetic justice. They've trapped me down here, trapped me like a rat, I think, as a bubble of hysterical laughter tries to burst out of me.

I take out my penlight and look around. The sewers are an impossible maze of tunnels and churning water filled with undefinable debris. Then I look up and find the rat peering down at me with those intelligent eyes. It makes me think of a movie I once saw as a little girl before the plague, when I still had a name, about a white mouse who was adopted by a human family.

The hysteria is still near the surface and I let out a sharp laugh as I say, "Well, Stuart, may I call you Stuart?" The name suits him, and he seems to perk up at my words. "I don't suppose you'd be willing to show me another way out of here?" To my utter surprise, Stuart starts down a tunnel and as before stops to look back at me. This time I don't hesitate; I follow Stuart through the winding tunnels for what seems like hours. He finally stops in front of a rusted ladder. I climb it and shove my way above ground.

The night air is freezing, but I suck in lungful after burning lungful. It has started to rain and I know I should get up, but I continue to kneel, alternating between fits of crying and laughter. Stuart watches my antics with weary disapproval, but he doesn't leave my side. Shakily I get to my feet. Stuart is on the move immediately and I hustle to keep up. He stops, and I launch into another bout of tearful mirth when I see that the beautiful creature has led me to an abandoned supermarket.

I peel off my putrid clothes, leave them in a dripping pile, and pull on clean jeans, thick socks, and a hoodie that is only slightly too large. All of the jackets are gone, but I do find a sleeping bag, and a sturdy backpack. I stuff the pack full of food and water, as well as a change of clothes. I've become an accomplished scavenger since the outbreak. The most important rule in my view is, you grab what you can when you can. Clothes and fresh water are more precious than gold and I scoop them up with all the wild glee of a forty-niner hitting pay dirt. With my new acquisitions in order I regard Stuart.

"*We* got it wrong," I tell him as I toss half of my beef jerky in his direction. "Diamonds aren't a girl's best friend; you are." He doesn't argue and we eat in comfort. I unroll my sleeping bag and for once fall into a deep, instant sleep. The next evening I pack up and head out, Stuart falling easily into step beside me as if it were the most natural thing in the world.

By the third day, Stuart lets me put him in the backpack. I talk constantly, pouring out everything I've held in since the outbreak. Stuart pokes his head out of the pack and rests it on my shoulder occasionally. The irony of our fledgling alliance isn't lost on me. The survivors are convinced that people like me somehow triggered the plague, controlling the rat's behavior, and once every rat person is killed they believe things will return to the way they once were. I wonder what they'd say if they could see Stuart and me now. And, I wonder what it says about me that I was so easily charmed into adopting one of the creatures that destroyed my civilization and made me an outcast. I have no answers so I focus on the road ahead, and leave my tangled thoughts for later.

We come across more and more rusted cars and neglected houses. Many of them still have their former occupants inside, half liquefied and chewed. Just as many, however, lie abandoned. Stuart and I stop to investigate, or take shelter within them whenever the mood strikes us. I consider trying to use one of the cars, but quickly dismiss the idea; it would bring too much unwanted attention. A bicycle might work, if I can find one, but for now I'm content just walking with Stuart.

We haven't seen any sign of survivors in days. The sun, wan as it is, proves too great a temptation, and I decide to risk traveling during the day. It feels glorious to turn my face up to the sky and let it wrap me up in all the warmth it has to offer. All too soon, however, the wind springs up, bringing with it depressingly dark clouds that smother the last of the light.

"Looks like another big storm," I inform Stuart. His only response is to burrow deeper into the backpack. When the rain finally begins to fall the wind picks it up and hurls it like darts in every direction. I unzip my sleeping bag and pull it over my head and around my shoulders like a hooded cape. Even so, the rain finds its way through, and the sound of approaching thunder lets me know it's only going to get worse.

"Time to make camp," I say and look around for a place to hunker down. There is what might have once been a small shopping strip just ahead. All of the stores seem to have been looted. The windows have been shattered, the glass mixing with the trampled garbage the looters dropped or left behind. There's a tractor trailer smashed into the front of the liquor store on the far side of the street.

"Slim pickings." I sigh as we come up to the first sagging storefront. As with all the others the windows are broken in, but the sign on the door still reads, "Paul's Party Palace: where your fun is our business," in bright confetti colors. It's as good a place as any, I decide, and climb through the window, careful not to step on any glass. I stop just inside, trying to sense if anything else is taking shelter here. Stuart jumps out of the pack and heads down one of the aisles. I take this as a positive sign and follow.

Most everything has been ripped off the shelves. Colorful wigs, masks, deflated balloons, and cans of silly string clutter the floor. I make a quick circuit around the shop, spotting a bag of assorted candies and snatching it up before continuing around toward the cash register. As I inspect the desk and the displays around it, hoping to find more junk food, a shriek splits the air and nearly stops my heart. I whirl to face whoever made the sound only to find a grinning skeleton with a plastic ax sticking out of its skull. Feeling like an idiot I continue my search and avoid the screaming skeleton. There's nothing else of use, but there is an open manager's office in the back that Stuart and I use as our sleeping quarters.

I come awake with a start; something is wrong. I'm up in an instant gathering my sleeping bag and shrugging into my pack. When you're a rat person you learn the value of being prepared to escape at a moment's notice. Still, nothing seems out of place.

Then I hear something, the sound that must have awakened me, the sound of motors. Crouching down, I ease toward one of the front windows making sure to avoid the grinning skeleton. Peering over the window ledge I see three motorcycles tearing down the street. Happily they are headed away from us. The riders are huge wild-haired men that might have stepped straight out of one ice age or another. The man in the lead seems to have decorated his upper body as well as his bike with an assortment of bones. It's hard to be sure at this distance but some look suspiciously human.

"Time to go," I announce and Stuart leaps obediently into the backpack. I wish the skeleton luck as I climb back out onto the street. I start off in the opposite direction from the Neanderthal bikers. A moan of absolute agony floats out from one of the buildings, freezing me instantly. I almost expect to see that damn grinning skeleton lumbering out of the party supply store to follow me. But, the street is deserted and the moan was anything but artificial. Stuart begins chattering in my ear, a sure sign that he wants to move on. Usually I trust Stuart's instincts, but there is someone sobbing pitifully somewhere close and I hush Stuart so I can pinpoint the source.

The crying is issuing from the liquor store. I approach the ruined entrance and peek warily over the side of the tractor's rusted hood. Even with the coming darkness I can see that the interior has been trashed. Bottles of every variety lie smashed all over, and the walls are smeared liberally with what I'm certain is fecal matter. I can smell it even over the nauseating mixture of spilled spirits on the ground.

Nothing good can come of going in there, but before I can back away the moaning comes again. A form moves in the back corner of the store, crying out as it does. I squeeze past the trailer and step inside the building, feeling like the stupidest bimbo in a bad slasher film. My boots stick to the filthy floor, and although I move slowly it is impossible to move silently in this mess.

I jump as I realize that this establishment also boasts a hanging skeleton; of course this one doesn't scream as I approach. It's beyond screaming now. He, at least I assume it's a he, is still wearing a pair of tattered pants although only one leg pokes out of them. The other leg is missing from the knee down, and I suddenly remember the biker with the bone accessories.

There's a shopping cart half filled with unbroken liquor bottles by the skeleton's side. I heft a bottle of tequila trying to gauge how effective it might be as a weapon. I decide it has to be better than my bare hands and I hold it by the neck, ready to swing it like a club, as I inch toward the figure in the corner.

Turning my back on the skeleton doesn't bother me all that much—it's dead. Only the survivors can make my palms slick with terror, and yet I can't walk away, can't ignore the sound of a suffering person, because no matter what anyone might think, I am still human.

The woman lying in a ragged heap in the corner doesn't seem much better off than the swinging corpse. Every visible inch of skin is a patchwork of bruises in a variety of startling shades. She is practically a skeleton herself, and as I watch the feeble flailing of her emaciated limbs I know that there's nothing I can do to save her.

The woman's eyes are closed, perhaps swollen shut, not that I fear her recognizing me. She'd only gotten a fleeting glimpse of me in the dark the night we first met. I have no trouble placing her, however, even now in her debilitated state. I remember her sitting by the glow of a bonfire, I remember her voice that drew me in, and I remember her shouts that called for my annihilation. I wonder if the dangling dead man is Jimmy. I crouch down beside her, moving slowly so as not to startle her.

"Can you hear me?"

"Co-cold," she stammers through chattering teeth. She does open her eyes a fraction, although it seems to be only by extreme effort. I unzip my sleeping roll and lay it over her like a blanket. I pull out a water bottle from my bag and hold it to her cracked lips.

"Try to drink some of this," I encourage as I gently lift her head. Most of it spills down her chin, but she does manage to get some of it down.

"Good," I say, wiping her chin with a corner of the sleeping bag.

"Who are you?" she asks. It takes me a moment to remember, but I finally tell her, "My name is Adriana."

"Thank you, Adriana," she says. I want to tell her that hearing my name is the greatest thanks anyone could give me, but just then, Stuart pops his head out of my backpack and she screams.

"You're one of them," she shrieks in a voice that is surprisingly fierce in intensity. I try to explain that I am just a survivor like her, but this only causes her shrieking to grow in volume and desperation. Her outrage must have lent her strength, because suddenly she sits up and faster than I could have thought possible her hand shoots towards my face, fingers hooked into claws. I throw my own hand up to protect myself and scream as her ragged fingernails sheer my skin from my palm to halfway down my wrist.

I stumble backwards watching dumbly as my blood drips onto the filthy floor. The woman is still keening, wordlessly now, like some kind of maddened animal. Stuart leaps out of nowhere to clamp onto the hand that is reaching for me again. Her yells turn to howls of pain and terror as she tries fruitlessly to shake Stuart off. Suddenly rats of every size and hue emerge from every direction, and converge on the woman. I turn and run, too horrified to even glance back, but the dying groans of the woman chase me like a final accusation.

I run through the gathering darkness, hardly noticing when I fall. Stumbling to my feet I keep moving, ignoring the pain blooming in my chest, until I reach a highway offramp where my legs finally buckle beneath me. The full contents of my stomach go sailing over the side of a guardrail in a hot stream of misery. Even then I continue to retch and sob, as if despair could be so easily purged.

It hits me that I am alone again and I consider throwing myself over the guardrail and into the ditch below. Instead, I open the bottle of tequila, which is the only thing I managed to hold on to, and after taking a swig I pour the rest onto my scratched hand and wrap it with torn strips from my shirt. Neither experience is pleasant, and I hurl the bottle over the rail where it breaks with a satisfying sound.

Only now does my body start to register how cold it's gotten. Standing is a struggle, my legs wobble alarmingly, and I have to clutch the door handle of a nearby pickup truck to keep from sprawling on the pavement. Peering into the window I see the driver face down on the steering wheel; he almost appears to be sleeping except for the fact that his entrails are spilled over his lap. I recoil, my stomach does a little flip, but there's nothing left to throw up. The highway is clogged with vehicles; most likely, however, they contain passengers like this one. As it is I barely have the strength to climb into the truck bed. There's a bald tire, battered toolbox, and dusty tarp on the flatbed. I wrap myself in the tarp and try not to think about my sleeping bag.

Looking up at the heavens I'm struck by how dazzlingly bright they seem. Without the lights and smog of the cities the stars parade across the sky and captivate me the way they must have done my ancestors. I look out at the sea of vehicles, and wonder how many of them have become caskets for the dead. Death has come and blown down all the glittering constructions that man erected to keep them safe. And, the survivors are hopelessly deluded to think that anything can bring back what has been lost.

For the first time I wonder if maybe they got it wrong. Perhaps, humanity has not been doomed but given a do-over. I flex my stinging hand and think about all the survivors that yearn for my blood. But, what if rat people are not the cursed but the chosen ones? In that case, maybe I was meant to do much more than simply survive.

Stuart lands in the truck bed with an audible plop. He gives me an uncertain look. I hesitate for just an instant before extending my injured hand to him. He rushes forward, rubbing himself against it like a cat. I glance at the sky again; it's lighter now. Most of the stars have disappeared, outshined by the coming sun.

"Time to get started," I tell Stuart. My legs are steady as I move down the road. I pause to watch the sun turn the heavens into a kaleidoscope before finally bursting through and illuminating everything it touches. Stuart sits on my foot and looks up at me with the same kind of rapture. Smiling, I continue on, moving past wreckage after wreckage knowing that my days of traveling in darkness are behind me. Stuart and I have finally stepped from the shadows and inherited the earth.

PART IV

THE KIDS

THE UNGUiDED

JOSH CHAFFiN

The dark purple horizon looked ominous above the four dirty, shadowy-eyed children squatting in a circle over ashy debris playing a game. It was a fitting background for the two blond-haired kids, probably brother and sister; the brown-haired boy; and the short-haired black boy. Their raggedy clothes and ashen skin gave them the appearance of the dead. They sang a song as they played a game that reminded Jordy of jacks. Except they weren't playing with six-pointed metal pieces and a ball. They were playing with teeth.

> *Jordy's teeth keep falling out,*
> *falling out, falling out.*
> *Jordy's teeth keep falling out.*
> *He's so ugly—*

The little spawns of Satan weren't very creative, biting off the "London Bridge Is Falling Down" tune and all. And his teeth never *fell* out. They were *pulled* out.

They laughed their high-pitched squeals of delight as the little girl won the game or something. He didn't know and didn't care.

"Can I ge' thome foo' p'eathe?" Jordy erratically rubbed the scars and few remaining patches of hair on his head as he expected the worst.

Little chuckles were given instead while they set up a new game. Everything he said was funny to them now. They didn't even turn Jordy's way. He acquiesced to their laughter and wondered if there were any other adults for the millionth time. And if there were, were they being treated like he was? He sat back down in his giant, portable bird cage and imagined that if any adults before the apocalypse could see him now, they would ask, "How in the hell does a forty-four-year-old man come to be held captive by children no older than nine?" By their insidiousness, that's how! is what he'd tell them. In the beginning they had seemed so innocent . . . then they turned into nightmares.

Jordan first observed everybody dropping dead in Washington, DC. Literally dropping dead. They'd be walking, and then all of a sudden they'd drop. Dead. All but him and children. Whatever it was, it was airborne. Jordan believed it was designed by the government to be a weapon and got out of control.

Seeing the children and himself not affected, he knew the weapon was doing something to people's brains. He had heard that the brain grows and goes through developmental stages all the way into adulthood, and it appeared to Jordan he was a lucky son of a gun to have had a tumor removed from his right temporal lobe when he was seven. Ever since the surgery, he had to have Shaggy's haircut from *Scooby-Doo* to cover the scar on the side of his head. But he figured that whatever had left with his tumor is what prevented him from developing the part of the brain that was triggering the deaths in people.

As soon as Jordan saw everybody was dying, he

immediately drove to his son's house, speeding the whole way. When he opened the front door and saw his four-year-old granddaughter, his keys slipped through his fingers and hit the floor. She was standing over top of his son's and daughter-in-law's bodies on the couch, crying. Her auburn hair and rosy tear-stained cheeks gave her a ruddiness that would blend in perfectly with his breaking heart.

"Pop Pop," Baby Kaitlyn cried, her raised arms beckoning him.

Jordan ran to fill that void in him, scooped her up into his arms, and pressed her against the source of his anguish. He wanted to say it was okay, that everything would be all right. It wouldn't, though. So he said nothing.

He didn't even cry. Everybody's different. And he *was* affected by Baby Kaitlyn's tears, by her little raised arms—needing love and comfort—and by his only child sitting next to his loving wife, both dead on the couch. On the outside was a small frown. On the inside, his grief was a raging storm. Where violent gales battered against his knees, making them buckle. Where lightning mercilessly struck his heart, making him cry out in pain. To the core he was on his knees, clutching his chest, and wailing. Oh, he knew grief. They knew each other very well.

When Jordan's wife Shannon had died six years ago, people who didn't understand him had thought Jordan a callous man at her funeral. Only years later when they saw how he turned down dates and offers by friends to "hook him up" with smart, attractive women did they realize that Shannon was everything to him. And in passing, she had left with a part of him he couldn't give any other woman again. He didn't want any other woman anyway. They didn't get that. Move on, they said. They obviously had never experienced true love.

Jordan shook his head while bouncing Kaity and patting her back.

She pulled away and looked up at him. "Wha' happen',

Pop Pop?"

"I don't know, Kait . . ." His voice cracked on saying her name. In a strained voice he continued, "But I'm going to take care of you now, okay?"

🐦 🐦 🐦

The first three days were the hardest: burying his son and daughter-in-law, finding stranded children, wanting to save them all. He got a bus and drove around looking for survivors, hoping to find at least one other adult. There were none. But there were dozens of children, all of them under the age of ten.

Jordan was oppressed by the children fast. He was a simple man, a freelance photographer. Kids were never his thing because he didn't talk much to begin with, but they always wanted him to look at them ("Look at me! Watch this!"), to play games ("Pretend to be a monster and chase us!"), and to dance ("Dance, Jordy, dance," a boy would say while firing a cap gun at his feet). He wasn't much of a performer, so they threw things at him for their amusement. Because of his lack of outward emotions, namely anger, they found throwing things at him to be just fine. It didn't matter if he didn't react to one of their toys bonking him on the head. Didn't matter if he got the occasional bloody nose, either. Heck, everything was a hilarity to them.

They were so out of control Jordan had to store all of the food and drink in a double-locked room that only he had the keys to. If he didn't have it that way, they'd waste it all by eating and drinking in excess. He couldn't even allow the kids to help cook, prepare, or serve food because everything they touched seemed to burn, disappear, or spill. And food and drink were precious nowadays.

By no means would he desert them, though, even after he caught a little one lighting his pants on fire (while they were still on him, by the way). They were the future, and he understood that it was his responsibility to guide these children in order for them to create a better world than the previous one. For all Jordan knew, they would be the only ones to do so. He had an obligation to preserve the human race. It was a disheartening thought.

There were all types of personalities among the children. Some good. Some bad. It was quite interesting to observe. In stereotypical fashion, the really bad ones preferred night to day. And they were self-reliant. They housed themselves. They fed themselves. They drove— although Jordan tried over and over to stop them. They refused his guidance. They had their own society that had no rules. But they did stay in the photogenic community he had created. He knew they'd eventually stop finding food, and Jordan would be there for them, only on *his* terms. Until then, what could he do? The only thing he did was label them: they were the Unguided.

❧ ❧ ❧

"I wanna help you, Jordy," Brandon O'Brian said. He was the only child Jordan had ever met who preferred to be called by his last name.

A corner of Jordan's mouth curled up slightly. All the kids wanted to "help" with one thing or another. "Pull up a chair to stand on, and you can help me dry off the dishes."

"No," O'Brian said, slicking his brown hair back with both hands. "I gotta idea. I know I'm only a child, but I want you to be open-minded about what I'm gonna tell you."

All the more amused, Jordan rinsed off a plate and replied, "I'm listening."

"I believe if we throw a fun party for Tasha's birthday tomorrow, I can get the others to be thanking you instead of harassing you." He paused, allowing Jordan to absorb what he said. "I could tell them to stop being mean to you because you may stop throwing us parties. I could even tell them how great you are for throwing us the party to begin with. All they need is a good reason to stop treating you like a play toy, and I can help get that message across to them. *If . . .* you'll allow me to be the party planner."

While he was making his pitch, Heather had come from behind him and heard his spiel. "You stole my idea, Brandon!"

He turned around. "Please, Heather, it's O'Brian."

"I'm not calling you that. That's stupid!"

"You're stupid!"

She ignored him and glanced up at Jordan. "Jordy, *I* want to be the party planner. I'll be better than Brandon—"

"Brandon O'Brian."

"Shut up! *I* can keep the other kids from lighting you on fire. *I* can keep them from throwing things at you. *I* can keep them from hurting you. They listen to *me* more than him!" She stabbed an angry finger in O'Brian's direction.

The two of them campaigning against each other would've been comical to Jordan only a couple of months ago, probably to any adult, but he had been desperate for some relief after only a week of taking care of the kids. Their idea of controlling the children through parties was less of an idea and more of a gem. He stopped washing dishes, grabbed a hand towel, and focused on them. O'Brian and Heather were highly influential to them. Both of them had different styles. O'Brian was subtle. Heather was aggressive. He wanted them both. "The *both* of you can be my party planners."

"No!" they both shouted. Jordan tried talking to them, but they put their hands over their ears and wouldn't listen.

"No. No. No," Heather chanted while O'Brian hummed.

Suddenly O'Brian's eyes lit up. He pulled his hands away from his ears and said, "I can provide a lamb for the party! Heather's too bossy anyway. They'll turn on her, Jordy. I'm more of a friend to the others." He brought his hands together like he was praying. "Pleeeeeease, Jordy?"

"I have friends!" She spun on Jordan. "And I can get a

lamb for the party, too. I'll also be there at three o'clock in the morning when those nighttime troublemakers come."

O'Brian had made such a strong point about Heather that Jordan was compelled to choose him. And Jordan knew Heather would be asleep like everybody else if the Unguided came at that hour. He suddenly thought of a good excuse to go with O'Brian. "I'm sorry, Heather, but O'Brian asked about being a party planner first. I have to go with him if you two can't work together."

She stared up at him, face beginning to scrunch, eyes getting shiny.

"You made a wise decision, Jordy," O'Brian said, completely ignoring the girl that just ran off crying. He stuck out his hand. "I won't let you down."

He stared at the stolid boy and reached out to shake the small hand. It all felt like a big charade to him, but he had to admit he was optimistic.

The following morning, party day, Jordan was buttering toast for the kids. Slow and steady wins the race was his motto. The children didn't understand that, of course. They always wanted things now. When they couldn't get it now? They wanted entertainment. And while he was making them breakfast, they threw stuff at him. And O'Brian was nowhere in sight.

"Hey," Jordan said in his always calm and always controlled voice. "Don't you all see I'm fixing you breakfast? If I can't make you some food, we can't quiet those rumbling—"

SWOOSH!

Bang! Clang. Dechang.

Was that a knife? That thing came close to hitting him in the head. He picked it up. The sun's glare from the window reflected off the blade's stainless steel and hit him in the face as he gaped at the kids. His shocked expression sent shrill giggles chorusing in the kitchen by over four dozen children. Last count was fifty-two, but more showed up every day.

They all looked around themselves. A pang of terror

swept through him. They were looking for something to throw, and they were apt to throw something dangerous to get that same slapstick show on his features again. He tried to keep all of the hazardous objects away from them, but the world was theirs now. Just yesterday he saw a lamb tied to a living room chair. A lamb.

They found several more things to throw at him before he could find the words to explain that what they were doing wasn't wise. He ducked behind the kitchen island. More laughter. Their sweet little giggles were beginning to sound more like bleating goats—the ones with horns, hooves, and a tail; and can't forget those demonic-looking eyes. He thought he was safe until a ball of fire flew over the island, landed on his back, and fell to the floor. He didn't catch on fire, thank God.

"Awwwwwww," some of the little ones chided, but seeing Jordan dart out of the kitchen ignited that bleating again. Before he ran out of the house, a cup of orange juice was thrown at him with a shout following it. "Come back, Jordy! We need feed!"

Little demagogues.

He ran out of the house and didn't look back. What the heck was going on?! Jordan had heard laughter was good medicine for coping with a loss, but this was insane. Things were even worse than they were before! O'Brian needed to get those kids looking forward to the party again. Maybe it just needed to get under way quick, fast, and in a hurry. The quicker they were having fun, the faster they'd want more parties, and hurry to be *nice* to Jordan.

"Hey!"

Jordan spun around. It was him.

"Jordy, what happened?"

"You lied is what happened. They tried to kill me in there."

"Impossible." O'Brian flashed Jordan a winning smile. "Look, things don't change overnight. You have to be patient. Everything will be okay. Trust me."

Jordan shook his head. He'd heard enough lies already. "Just get that party started, O'Brian." Jordan turned his back on him and walked away.

"We need snacks for the party," O'Brian called after him, but Jordan didn't even look back.

He had to get away for a few hours. Baby Kaitlyn was fed before any of them, so she'd be all right. And he really did need a brief reprieve. As long as the party was going when he got back, he should be fine. They'd see how much fun he could bring them *without* having to be hit over the head. He hoped O'Brian would get the party together. This party business felt like his last hope. But it was either this or conform and start "playing" with them, which didn't sound like a bad idea anymore. It sure beat having knives thrown at him! The fact was, he could do both: conform and throw parties. But if he were to play pretend in that sense, he might as well put his foot down and say enough was enough. He could show anger. He could shout. He could refuse to play *any* of their games! That would work. And he knew it. He just hated the idea of fighting against the kids. It felt wrong. All the what ifs scared him, too. What if they fought back? What if it brought *more* trouble? No, he had to play along. Play along to get along, right? Yeah, he'd throw them parties and let them "play" all over him. It wouldn't be that bad. But for now, he needed a break.

Inside an upstairs bedroom of a neighboring house, Jordan sat down in a comfortable chair and picked up George Orwell's *Animal Farm*. Farming wasn't really his thing, but a book and quiet, he found, were pleasures he had truly missed. It was only a little over a month ago when he did this very thing, but it seemed like years.

A faint sound of whispering and giggles came from downstairs. He leaped out of the chair, closed the bedroom door, and locked it. He turned back to his book and noticed an MP3 player beside a large, hardened wax puddle on the nightstand. He grabbed it, put the earbuds in his ears, and fingered through the playlist. "Come

Together" by The Beatles. Classic. He and his book reunited. In the back of his mind, he thanked God for not allowing this house to burn down like so many others had. By the looks of the melted candle on the bedside table, it came close. The woman on the bed beside it was lucky, too, though it'd only be cremation to her now.

He heard a knock on the door and turned the music up, full blast. After five minutes had gone by, he got into a good zone in the book. An hour or two passed before he decided to have a break from the talking animals. He pulled out the earbuds and looked down at his watch. 10:45 a.m. He almost felt rejuvenated. A smile crept to his lips as he thought about taking on the little tikes again. He even decided now was a good time to step outside his normal habits and have some fun with them.

"Who's out there?" Jordan shouted playfully. The little ones burst with excited screams, followed by giggles. He stomped toward the door slowly. "Here!" Stomp. "I!" Stomp. "Come!" Stomp. He opened the door and gleeful shouts met him.

Horror Jordan had never known existed in him clashed with his rational mind as he saw Baby Kaitlyn hanging by her neck, chest high, from the hallway's light fixture. His jaw hung and his face appeared to be screaming, but no sound came out. Rope was tied to each of her tiny ankles, wrists, and forehead. The boys holding the ropes were forcing her legs and arms to dance, making their human puppet come to life. The rope on Kaity's forehead was pulled, springing her little head up. Her bulging dead eyes stared at him.

"Nooooo!" Jordan shouted, but it came out more like a shriek. "God! No! No! No! No! No! No!" He grabbed Kaity with one arm to support her weight. His free hand yanked the ropes away from the kids fiercely. "Get outta here!"

They fled.

With a savage pull on the last rope, he snatched the whole light fixture down. The knot around her neck was just a bunch of loops and tangles. He attempted to untie it. Every twist and tug got him nowhere. He screamed with frustration at the chaotic tangles and his shaking fingers. He needed a knife. He jumped up and ran and tripped over a stepladder that was near the stairs. Jordan went tumbling down them. Upon hitting the floor, his adrenaline-fueled body rolled and sprinted for the kitchen as if the tumble was what he intended to do. He was swooning and out of breath when he discovered he was back over his granddaughter cutting the loops of rope from around her neck. He couldn't even remember where he found the knife. He was simply back in front of the bedroom, cutting.

The rope off, he breathed into her mouth. He pressed on her small chest over and over and over. It was eighteen chest compressions now, right? *God, help me!* He breathed back into her mouth. He repeated the sequence . . . and repeated . . . and repeated . . . and repeated . . . Sweat was dripping from his nose, cheeks, chin, and forehead when he finally gave up. He shouted . . . then noticed children were everywhere. Including O'Brian.

"Sorry, Jordy," he said sympathetically.

"Sorry, Jordy!" Jordy mocked. "Sorry, Jordy! Sorry, Jordy!" The kids began crying. "Waaaah! Waaah!" Jordy taunted. "Waaah! Waaah! Get outta here before I kill you little demons!"

They quickly walked out on him.

He wept.

His granddaughter was dead. The one child he *needed* to protect, the only child from *his* only child, was dead. His fear had caused it. His neglect had caused it. His desire to have time for himself had caused it. His selfishness . . .

2:37 p.m. It was party time, and he needed to feed the kids . . . kids . . . kids feed. Jordy moved zombielike back to the Fun House. One happy little thing began spraying him with cologne as he stepped through the front door. Music was blaring, and the kids were shooting each other with things. He ignored them all.

"This is for the dead," the redheaded boy said. The child continued spraying him.

Jordy said nothing. He just plodded through the hallways. He didn't trust himself anymore. Was he himself anymore? Who's Jordy?

Wait. Did he leave Baby Kaitlyn in that house? *Dear God*. But he needed to feed the kids. Kids. Kids feed. He grabbed a bunch of sandwich materials out of his double-locked room and started for the kitchen. Bread. Bologna. Cheese. Easy. Bread. Bologna. Cheese. Easy. Bread. Bologna. Cheese. Easy. He needed to feed the kids, kids, kids feed. Wait. They were in there. They could hear him. They were listening. Always listening . . . From a place far, far away, Jordy could hear a spraying sound. And then a clicking noise.

WHOOMP!

Jordy instantly knew he was in flames and fell to the floor and rolled.

Laughter.

Rolling. Rolling. Rolling.

Laughter.

"Aaaghh!" Jordy screamed as realization burned through his scalp, skull, and *finally* into his brain that his fucking hair was on fire too! He smacked at his head.

Laughter.

He rolled and slapped. Rolled and slapped. Rolled and slapped.

"Jordy, you're not on fire anymore, silly!"

He may not have been ablaze anymore, but it still felt like he was. He rolled one last time and looked. He was smoldering. His face burned. His scalp sizzled. Jesus, he was in agony. He took one deep breath.

And passed out.

Later on that night, through sticky eyelids, Jordy saw more than felt (there was too much pain to feel anything else) that he was wrapped in rope. Tied up. Chaotic knots everywhere. They thrived on chaos, didn't they? He burned. God, did he burn. It felt like he was being scorched by a giant blowtorch that only God's hand could hold, and he was roasting Jordy's upper body as a kid does to a marshmallow. He needed help. Every time he blinked, his eyelids melted together again. He looked around him. Kids were everywhere. These hadn't gotten much sun in a while. And they didn't appear to be getting much sleep lately, either. Fear ripped his pain away—but for only a moment. He tried to speak, to help them understand that if he's not able to treat his burns, he'll die. That if he died, they'd have no one to take care of them. Except, the Unguided took and did what they wanted. So what he did instead was go unconscious as their doll-like hands reached toward him.

Jordy slipped in and out of nightmares throughout the evening. During one of those conscious lapses, he had enough time to comprehend the fact that his mouth was inflamed, and then he slipped back into his dream world. There was sunlight during several of his awakenings, and O'Brian had just enough time to tell him his being tied up was for his own good before Jordan's eyes closed one last time. When he obtained a strong grip on consciousness, it was night again. His mouth was still swollen, and it and his throat were parched. The Unguided children stared at him. Their pale skin and dark circles around their eyes made Jordy feel like their cold little fingers were crawling all over him.

"You bit off Megan's fingies and we had to pu' out yo' teef," a black-haired boy said and grinned.

I didn't do that, he attempted to say. His demeanor must've shown his incredulity, for the boy summoned Megan.

"No!" a girl exclaimed from somewhere Jordy couldn't see. "I don't wanna go!"

"He can't hurt you anymore, come on!"

That one sounded like a boy.

"No! I'm scawed! Stop!" The girl was pushed around a corner and into the living room Jordy was just now sensing he was in. Her confidence rose with each second she had to take Jordy in. She stopped resisting against her oppressor. His fat mouth, his lack of strength, his look of defeat. Her reaction went from panic, to puzzlement, to amusement. She was holding up her hand. Band-Aids were all over the two finger stumps. Simply by her fear, he knew he was the cause of those stumpy fingers. He must've blacked out instead of passed out like he had thought.

He cried.

"Wook at you, you ugwy monsta," she said, stepping closer. "I'ma make you pay, monsta. Whudda ya think about that, cwybaby?" She grabbed a box of crayons sitting beside the couch he was on and approached him.

"You bewieve now," the Unguided boy said, still smiling at Jordy.

The girl took one of the crayons and shoved it up one of his nostrils. "Make you ugwia," she mused, as if she were Michelangelo, merely creating an ugwy masterpiece. She continued shoving crayons in all the holes of his head. He thought the crayons crammed in his ears hurt the worst until she decided to stick them into the holes where his teeth had been.

The other Unguided boys and girls chipped in. Beyond the tiny hands and arms, Jordy caught flashes of O'Brian standing off in the background smiling.

"No," a bigger one said. "Break 'em up and put 'em in there, like this."

"I wanna do one!"

Giggle.

"Me too!"

Giggle.

"Me first!"

"Aaaagh!" Jordy's scream wasn't very loud. There were too many little hands in and around his mouth suppressing his cries.

"Aww, man! His new teef keep fawing out!"

"Wet's see how many we can fit up his *butt*!"

"Ewww! Gwoss!"

Giggle.

"Yeah, come on. Roll him over."

Jordy fingered the bars of his cage thoughtfully. How he had survived it all, he didn't know. God must've found it all quite amusing. Deep down he wished he would've taken a stand against the children's behavior from the very beginning. He let it go on for far too long, he knew. And now the future he pictured was but a burning, voiceless nightmare. Not that much different from before, really. They did whatever they wanted, they didn't provide for all of Jordy's needs, and they didn't listen to Jordy's cries when they abused him, either. They were just as bad as the kids he originally named the Unguided. But after seeing what O'Brian and the others were capable of, they all were the Unguided in his eyes now.

PLEASE

CHANTEÉ HALE

I can practically smell the man, below me. His battered shoes shuffle across the moldy barn floor. It looks so vacant, so empty, down below. The weak light of morning caresses the still-warm carcass of a rat and it lures him closer. I am a shadow lurking overhead, unnoticed, as he closes in on the thing he thinks he needs. But I know the truth. They always say please, in the end.

It scared me at first, like it did everyone else.

I remember those early days, after the world as we had known it crumbled. There was always fear—for our lives, for our hungry bellies. It wasn't until our family stumbled on a ragtag group of men that I began to suspect that those two things were one and the same.

The men smelled of shit and blood and fingered weapons covered in black filth. My little sister whimpered, clinging to the hand I offered her while my parents gave smiles as thin as our gaunt frames. The men's voices were rough, their laughter as sharp as the tools of death they carried as they mocked my parents' insistence that they had nothing to give. When our parents fell to their knees, begging, I turned and ran,

Elena's small hand clenched in my own.

It took an unbearable minute for their laughter and my parents' screams to die, but that was enough. We hid in the darkness of a nearby building's remains, choking back tears and sucking at air—grateful to escape. Eventually, the men gave up searching—or something found them the way they found my parents—but still we hid, crawling through the darkness and the remains of our parents' world.

It felt as if the whole world was in hiding, back when it began. Little more than two waning points of light staring out of the darkness. Eventually the hunger gets to you, though, and you take your little sister's hand and pull her into the sunshine. That's when you realize that sunlight can't fill your aching belly anymore than darkness could. That's when you realize your parents were the lucky ones.

We lived like rodents, back then, scurrying under the feet of the grown-ups. Hiding in shadows while they killed each other, and picking at the scraps they left behind. They seemed driven to war and I couldn't help but think that was what ended things in the first place—their need to destroy. Eventually they were almost all gone. Eventually there weren't any scraps left—the adults had consumed everything they didn't destroy. Elena had grown, but her hand was still small in mine, and she was getting frailer with every passing day. That's when the talk of death started. "Do you think we'll see Mom and Dad again, when we die?" Elena would ask. I never answered, not even when it's all she could say. She'd lie curled in a shopping cart, half buried in tattered blankets, and whisper their names.

Once, I found a dead rat. It was stuck, flies buzzing as they kissed its lips, in a spring-loaded trap. It was the first thing we'd eaten in a week and tasted like heaven. As I licked its fat and blood from my fingers, I envied that simple trap, coveted the ease with which it caught its prey. I scraped the last shards of flesh from its mangy pelt and wondered what tiny morsel an animal like this would risk its life for.

Elena's tiny whimper, muffled by the thick hunk of rat meat I'd been forcing her to chew, saved us. I looked up to see the man, knife thin, twisting his way over the tangle of rotting wooden benches. There were yellow grass stains on his shirt, and it's all I could think of as I scooped Elena off the ground. "Daddy," she whimpered while I darted across the empty space between us and the cracked pavement where her shopping cart awaited us. I could feel him, his fingers inches from my shoulder blades, as I dumped her into the basket and began to push. I ran, the cart threatening to topple and spill my sister across the concrete, and marveled at the trap's complexity: a rat-trap that catches an unwary passerby. Luckily, it was only one man chasing us, and when the cart toppled, it was by my own hand.

I grabbed Elena and shoved her down the gaping storm drain. It was harder for me to follow after her, but not by much. She didn't even lift herself out of the wet muck into which she fell, waiting for me to do it for her. Still, I carried her. Maybe he would find a way down, maybe he wouldn't, but I wasn't going to let her die that way.

A week later, she started saying please. "Please, Jordan, I'm so hungry." I fed her bugs, dirt, whatever I could find to fill her belly. It was never enough, but I couldn't give up. I'd taken care of her for too long.

It took me a month to understand what she needed. At the end, all she could do was beg me: "please." In the end Elena wasn't hungry anymore, and after my tears stopped, neither was I. By morning the whole world felt changed. The fear left with the hunger, but while hunger returned, the fear never did. I never had to run again.

Even though morning makes the weathered barn feel almost peaceful, the man below me eats in terrified haste, his body shaking and trembling. While he licks the last drop of blood and rat grease from his fingers I drop to the floor.

My feet touch the floorboards and they heave a muffled sigh. Like him, the boards are ready to give in and crumble back into the earth. The man twists around, knees grinding on the soft wood as he spins. He doesn't bother to rise. Already I know he won't run. They never do.

He says "please," his voice nearly desperate with hope. He doesn't have to tell me he's hungry and tired of living. I already know.

I give him what he wants, and then I eat.

WEATHERVANE

PETE BOGG

The worst flood the world has ever known happened when I was eleven years old. The flood that wiped out the sinners and lasted forty days and forty nights may have been worse. But not by much. I was home alone at the time. My parents, Robert and Emily Sherman, had gone out for the night, trusting that I could handle whatever our quiet neighborhood had to throw at me. Had the clouds been gathering ominously, had there been a hint of destructive rain, they might have thought better of it. But seeing how the sky was blue, the birds were singing, and I was an only child who had never been anything but absolutely responsible when it came to being left alone, they each gave me a kiss and a hug, walked out the door, and that was the last I ever saw of them.

Cold weather aggravated an old war injury my father had. He walked with a cane during the winter months and limped around the house in thermal pajamas constantly. It's one of the few clear memories I have left of the man. The only indication of what was to come that day was that my father had decided to take with him the flashy walking stick with the polished eagle head handle. Even though it was summer and the weatherman forecasted uninterrupted sunniness for the foreseeable future. My father never complained about his injury. Never even grimaced when the limp became pronounced. My mother and I thought nothing of it. Even though he had told us on occasion how his magic leg could predict the weather.

How it had never been wrong, not once in twenty years. I thought nothing of it as I stood in the doorway, watching my father escort my mother to the car, hobbling, and leaning heavily on the long polished stick.

I fixed myself a dinner of boiled hotdogs and a chocolate pudding cup for dessert. I settled on the couch, prepared for a quiet night at home, and ate my hotdogs bunless with ketchup and relish. A big tall glass of chocolate milk went down nice. On the extreme sports channel, guys and gals flipped and turned in the air and made it all look so easy and natural on the gargantuan half-pipe made entirely of ice. Extreme sports reruns were my latest addiction. I'd been surfing since I was six years old, but had somehow never made the transition to snow. Snow was just so much more intimidating for some reason, even though the rational part of my brain knew that a wave traveling fast enough could hurt just as much, if not more, than the icy side of a mountain.

At some point during my extreme sports television marathon extravaganza, I drifted off to sleep.

I was awakened by a peal of thunder. I had never been one of those timid boys who hides under his bedsheets during a lightning storm. But on that occasion, I awoke screaming because it was so loud. Imagine three-inch plate steel being ripped down the middle on speakers loud enough to pacify even the most discerning death metal junky. I awoke in a darkened living room, in a completely darkened house. We lived in one of those old-timey jobs. Three stories with a wraparound white porch and a basement that served as a storm shelter in a pinch. Of course, I wasn't thinking about stuff like that then.

What I wanted to know, in my half asleep mind, was who had just screamed and why the television was off. I couldn't remember leaving the kitchen light on, but that was off too. And I felt nowhere near rested enough to explain how I'd slept through the better part of the afternoon and some of the night. My parents were home. They had to be. And from the eerie quality of the house I judged that they had gone to bed and been asleep for hours. But even this didn't feel right. I don't know how to explain it other than to say a house with only one person in it has a different feel than one with multiple people sleeping.

A lone sane house just feels—colder. And that's how this house felt. Besides, if my parents were home they would never have left me asleep on the couch, lips crusted with ketchup, relish, and chocolate pudding. They'd have woke me up. Made me take a bath. Scolded me for leaving a mess. All the things good parents do. Their absence was a swift kick to the adrenal gland.

I got up and ran over to the light switch on the wall. Like the one in the kitchen, it refused to cancel out the all-consuming blackness. My mind reeled, wanting to convince myself it was late. That I'd slept for many hours. But my body knew better. It told me that my muscles weren't stiff enough yet from sleeping at that awkward angle. Not by a long shot. If I had slept propped up on the couch for that long I'd know about it. Fact was, I'd only been out for a little while. That explained why my parents weren't home yet. But not why the view outside my living room window was black. That would come a moment later as the sky erupted in pink electrical fire.

In that blinding instant, I had a half-second glimpse at

the geography of the land and sky out of my kitchen window. Clouds like a hideous pink and gray writhing brain on the cold steel autopsy table is what the sky looked like. And the neighborhood—the old boring neighborhood where nothing ever happened—it was as still as death. Our neighbors, the Jensens, had a flagpole in their front yard, and on their roof, one of those rustic weathervanes shaped like a rooster. Neither stirred. There was not a breath of wind outside to be had. It was as if everything, including me, was in stasis, only to be returned, a moment later, to crashing darkness.

The thunder that followed rattled our windows and my teeth simultaneously, all at once transforming the very ground I stood on into a tuning fork.

You know that voice inside that tells you when to run? Mine had gotten a glimpse of the sun, smothered like the last lingering campfire ember, down till it was no brighter than the cherry of my mother's cigarettes when I'd peer into my parents' darkened room late at night. The glowing red ember told me she was awake, and that she saw me looking in, even though she never spoke. The inner voice had seen the dying sun look back from its impossibly high position in the sky and it wanted me to turn around, get away, go anywhere but here. It wanted me to get lost, or even hide in the closet, as so many dead children did during a house fire.

Somewhere safe and familiar and had I listened to it there wouldn't be much of a story to tell. Just as surely as I know the blackening hatred I looked into also looked back into me, I know I would have died that day had I listened to my instincts.

Instead, I did the worst and stupidest thing I could have done. One look at that sky and I knew it was coming for me. So I grabbed the wireless phone off the charger and ran downstairs, into the basement. Of course, the phone didn't work. I had already tried that. But I held onto that inanimate piece of plastic like a plush teddy bear. I prayed to it. I rubbed its smooth side unknowingly against my cheek, willing its bright orange screen to come alive with an incoming call. Had I hid in one of the closets upstairs I wouldn't have seen the flood waters rise until it was too late. My rashness, and my stupidity, saved my life that day.

                                        ⇃ ⇃ ⇃

I didn't have to wait long for the flood waters to come pouring in. Through the letterbox windows high upon the basement walls, it slapped the concrete floor below like an abusive husband and immediately began filling the dark, square space. I felt it up to my ankles in an instant. It was frigid as a skeleton in a graveyard in October. I knew it would be above my head in no time at all. So I ran back upstairs, clutching my phone. Only this time I didn't stop at the living room where the front door was. I ran right up to the floor where my parents' bedroom was. Despite what I knew to be true in my heart, I ripped back the comforter on their carefully manicured bed, checking to see they weren't in it.

Seeing only bed sheets, I ran down the hall to my bedroom and started slamming fistfuls of clothes, socks and underwear mostly, into a light blue nylon Transformers backpack. But first, I upturned it, dumping out all the useless school books, papers, and number 2 pencils. I would be leaving soon, with no idea if I'd ever return. The last thing I wanted to take with me was homework. When I was done emptying my sock drawer I looked out the window and by the next great pulse of lightning saw the flood waters.

It was a sight maybe seen only once before by Noah himself. Except he was afforded the luxury of seeing it from the bow of a boat in the company of two of all the world's animals. I was just a terrified boy, alone, looking at it from a second-floor window, as a lake the color of chocolate milk materialized from every direction. It crawled up the side of my house and shattered the first-floor windows. It swirled and undulated with tiny whirlpools; and in it, pieces of my neighborhood bobbed in and out of sight, like motes in a focusing eye. Mailboxes, telephone poles, minivans, and people, presumably.

Of course, any human debris I saw I immediately convinced myself was something else entirely—mannequins perhaps, from one of the boutiques in town. I willed myself away from the window, heart pounding as water rushed into my house. I heard it downstairs, clanking around like an inept intruder, fumbling loosely around the cavernous space, making noise like a jet turbine, all echoes and howling air being displaced by furious waves. I had minutes at best yet to live. No one ever thinks to include life boats in a list of emergency supplies. Back then, very few people even carried flood insurance.

❧ ❧ ❧

For reasons I've never been able to fully explain, least of all to myself, I had a knack for remaining focused in a crisis situation. In a different world, I might have grown up to be a fireman or a police officer. If I had the steady hands to go with my talent for remaining calm, I might have even become a surgeon. But it was not to be. Many times in my life since, this talent has proven itself useful, but never in the aforementioned capacity. As I watched wave after wave lap against the bottom rungs of my staircase, inching their way toward me like a specter in my nightmares, a curious thing happened. The voice inside went from an urgent roar to a soothing whisper. It whispered to me like my mother had when reading bedtime stories to me as a boy. It told me just what to do next. And I listened. Oh, for the life of me, I listened.

I ran back to my parents' room and took my father's old service pistol out of the drawer of the nightstand beside the bed. I checked to make sure it was loaded. Then I grabbed a box of bullets from where he kept them stashed in the pocket of a suitcoat he never wore. I also took an umbrella, even though there had not yet been a drop of rain. The sleeping bag I went back to my room for. And by that time, the carpet in the hallway was damp, spongy beneath my bare feet, and where I ran it shot up fountains of brown cold filth up my calves. I was nowhere near ready to go for a swim. But time was running out.

I was able to grab a flashlight, some extra batteries, and an unopened soft drink from my bedside table before an ominous rumble jerked my attention back toward the window. I would have convinced myself it was thunder had there been lightning. This was the thunder of a thousand timbers breaking at once, splintering like stick matches. Of brick and mortar peeling away from a foundation slab. Detaching from the umbilicus. Of our neighbor's home reduced to driftwood. I watched it separate from the ground and rise up on a wave like a slumbering giant aroused to anger, lurching awkwardly towards our house. My house.

When I was certain my neighbor's three-story home would hit us, I closed my eyes and braced for impact. This was it, I thought. And I was dead meat, I told myself. I closed my eyes and bit my lower lip and when a few moments went by and nothing happened I partially peeled open one peeper and saw the empty lot where the house had been. Then both eyes shot open, and I stared in wide-eyed wonder at the mountain of lumber with the rooster weathervane atop the roof moving by as gingerly as a fat woman in a grocery store aisle. If I had to guess, I'd say it missed hitting our house by mere inches.

I'd had all the excitement I could handle for one day and then some. Before anything else crazy could happen, I shouldered on the blue Transformers backpack, grabbed the umbrella, and threw my leg over the ledge of my window. Just before I ducked out onto the shingled roof, something in the corner of the room caught my eye. It was my surfboard, propped up in a corner. I don't know why I brought it with me. It just felt wrong to leave her behind.

With surfboard and umbrella in hand I climbed up onto the highest point of the roof and waited.

A house made entirely of bricks would have sank to the bottom immediately. Goes to show that either the three little pigs didn't know what the hell they were talking about when it came to the finer points of home construction, or the risk of flood was the furthest thing from their little piggy minds. My neighbor's house had been half brick and half wood, which was why it bobbed for a time, like a wine cork, drifting out away from where it had sat undisturbed for decades, before slipping below the waves. Until all I could see of it was the brass rooster weathervane, which had yet to so much as turn.

Our house, on the other hand, was built entirely of wood and stucco. A glorified chicken coop. The stucco made it light, and the wood made it buoyant. It might not have fared too well against the big bad wolf, but for my purposes it would do nicely. Unless, that is, it decided to dissolve like an effervescent tablet in a glass of water. Saddling the highest point, with a leg draped over either side of the roof, I awaited death with an alien sense of calm. Nothing could have been more beautiful. Humid misty air peppered my cheeks with spray, and every once in a while, the sky would alight with an incandescent heartbeat, giving pause to the chaos abounding.

In those instances before the thunder came and nearly swept me over the side, I would get a picture of the world so clear it may as well have been a photograph. Partially submerged cars passing by like schooners. Uprooted trees, some as old as a hundred years, nearby. Trash, refuse, plastic containers, everything that floats, up to and including human bodies, was frozen in those moments of intense pink light.

When your house separates from its foundation you just have to grip the terra-cotta roof shingles with your thighs and scream to God. The initial jolt is the worst part. When concrete and support beams and a whole host of other immoveable fixtures give way to the not so subtle influence of water, you have to hang on for dear life, that's for sure. But once the home detaches and the wood beneath stops groaning in protest like a mortally wounded sperm whale, there is a long moment of peace that follows.

Sure, my nerves were frazzled. What kid's wouldn't be? I worried about my parents. Wondered if maybe, by some miracle, they'd managed to climb to the roof of the restaurant where they'd been having dinner. My father, after all, was a war vet, and he had a certain intuition. I convinced myself, as our drifting home on Watermelon Street picked up momentum, that his leg had ached so intensely, it had been enough of an early warning system that they had gotten out to somewhere safe.

The air was so warm I basked in it, sleeping under a roof awning, completely exposed that night. If I closed my eyes I could almost pretend the gentle pitching of the bow and stern was my mother rocking me to sleep. She hadn't rocked me like that since I was a baby. How desperately I wanted her to then. Somehow, even with irregular thunder, sleep came.

You'll buy a house and you'll fill it with stuff. That was the philosophy at the start of the twenty-first century. And when it's gone, what you'll miss most, besides the people and what they contributed, like the smell of bacon and eggs frying in the kitchen, or the wood varnish scent of my dad's old workshop, are the photographs. I sat in a nook, on the shady side of the house, the next morning, wishing more than anything I had thought to bring our photo albums. I had to fight off a real compulsion to climb back in through the window, dip into the dark murky water and go searching blindly for them.

Instead, I focused on what I did have. An LED flashlight, a sleeping bag, an umbrella, socks of all colors, and absolutely positively no hope whatsoever.

Eventually though, sunlight pierced the clouds. They

were like nothing I'd ever seen or have seen since. Only now, many years later, do I know the truth of it. They were steam clouds. Steam from the top of the world where the ice is thickest. That I could see them from atop my roof should clue you in to just how massive they were. We still don't know what caused it. Two of the most widely circulating theories are that a supermassive volcano underneath the ice cap spontaneously erupted or that we were grazed by a passing asteroid and that the friction in the earth's atmosphere was enough to flash fry a couple billion tons of ice.

But these theories don't come from your run of the mill scientists. They come from kids like me, raised on MTV, the Discovery Channel, and countless hours surfing the net. Kids who knew of the Bible but had never actually read it. They would make up quotes from it to scare their little sisters. And I'd roll my eyes. They had absolutely no idea what they were talking about.

It was my desire to find photographs that sent me back into the house. It had been what I'd found instead that sent me back for more. Despite having been jerked free of the ground, the contents of our house on Watermelon Street stayed relatively where they'd last been. I had to go diving for them. Hold my breath and swim down the hall, eyes pinched shut. But there were air pockets and if I felt around with my hands long enough, eventually I'd emerge with treasure. That first day I recovered my parents' bedsheet and also a box of markers from my room.

With them I fashioned a flag. My original intent had been to make a distress signal that someone could see from a long way off. Instead, I drew a smirking skull and crossbones on the white sheet. I was the captain of this ship after all. And if any potential rescuer couldn't take a joke they weren't worth being rescued by, I decided. My dad's tools were somewhere on the first level, along with the camping gear and most of the other usefuls. But I hadn't the guts yet, on that first day, to swim that deep.

★ ★ ★

I saw other kids on rooftops. At night, their little fires were the only sources of light, other than the stars, for miles. In the day, they'd see my flag and wave hello if we drifted close enough. When I was hungry and thirsty, I mustered my courage and swam to the first level of the house on one lungful of air. In the kitchen there was a large pocket above the stove that I had to feel for in frigid darkness. I gasped, emerging in the smoke vent, clutching my LED flashlight. Shadows reflected off the jostled brown water. And each looked like it could have been a hand reaching up to pull me back under.

When I came to my senses I searched the kitchen. Found soggy salami in the fridge, and a few non-perishables in the cupboards that wouldn't require a can opener. My backpack was half full by time I swam back through the living room. Ultimately, I found what I was looking for in the hall closet: All my dad's fishing gear. Multiple poles and a tackle box. I couldn't take all of it with me and still swim. But I managed to drag three poles, a tackle box, and a full backpack upstairs without drowning. Not bad for an eleven-year-old kid raised on MTV.

★ ★ ★

I traded one of my fishing poles with a kid who looked far worse off than me. He was a couple years younger. And it was just him and his sister huddled close together on the roof of a small apartment building. I traded him my fishing pole and a couple bottles of water for a camp stove that still worked and the fixings for s'mores the kid had with him that had somehow miraculously stayed dry. All that day, we splashed and played in the water together, our houses on a similar trajectory. Then at dusk, I shared my dinner of s'mores with them. And the little girl actually turned and produced a big chocolaty marshmallowy smile for me before they swam back to their house.

In the morning they were gone. Then there were two days when I saw no one, and nothing except murky, fast-flowing water as far as the eye could see.

On the third day there were seven floating coffins. Must have been a funeral home upriver, I thought. Lids were still shut, and I didn't have the nerve to swim over and see if they were full or not. Lacquered wood had seen better days. So had I, by that point. I went to sleep early, feeling truly scared for the first time since this whole fiasco began, and when I awoke, they too were gone. But I've had nightmares about it ever since. Always that some watery corpse emerges out of a pill-shaped vessel, climbs up a rain gutter, and gets me when I'm not looking. Always the same dream.

Truly, the most amazing thing happened shortly after sunrise on the fourth day. You won't believe it if I tell you, but I feel oddly compelled to keep this account as accurate as possible. I awoke to the sound of splashing and I scrambled, nearly falling off the pitch slope of the roof, thinking it was the undead come to get me. Instead, what I found was a German Shepherd paddling wildly, exhausted to near death, trying to climb up onto the awning of what used to be our porch. Without thinking, I dove in head first, and swam to him.

He nearly drowned me, and his claws cut me up something fierce, but I managed to get his front paws over the ledge of the rain gutters. Then, when he stopped thrashing, I dove below and shoved with all my might till his hind legs were up too. He gave a couple violent shakes that would have covered me had I not been as wet as I could get. He licked my hand and we became fast friends.

The name on his collar said Brutus, and I thought it was some kind of cruel joke. Brutus was anything but what his name implied. At night, he liked to curl up by my feet. I shared the fish I caught with him. And he alerted me every time we came up on another floating house. Even in pitch black, he would whine and get agitated if one came too close. Someone must have been taking him for a walk when the water came and swept them both away, because a leather leash was still attached to his collar when I found him.

It became apparent pretty quick that we couldn't rely on the contents of our house alone if we wanted to survive. I'd taken all the camp supplies, all the bottled water, and whatever else Mom had in the cupboards. It must have been close to grocery day when the event occurred because the pickings were threadbare and what I did manage to scrounge was mostly spoiled. We would need to search another house, I knew, but the thought of what was in there scared me nearly as much as the prospect of dying of dehydration and exposure. People who hadn't made it out in time. Strange floor plans I didn't already know by heart.

I'd have to feel around in pitch blackness, and do it quickly before hypothermia set in. But there was nothing else for it. If we wanted to live we would need more than the slim artifacts my house alone had contributed.

I couldn't be too choosy, of course. Houses were fewer and farther between. But I knew what I needed: a wooden, single-story home, preferably one with an open living room area and a lot of windows so in case I got lost inside I could escape quickly and not drown while searching for a way out. It just so happened that the next house we saw was close enough for horseshoes and hand grenades. The great thing about single-story homes is that if they're small enough, they tend to ride high in the water. Just like a dingy compared to some epic barge, like our house on Watermelon Street was. If they're light enough there is a cushion of air inside to breathe.

I told Brutus to stay. But we were friends. And friends don't tell each other what to do. He barked once as I dove off the roof. Then he dove right in after me. I have to admit, it made me feel better swimming toward that eerily deserted house with him paddling along beside me.

At one of the windows I helped hook his front legs over the ledge and told him to wait. This time, he listened. Inside, the water rose to my chin, and if I stood on tiptoes I could feel the squishy carpet below. Shoes don't work so well for swimming, and I cringed at the thought of accidentally stepping onto a corpse with my bare feet, or, more accurately, stepping into.

A body that waterlogged would be the consistency of cream cheese, I knew. Unless it decided to reach out and grab hold of my leg, I thought wildly. What is it about the mind that enjoys self-induced torment?

Brightly colored toys bobbed listlessly in the living room—wooden blocks with letters of the alphabet painted on one side and a number between 1 and 9 on the other. Below the surface I stubbed my toe against what felt like a coffee table and yelped. Toys encircled me, hungry for my blood. With a sweep of my arms I cast them aside, trying not to think about who they belonged to. I filed it away with all of the other dangerous questions: How deep is the water? Where does it flow? Where are my parents?

I stuffed my backpack full of unopened, unbroken jars of baby food. Then went in search of a tiny spoon. Awaiting me at the window, Brutus looked anxiously in. His ears were pert and his eyes tracked something in the water. Something just beneath the surface. I didn't look back to see what it was.

We ate our baby food in silence and it was about this time I decided I needed a weapon. The kids I had met so far were nice enough for the most part. But there had been that one older boy who had cursed at us from the roof of a house a long ways off. Binoculars from my dad's camp gear provided a close-up view of what had been a filthy and emaciated boy hugging a brick chimney as if it were his last and best friend, screeching obscenities in our general direction. As a boy, I had never even been in a fist fight. His eyes convinced me that had there been less water between us, he would have had no moral dilemma with killing me and taking my stuff.

The best I could do was an old skinning knife my dad had. Guns were worthless, if only because every bullet on earth was wet now from a weeklong soak. Dad's old service pistol had been one of the first casualties of this new alien environment. I had never been a fan of guns anyway and would have just as soon they were all at the bottom, so long as no one else possessed a dry box of ammo anywhere. With the knife I prepared our dinner that night: sautéed carp in a cast iron skillet with a side of pureed carrots.

🦋 🦋 🦋

I'd taken to collecting drift wood, letting it dry, and then burning it on cold nights. I sat in a lawn chair one night about dusk, warming wet calves over a driftwood fire, when I heard the rattle of an outboard motor. Brutus heard it first, long before I did. He stepped to the edge of the roof, head cocked curiously out over the water, due west. I slipped Dad's skinning knife into the back of my jeans and watched as a boat approached. Three occupants. Two boys and a girl. Spread out in the middle of the boat, a canvas tarp under which presumably were all their worldly possessions.

"Hey, kid!" the one at the front yelled up. Something about the smirk on his face made me think he had been a schoolyard bully in a previous life, and had since gone on to bigger and better things. The girl, if you can believe it, was in a yellow sundress, and looked freshly bathed. She looked up as well, eyeing enviously the umbrella I had open to keep the sun from toasting me mercilessly. The floppy hat she wore looked to be doing an acceptable job, but I knew envy when I saw it. "Got any food up there?" The kid in the front asked.

"No," I lied flatly. Even with grappling hooks they'd have a hell of a time clawing their way up the terra-cotta shingles. Especially with me stabbing at them the whole way. My hand crept to the rubbery handle sticking out above the top of my jeans at the small of my back.

"Want some?" the kid asked. I blinked, not knowing what he referred to till I saw the can of beans in his hand. "We were out on patrol and came across a bunch," he said, prideful-like. "More than we can eat. Here," he said, and tossed the can up to me. It glinted in the sunset, turning end over end.

I caught it in midair.

Beneath the rumble of the two-stroke engine, very faintly, Brutus was growling.

Turns out, they had all the canned goods they could eat and no can opener. In exchange for using the one I'd taken from my mom's kitchen, they shared their bounty of delectable tin treats. We sat eating pineapple chunks, looking out over the water, at the moon as it rose. Brutus regarded the three with a wary uncertainty and refused to leave my side the entire night. The oafish one who had been steering the boat was the girl's boyfriend, and the smirking one was her brother, or so they claimed. I gave them some sleeping bags and a tent to sleep in, thinking that by morning they too would be gone.

When morning came they were there, groggily stretching, and shivering in the briskness. "What did you mean 'on patrol'?" I asked him.

"It's exactly what it sounds like," the boy said. "We go out and enforce the law. Now it's my turn to ask a question," he said. "Where did you come by all this stuff?" He gestured toward the gutted contents of our house on Watermelon Street, strewn over every square inch of available roof space.

"Easy," I said. "Swim down and get it."

He looked at me differently after that. He had been certain before stepping foot on my roof, when he saw the flag with its skull and crossbones. Now he wasn't so sure.

"You can do that?"

"Of course," I replied. "It's easy." It was my turn to be boastful.

"So what are we going to do when all the houses sink?" the girl asked.

The two boys looked at her, then back at their feet. She had successfully voiced one of those dangerous questions I hadn't even gotten around to truly considering yet. Neither had they, apparently.

"Don't worry about that now," her brother said. "Just worry about not burning lunch."

She absentmindedly stirred a pot of beans over a driftwood fire. She stuck her tongue out at her brother.

"You use that thing much?" her brother asked, nodding to the surfboard I had stashed in a shady spot.

"Not recently," I told him truthfully.

Before I knew it, they were pulling me behind the boat and I was surfing in their wake. We used the long leather leash that had been attached to Brutus when I found him as a tether. We spent all afternoon like that. Splashing and yelling in the sun. Taking turns on my surfboard. Seeing who could stay on the longest.

"We should be going," her brother said.

"Do you have to?" I asked, plaintively and out of breath.

"You should come with us," she said, as if she had just had a brilliant idea she had never before considered.

"Yeah," her boyfriend said. "Why not? A guy who can surf like you."

"But where?" I asked.

"Only place left that's safe," the girl's brother said.

Come to find out there were more kids adrift than just us. They had attached tow ropes to houses so they drifted together like one big mother ship. They had been busy devising ways of keeping the homes afloat indefinitely, which was why they needed the law, he explained.

"You can keep a house afloat forever and it won't matter if chaos reigns." He pulled back the tarp in the middle of his boat, revealing a pile of canned goods. Lying atop it there were three AK-47s and a corpse bound at the wrist and ankles that had been shot in the head.

"We tried bringing him back alive," the brother explained. "But somewhere between there and here he tried overturning the boat. If you look at it in those terms, we really had no choice."

I had yet to take my eyes off of the dead man. He had been older, with salt and peppery hair. He had a thick, coarse mustache and appeared to be thinking. The hole above his right eye gave no indication of the mess at the back of his head. It didn't even leak blood. I felt my knees getting weak.

"Don't worry," her brother said. "Our dad was a cop. These were his guns and he taught us how to shoot."

"Who is the guy?" I ventured, testing my tongue to see if it still worked.

"Him?" the boy asked incredulously. "A nobody. He tried touching one of the girls. Then stole a boat to escape the night before the execution."

Guess he had it coming, I felt like saying. Words rose in my throat. Then settled back like curdled chunks. It was something cold that a true gunslinger would say. But I didn't feel very much like one of them at the moment.

"Come with us?" the girl repeated.

"You could be part of the salvage crew." I looked inquisitively at her brother, who answered. "They even have real diving equipment. Oxygen masks, goggles. The works. You been going without so long I bet you'll swim circles around them too."

"What about my dog?" I asked, rather lamely. I was still mindful of the corpse in the boat. It was the first dead body I'd come up close and personal to.

"Bring him! Of course!" the boyfriend crowed. "There are plenty of dogs there. Great early warning systems. They also help us find things in the dark."

"Sounds good, I guess." I believe those were my exact words.

PART V

THE LOST

SHADOW PEOPLE

SCOTT CLARK

These days, waking up wasn't really waking up. It was merely opening his eyes to what he could already smell and feel: smoke wrapping itself around him every waking second of the day. Greasy coils clinging to his every move, hanging on his every breath. Stinging him in his guts. Choking him.

After the fires started, there had only been the smoke.

It was heaviest at the ceiling, where it gathered in a hot reeking cloud, so he did his best to keep low. Some days, his back ached and he gritted his teeth mercilessly. Only a few months ago, his tooth had cracked and a sliver of yellowing enamel had disappeared down his throat.

Though he knew he was surely one of the few, or *only*, left he took care to lock the door behind and before himself. The wooden door had been patched and nailed a hundred times and it rattled noisily with the slightest movement. The gray haze seeped through every crack and hole, riding an invisible breath of stale, roasting wind. When the smoke bellowed in he would curl up in a ball and clamp his eyes shut. This was sleep. There was no

189

one to say otherwise.

He shared his bed with charcoal snakes that disappeared mischievously at the wave of a hand. Figures danced through the smoke only to vanish when he approached. Faces burst out of the shadows, speaking nonsense, sometimes smiling, sometimes not. He knew he had been alone too long. A few years ago while shaving in the shabby bathroom, he had sworn he saw someone watching him from the bedroom window. He had seen, clear as day, the impossibly dark form of a man, still as stone, watching. He had hidden.

After that, he smashed all the mirrors in the cabin and boarded all the windows.

Cabin. Only once had the man used that word, but it didn't feel right. There had been a cabin before, but it had happier memories than this place, family memories. Shack wasn't the right word either. Some nights he fooled himself into calling it home, usually after a few nips of the whiskey he kept wrapped in jumpers and stuffed in an old welly under the counter. The whiskey was only half of his valuables, the other half being a tightly wrapped package under his bed—a souvenir from the old days.

He hated waking. Moving at all in his filthy clothes was worse than uncomfortable. The sweat and the smoke, they formed a thin layer of black ooze on his stinking skin. The rags he had gathered on his travels did little to help; they were matted beyond comfort.

First thing after waking was to check the door. He swung his legs over the edge of the old bed, slowly and carefully. Once on his feet he assumed his hunch, breathing slowly, and approached the door. It was shut tight. He staggered to the tiny kitchen, an old t-shirt wrapped twice round his grimy face. He pushed his long, sticky black hair back into a ponytail and, after rooting around in his crowded pockets, produced an old worn elastic band to secure the strands. He surveyed the cabin: old, crumbling, eternally dark with plumes of fog. Even after all this time, empty.

He hadn't had much time when he left his last haven. The earth had started grumbling, a noise he could never forget. The walls had cracked, showering him with white plaster. Mud poured in by the ton, pushing years of work into the concrete floor. The tin openers, hobs, gas bottles, clothes, torches, even a stationary bike, all disappeared in seconds. Then the fire had clawed its way in, and the underground room became a crematorium. All he could do was snatch the closest bag and race up the exit ladder.

He collected one of the few remaining cans from the kitchen worktop and put it in his pocket, then shuffled back to the front door. Next to it, a large collection of torn fabrics hung on a nail on the wall. This was a jacket once, he thinks, someone *made* it. Someone worked on it and for it. Sometimes he thinks he can smell the previous owner on the lapels, deep in the weave. Sometimes he thinks someone left it here, just for a moment.

Next to the door, in the corner, lay a long pole with a chain net on the end. The man picked it up and slid the door block aside with his boot. The door slowly creaked inward, a gust of black air pushing inside. Black feelers rolled over the door edge and the man's grizzled face. He pulled the t-shirt farther up his nose, so that his eyes were barely free, and started out the door. Things never get better out here. He has learned that.

The red fields stretched for a thousand miles in every direction, flaring and burning constantly. Swirls of crimson exploded up from burnt orange rivers. Islands of black rock wobbled slowly, toppled, and then bobbed back smothered in fire. Black smog erupted from cracks in the burnt parts of the lower hill; every now and again a fresh spurt of arterial fire sprayed out into the never-ending night. The smoke choked him, even from behind the makeshift mask, so he worked quickly on the roasted earth. The hillside he has found provided all he needed.

Carefully, he crept across the grass, down toward the fires. His hands out to steady himself, he watched his footing. One slip is all it would take. He noted his small flag, erect in the charcoal earth, and carried on past it. When he was about seven feet away, the man squatted on his haunches and put the pole down next to him. From his pocket he took the can, and from his belt he removed a sturdy, thick, butcher's knife. A few seconds later and he had half-decapitated the can, the sweet smell of plum tomato just bursting through the smoke that blackened his nostrils. He stabbed the knife deep into the black ground then placed the can carefully into the net at the end of the pole. Steadying himself by holding the knife he reached out slowly, extending the tin closer and closer to the angry flames until they licked and bit at his meal. When bubbles appeared at the gash in the tin, he retracted the pole and, with a sock over his hand, set the can back in his deep jacket pocket. He picked up the pole, put the knife back in his belt, and made his way up the hill.

The man stopped only to pick the flag out of the charred soil and place it carefully in the new line between the burning and the burnt.

Back in the cabin the man removed all of his blackened clothes and sat on the floor, naked, legs crossed, eating boiled tomato with a dirty spoon. Once finished he looked at an old photo of himself and pretended it was a mirror. He laughed. Then he coughed. The moment disappeared when he stood to put another rag into another crack in the wooden walls. The wind had changed to blow from the south. The southern slopes were where the apple trees were. The last of them, too. But right now he made a point to himself.

Got to eat, he said.

Got to eat.

He took a long gulp from a bucket under the sink. There was little water left, so he must venture up the hill. He noted what he ran out of on a yellowing scrap of card and replaced his dirty rags. He bolted the door and heaved his weary body through the swirling smog.

The south slope was ruined by the time he arrived.

The fires were quickening. The last of the apple blossoms stood charred, their great thick branches reduced to black bony spider's legs, grasping desperately at the sky. The man collected the few grubby apples that survived the scorching, and turned toward the summit.

At the summit lay a corrie. Water from one of the rainstorms, a week or so ago, stagnated in the pit of its bowl. He had done his best to protect it from the smoke and ash by pulling a tent cover from one shore to the other. On the little beach, under a rock lip, he kept the provisions he found on the hill—boxes of browning apples, bottles filled with the water when it had first fallen, and some meat he had salvaged from a sheep, half roasted by the fires. The few condiments that had been abandoned in the cabin were wrapped and double-wrapped in plastic bags and kept under the food.

He filled a bottle with the water and then replaced the cover, finally gathering the last of the mutton. Climbing out of the summit, he started toward the north slope, where he kept the few vegetables.

The fires had not managed to ravage this area yet. He muttered thanks. The blazing pools had a long time to go if they were to get this far. The south side of the hill was an easier contour; the fire had had no issues rolling up it. The north face, however, was much steeper, and patchy; there was little for a fire to grab at. But he knew in time everything would burn.

Suddenly he stopped, staring into the smoke. His eyes squinted and strained against the abrasion of the winds until the image became clear. There was a man in the fire, clear as day. Black, his skin fried so that it had shrivelled up in patches to reveal the pink glistening flesh beneath. The burnt man stared silently, eyes red as rubies, at the hunched man in the rags. The burnt man started forward slowly, smoke flapping around him like leathery wings. His boiled skin ripped and tore, fresh streams of crimson appeared all over his body. The man in rags reached for his blade, dropping the food and water. He fumbled blindly in the thick smog, his t-shirt mask fell away, and immediately he started to cough desperately. Still, the ghoul advanced faster and faster. He had crossed the vegetable patch now and was only meters away. His hands outstretched, his face contorted with rage, he tore forward as the man in rags fell back, choking on the smoke and watching the advancing horror with wide, terrified eyes.

The burnt man screamed when he started to run, for his skin tore worse than before. The stench of blood grew thicker, thicker than the smoke, and the man in rags gargled a scream through his chokes. The face, cracked with hate, and fire, stared down at him, then lurched forward. The man in rags closed his eyes and waited to die but it did not come. He opened his eyes to the smoke.

There was nothing.

Shaken, he gathered his things quickly, not sheathing the blade, and plucked a few carrots from the soil. He ran back to the cabin where he bolted the door and sat, panicked, in the corner of the room.

He had not always been alone. Back before the air had caught fire, and the ground had blistered in the heat, he had travelled with others. As resources grew limited, it became dangerous. Very dangerous. He had found an old tailor, deranged and lonely, and found himself resting for a while. Within a week the old man had stopped calling names to the night, his madness stayed by the comfort of company. They had lived in peace for months; an underground vault, hidden from the rampaging fires, protected them. The man in rags had shaved, washed, and cared for the old man, and the old man had made him clothes in a makeshift workshop.

Then the fires had broken through, the angry earth had found them. The man in rags had fled. It happened too quickly, he left all the food, one package was all he could carry. Running was all he could do. Besides, the old man had a hundred tunnels out of the vault. He could have escaped.

He buried his head in his hands and let out a soft moan. How long before worse things came from the fire? He had asked himself that for years. There were a hundred horrors born of the smoke, he knew that now.

A yellow white flood poured through the mucky windows, obliterating the smoke and painting the floor. It warmed the man's face. He closed his eyes and smiled in the sun. It had been days. The wind had stopped, the smoke had drifted. Perhaps the vegetables would survive a little longer. He washed, in the last of the water under the sink, then stood at the window, watching the fires. The sun dried his skin slowly, washing over him in bright waves. He giggled once, a strange alien noise. It had been some time. He let it take hold. It evolved, somewhere at the bottom of his throat, then went deeper until his whole chest was convulsing with a full-hearted laugh. He held his chest and laughed out loud, the sun nipping at his skin.

The laugh cut short.

The shadow of a man had cut into the golden cascade. A black presence projected over the naked man and a new nipping started. Cold stung his skin, pushing pinpricks up all over his damp body. The thing outside stood, awkward and cramped, a thin red line framing its shape. The naked man stood with his mouth wide and his eyes wider. He hunched to get a better look, the smoke clouding his view.

The form had disappeared.

He ran to the door, bolting it and pushing the block back in place. He scurried over to the pile of stinking clothes and snatched up the knife, then retreated to the corner, the knife held in two hands pointing at the door. He trembled. The door rattled lightly, testing the lock. His breath caught in his throat. It still tingled from the laugh. The door stood still and quiet as the wind whistled through the cracks. He slid to the floor and let the knife fall from his fingers. He lay still and let the smoke fall on him like a ghostly blanket, then he shut his eyes and thought of the smoke.

When he opened his eyes it was a new day. The winds had obviously picked up and pushed the fires on, for he could smell burning wood. The wind was pushing the smell of the apple trees in his direction.

No. It was closer than that, he thought.

When he rose to his squatted position, he saw that the side wall of the cabin was being eaten slowly by flame. He cried out once, a guttural noise, snatched up the butcher's knife, then dove for the package under the bed. Once he had wrapped his arms tightly around it, he grabbed the welly under the sink and quickly escaped the cabin as the flames wrapped themselves around his home. Home, he said. Without reconsidering this, he turned and took off up the hill.

He hadn't had the time to grab his mask, and so the smoke wrapped its tentacles around his throat and pushed its way into his lungs, leaving sticky black taste on the surface of his tongue. It stabbed his insides and made him want to vomit, but he raced on, keeping his head as low as possible. He thought he might stop and make a new camp, but it became very clear very quickly that there was no need for a new camp. The fires had been at least thirty meters from the cabin only hours ago. The winds were stronger than ever, whipping the smoke at his face and stinging his eyes so that he kept them shut tight for most of the run.

On reaching the top of the hill, he surveyed the land and saw his fate. A blaze of red and black was devouring the hill, barbecuing the last of the grass. His vegetable patch would be gone now and everything else. The orange mass swirled and blasted around the lonely mountain in a hellish spiral that scored the ground again and again. Thick black smog followed this pattern, spiralling up and out into the night. The man stared quietly, waiting.

But nothing came from the smoke, except fire. He did not panic, did not rush, merely opened the package carefully and set its contents smoothly onto the little beach. He dropped the knife into the sediment, where it splurged and was slowly eaten by the ground. Next, he assumed the clothes he had just laid out, a shirt, trousers, silk briefs, and an old worn tie. The outfit was slightly grubby, but nowhere near as reeking and filth-ridden as his old rags. These he had saved from his journey, a present from the last friend he had known. These, he had rescued. He pushed his hair back out of his eyes, and it stayed.

The man walked out into the little lake, looking behind him only once to see a wall of flame creeping along in his wake: an army of ghastly shadow figures shrouding him. When he reached the middle of the lake, the water touched his chin. He took a breath and submerged himself, floating in the silent dark for what seemed like ages.

He let himself float to the surface where he lay on his back and was still. The water tickled at his ears and splashed quietly against his roasted face. He stared up at the sky and for a second he thought he saw a glimmer of sunlight through the smoke clouds. The crackling sounded a million miles away, but he could tell by the sky's orange glow that he was surrounded absolutely.

There was a splash back at the shore.

The man closed his eyes and breathed slowly. The wind howled and screamed above flames that crackled angrily. Bubbles appeared around the edge of the pool, as the water slowly boiled. The man registered nothing, for the water had filled his ears. The silence of the deep smothered him and for the first time in years, he dreamed.

THEODORE WAITS

JACK MATTHEWS

Theodore sits alone atop a cliff overlooking the angry Pacific Ocean and waits to be rescued. Gray clouds gather and swirl above the heaving water bespeckled with white-capped waves. A warm wind assaults Theodore's leather-worn face and blows through his thin, white hair as he squints and scans the empty horizon.

His joints ache and waves of nausea keep him from sleeping. It could be The Sickness, but he suspects he has the same cancer that ravaged Elizabeth. They would have been married fifty-eight years had she lived. Or was it fifty-three? Memory, his only companion now, has become unreliable. He does remember their wedding day, not so long ago in his mind: how Elizabeth, in her simple white gown, stood backlit by the warm, autumn light at the reception. It was at a seaside resort not far from here, but long gone now. Inspired by the champagne, she giggled effusively at her father-in-law's lame jokes and became part of the family that day, not just in fact but in spirit. They splurged on a short honeymoon in Napa Valley and settled down in Turlock where they both taught in the public schools. Elizabeth bore three children in the ensuing years; the second one—Paula Jean—was killed in an accident at the age of thirteen. She had been in a car with two friends and an older boy. Elizabeth was inconsolable and struggled with intermittent fits of depression afterwards. Theodore had grieved equally deeply but less visibly than Elizabeth.

A few harbor seals crowd together on a rock just off the beach and occasionally erupt into a cacophony of vocalizations that rise above the sound of the breaking waves. Theodore strains to remember how he got to this place. A couple of years ago he had learned how to turn on the gas pumps at abandoned convenience stores; but the power grid failed a few months afterward rendering the Toyota useless. He hasn't seen a functioning car in ages. It's a long way from Turlock across the mountains to the ocean; he would have remembered riding, even if it was in a carriage or buggy. He must have walked.

Other than Paula Jean, there were two sons. Charles and . . . Thomas, maybe? Charlie joined the army or the Peace Corps. Theodore remembers a picture of him holding a gun, or perhaps it was a shovel. A bomb had exploded in Cairo and Charlie went to Africa. He never came home. It would have killed Elizabeth but she was already dead.

Tommy is a chameleon-like ghost in Theodore's memory. Sometimes a son, other times a brother or an uncle. He was a champion athlete—a track and field star, Theodore remembers. He held the world record in the high jump. No matter, Tommy is dead too.

Theodore looks down at the beach five or six stories below. It would be so easy to lean over, let go, and be done with it, but they are coming to rescue him and he should wait. He needs to eat. He doesn't eat often these days and when he does, it usually comes right back up. Reluctantly, he reaches down into a tattered backpack and pulls out a box of saltines he picked up in a deteriorating supermarket. It's getting harder and harder to find food these days—most of the inventory has long since been pilfered, so he was lucky to find the crackers and a few ancient cans of vegetables in the storeroom. He opens the wax paper liner and finds the crackers have disintegrated into crumbs. He pours a small pile into his palm and contemplates putting some into his mouth; but he feels sick again and dumps them over the cliff. The wind catches the cracker dust and carries it back over his head.

A couple of years after Cairo, the storms started rolling into central California. The perpetual drought was broken and everyone rejoiced. But the storms grew in intensity and frequency and they kept coming; incessantly they kept coming. Joy turned to concern, concern to consternation, and consternation to panic. Crops died from too much of a good thing. They might have switched to rice, but they didn't. We didn't eat rice. We ate peaches and almonds and potatoes; and, above all, we ate meat. The almonds and potatoes died, as did the alfalfa that fed the meat. As the crops failed, so did the banks. The money vanished and along with it, civil behavior.

Theodore thinks about opening a can of beans but gives up on the idea of eating. He considers offering a prayer of some kind and wonders if that would bring them sooner. During the plague everyone had prayed to one god or another. The Sickness had started on a faraway continent but Theodore doesn't remember the specifics. At first, no one paid much attention as there were more urgent things to pray about. But in a few months the virus spread and touched every tribe and family on the planet. Weakened by famine, crippled by war, and hobbled by the disintegration of organized governments, few had any chance of fighting off the disease. Prayer hadn't helped then and Theodore decides it won't help now. Besides, pray to the wrong god and the rescuers might not come at all.

The clouds thicken, settle closer to the surface of the water, and change from the color of ash to the color of coal. Theodore looks again toward the horizon. He is unsure whether they will come from across the ocean or down from the heavens, but he knows that this is the place—so he waits. Another wave of nausea washes over him. There is nothing to vomit. He doubles up in pain as his body tries to rid his stomach of food that isn't there. The nausea passes. Theodore lies, belly down, in the grass a few feet from the precipice. His mind clouds with a montage of memory fragments, abridged and transfigured by the afflictions of age—a leather pouch full of cherished aggies, the organic, cleansing smell of the first rain of spring, a Pachelbel Canon and white lace . . . muffled sobs in the dark.

As the coastline slowly descends into darkness, a skein of pelicans glides effortlessly just above the water, their wingtips nearly clipping the tops of the waves. Beyond the birds, an orange light suddenly glows on the horizon, visible for just a moment before evaporating into the night. The rescuers are coming. Theodore closes his eyes, draws his final breath, and waits.

MEAN PEOPLE

DEMOCRACY

LARRY HiNKLE

The shelter had been well stocked at first, but we'd nearly exhausted our supplies, and poor Charlie, all sunken eyes, bony ribs, and jagged teeth, had been barking for ten hours straight.

The others took a vote; it took two rounds, but in the end they decided to feed Charlie to stop his barking.

They fed him to the group.

***

Eight months ago, I never would've thought us capable of sinking so low. I would've said we were better people than that. But eight months can make all the difference in the world in how you look at things. Especially when everything in your world has gone to shit.

We'd all been together for a couple months before we ran into Charlie. Things weren't so bad then. Certainly not like they got later. All things considered, I guess we were doing okay. We were still alive, which is better than what you could say about 95 percent of the general population from . . . before. Sure, there was never enough to eat, but at least we weren't starving like the people up north. Not yet. But it was coming. Things were getting worse as the summer wound down. The number of people we saw on the roads kept shrinking. And the few who would stop and talk all shared the same story—the militia was conscripting every healthy body they found. The men were given a choice: join up, or die. The women were given an even worse choice: put out, or die. That sound like the greatest country on God's green Earth to you? Right then I knew, if the world were looking for America to save it, the world was fucked.

Yeah, we thought we were kings of the castle once we found that shelter. And Charlie, bless his furry little soul, he'd led us to it. Shit, if it weren't for Charlie showing us that cave—which I'd like to point out, he was under no obligation to do—well, who knows what might've happened to us up there, above ground.

So just how did our little group, that last bastion of classic American democracy, repay Charlie for his bit of interspecies canine karma? Smashed his skull with a rock and stuck him on a spit.

And things only got worse for us from there.

Of course, Charlie hadn't been Charlie that first day. Six months ago he was just some stray who started barking at us from behind an old gate blocking a rutted path into the woods.

"Hey, boy," I said, bending and snapping my fingers. "Come here." I held out my hand like I was holding a treat.

The dog took a step toward me, then barked and trotted back down the path.

"Come here, boy," I said, stepping toward the gate. "I'm not gonna hurt you."

The dog stopped, turned, and took a couple steps back my way.

"That's right, come here. I got some yummies for you." I reached into my pocket and acted like I had more treats in there. That trick always worked when I volunteered at the Humane Society.

"Leave him be, Lisa. Last thing we need is another mouth to feed." That was Bud, of course. The group's resident asshole. He talked a lot of shit. At first there'd been a bit of a power struggle between Bud and Tim as they tried to prove whose dick was bigger. Tim was my on- and off-again guy, so of course he got my vote, but the rest of the group ended up voting for him as well. I expected Bud to skulk off like a little bitch that night, but to his credit he stuck around. Guess he figured second-in-command with us was better than El Presidente of Jack Squat. So now he spends most of his time taking digs at me to get back at Tim. Typical schoolyard shit, really. Like I said, he's an asshole.

"Don't worry, Bud, he won't eat that much," I told him. "Probably catches his own food, too. Besides, he might be a good guard dog."

"Whatever," Bud said. "But you're responsible for him. If he gets hungry, his food comes from your share."

"Don't mind Bud," I told the dog. "He'll grow on you. Like a fungus." I winked at him.

The dog barked and turned back down the path.

"I think he wants us to follow him," I said, turning toward the others. "What do you think we should do?"

Tim, our leader and my on-again, off-again guy, shrugged and called a vote. The ayes had it (except for Bud, of course), so we followed the dog down the path deeper into the woods. About forty, maybe fifty yards in, he veered off into the bushes. He continued for about ten feet before he started digging, throwing up a cloud of leaves and dirt and rocks.

"What is it, Lassie?" I asked. "Did Timmy fall in the well again?"

He stopped digging, looked up at me, and cocked his head. Maybe he didn't get my sense of humor. None of the others seemed to. Except Tim, of course. But then he'd had a few years to get used to it before all this.

I walked over to check out what had the dog so worked up. He'd uncovered a large square sheet of thick plywood, which I pushed with my foot, revealing the edge of a hole. I grabbed the wood and pulled it off to the side. A handful of leaves and rocks fell into the opening; a few seconds later, I heard the stones hit the bottom. There was enough sunlight filtering through the trees that I could make out the first steps of a wooden ladder dropping down into the darkness. The dog stood to one side, eyes bright and tail wagging.

"Guys, you better come take a look at this."

This part of Indiana is riddled with limestone caves. At some point, back when survivalism was still an abstract concept, someone had decided to turn this particular cave system into a makeshift shelter. Inside, there was more than enough room for at least twenty, maybe twenty-five people to spread out and have their own little place. Even more if they didn't have personal space issues. Fortunately, there were only nine of us, plus the dog, so it felt like a mansion. A musty, dusty, damp and dirty mansion. But it was ours.

Six metal shelving units lined one long wall, four shelves per unit, each packed with canned fruits and vegetables, plastic containers of rice and beans, and several dozen heavy-duty Ziploc bags of MREs. Tucked back in a side cave we found two Coleman stoves, six gas lanterns and a few dozen propane tanks, a case of those little portable propane canisters, a box of caving headlamps, extra LED bulbs and a few hundred AAA batteries. There were even a half dozen of those Russian crank flashlights. In another alcove was a large wooden crate filled with bottles of bleach and peroxide, plus ten cases of military-grade water purification tablets. And best of all, in my opinion, there was toilet paper.

Hundreds and hundreds of rolls of toilet paper. Sure, it was single-ply, but it was still better than leaves. We felt like we'd discovered a gold mine, which, in a way, we had.

Unfortunately, as Ponyboy once said to Johnny (by way of Robert Frost), nothing gold can stay. (And they said my English degree would be useless in a post-apocalyptic society.)

A few days and too many celebratory meals later, we took a vote and decided we should hole up there for a while. The leaves had already started to change and drop. Winter was coming, and with the way The Powers That Be had fucked things up, it might last for years. This was uncharted territory for those of us who were left. There was also the threat of conscription the longer we stayed above ground.

Before we could call the cave home though, the entrance had to be fixed. That door could barely keep out our dog; it needed some major structural reinforcements. First, we framed the hole with metal from the shelving units, then strengthened the plywood door by lining the bottom of it with a few of the metal shelves. Next, we camouflaged the opening with some brush and dead wood so it was invisible from the path. Finally, we pulled the door down snug against the newly reframed opening, attached some rope to the bottom, snaked the rope through the rungs of the ladder, and weighted the entire thing down with some very heavy rocks. Nobody could get in—or out—without at least two of us opening it first.

It was time for another celebration.

🐾 🐾 🐾

Tim started a rationing program for the food today. We should've started when we first found the place, but we were all so happy to have something to eat again that we got a little carried away. I don't think any of us realized how fast we were going through some of the supplies.

There's still a healthy number of cans and MREs, but I wished we'd been more careful with those. And there's plenty of rice and beans left. All told, we've probably got enough for the next five to six months, if we stick to our rationing schedule. Hell, contestants on Survivor *used to last over a month on just a handful of rice every day. Surely we can do better than those poseurs did.*

Tim had Bud set up some snare traps in the woods around the entrance. They think we can catch some squirrels, maybe even a couple rabbits. I hope so. It's been a while since we've had any meat.

🐿 🐿 🐿

The far back of the cave led down to a subterranean lake. I don't know where the water came from, probably a swallow hole or a spring, but it smelled fresh, more or less, and the level never changed much.

"We really need to see if there's anything on the other side of that lake," Tim said one day. "Probably just ends up against the back wall, but it'd be good to make sure. Never know when a strategic retreat might be necessary."

"You mean in case we need to hide like a bunch of bitches and let someone steal our shit? Is that what you're trying to say?" asked Bud.

"Well, Bud, I might have refrained from using the word 'bitches' but yeah, that's pretty much what I'm trying to say. There might come a time when we need to—"

"Let me stop you right there, boss," Bud interrupted. This was not going well. "There will never be a time, at least as long as I'm still here, that we retreat to the back of the cave and hide. If someone wants my stuff, they'll have to pry it from my cold, dead hands."

"That's great, Bud," I said, unable to contain myself. "But what about the rest of us? Those of us who are fond of our warm, live hands? I'd rather give up my food in exchange for my life. Tim clearly agrees with me, and I'm sure the rest of the group does as well. But just to be sure, let's take a vote: All those in favor of keeping their warm, live hands?" Everyone, except Bud, raised their hand. I raised both of mine.

"Easy to say now," Bud said, "while it's still all puppies and unicorns down here. But democracy don't solve everything, folks. Don't believe me, go take a look at what happened to Bloomington's stupid 'council.' I wonder if their bodies are still hanging from those telephone poles?" Nobody answered. "Look, all I'm saying is not every decision can be made by a show of hands. Sometimes it takes a show of force. And when that time comes, when we gotta protect what's ours, y'all'd be wise to follow my lead. Especially you, Lisa. I think you could learn a lot under my watchful eye and helpful hand."

"It's your hand I'm worried about, Bud. I already see the way your watchful eye stays glued to my tits."

"You caught me." He raised his hands and smiled. "No denying I am a breast man. And yours seem to be getting a little bigger the past few weeks. How is that even possible under these conditions?"

"Fucking perv!" I spat the words at him, then spun around and walked off before the questions could get more personal.

"All right, you two, just stop it," Tim said. "We'll talk about it some more later."

The group drifted off to their separate spaces and that was the end of that.

🐾 🐾 🐾

We never found the person who stocked the cave. If we had, the first thing I'd have asked is why didn't he pack any SPAM. It's meat. Sort of. It lasts forever, and it even comes with its own can opener. Dumbass.

Then I would've asked what Charlie's real name is. He didn't have a collar, so I had no idea what to call him. I went with Charlie because everything about him was shrouded in mystery, like the voice on the other end of the intercom on Charlie's Angels. *Of course, Bud thought Charlie was a stupid name for a dog. But once I told him my second choice was Little Buddy, he let it go.*

Finally, I would've asked why he didn't think to throw

a few cases of tampons or pads in with the toilet paper. Not that I needed them for the foreseeable future, but did he really have to take that whole "last man on Earth" thing so goddamn literally?

🌿 🌿 🌿

Bud and I kept our distance for a couple of days, at least as much as two people can in a limestone cave, and then Tim decided it was time to talk about the lake again. "We can't see the other side of it with our flashlights," he said. "That means someone has to take a swim. Who knows, maybe you'll get lucky and it's only waist-deep the whole way across. But we won't know until someone gives it a shot."

Of course, Tim volunteered for the job. That's what leaders do. But since we couldn't take a chance on losing him, I volunteered Bud. And of course, Bud refused. That's what assholes do.

"Why me? Why not you, Lisa, or any of the others?" he asked. "Hell, why not your stupid dog for that matter? I'm sure Charlie the Wonder Pooch knows how to swim."

"Because you're the only one who's not injured right now," Tim said, stepping in before things got any uglier. "Everyone else, including Charlie, has multiple cuts, sores, and scrapes. No point in anyone getting their wounds wet if they don't have to."

I thought it was nice the way Tim made a point of using Charlie's name, reminding Bud that everyone in the group was an equal. It was subtle, sure, but that's one of the reasons we followed him.

"But we have all these supplies now. If someone's little 'scratch' gets infected, we'll just dump some peroxide on it."

"We're not wasting supplies because you don't want to get wet, Bud."

Bud stared at Tim, jaw clenched, refusing to move.

"Fine," Tim said. "Let's take a vote. All in favor of Bud checking out the lake?"

We all raised our hands.

"All opposed?"

Bud raised his.

"Then I guess it's settled." Tim handed Bud a flashlight and pointed toward the water. The rest of us formed a loose wall with Tim at the center, blocking any chance of escape. Like there was any place to go. But it was important for the group to put up a unified front.

Bud sighed, then muttered something under his breath as he walked down to the lake. I heard Charlie, my name, and something that rhymed with 'hunt.' He took off his shirt, boots, and pants, then put his boots back on. He clicked the light, smacked it against his palm, and stepped into the water. The rest of us shone our lights out ahead of him as far as they would go. We could see another twenty, thirty feet of water, then everything melted into inky blackness.

Bud kept walking farther into the lake. He'd almost reached the end of our lights, and the water was now up to his armpits. Suddenly, he disappeared beneath the surface of the lake. He popped right back up, but it gave us all a fright. He splashed around a bit as he tried to regain his bearings.

"You okay?" Tim yelled.

"I'm fine, dickweed!" Bud snapped, his voice echoing throughout the chamber. He was standing again, and we could see him shaking the flashlight. It still worked, but it was noticeably dimmer.

Another few steps and Bud was out of our flashlight range; all we could see was the faint yellow glow emanating from his light. A few minutes later, even that was gone.

🦅 🦅 🦅

The snares worked at first, but once winter fully set in, the catches stopped.

On the plus side, if you can call having rats a plus, Mary found a big one trying to chew its way into the beans. Don't know how the little bastard got in here. We're gonna have to check that out, set up some traps. Hard to believe, but even a dirty ass rat sounds like Kobe beef at this point. I gotta hand it to Mary, though. She didn't scream or anything. At least not until after she killed it. Then she let loose a whoop straight out of the WWE.

It's embarrassing how much I salivated when they started handing out pieces of rat. Everyone got one teeny bite, even Charlie. Guess you never know what kind of shit you'll eat when you're hungry enough. And in case you were wondering, yes, they do taste like chicken.

Turned out the cave only went back another thirty yards or so beyond what we could see from the shore. Bud said he was able to walk most of the way, but toward the end the floor sloped down fast and he couldn't touch bottom anymore. Another few yards after that and he reached the back of the cave.

"Did you try swimming down to see if there were any tunnels?" Tim asked when Bud was back on shore. "Maybe they'd lead to another cave."

Bud laughed at that. "What, just swim around blind? I ain't opening my eyes in that water, and I sure as fuck ain't swimming around with my eyes shut and take a chance on hitting my head and drowning. You'd like that, though, wouldn't you? I know she would." He glared at me. "Well, fuck you! Fuck both of you! Fuck all y'all! Put it to a vote. I don't give a shit. No way I'm risking my neck like that when we just found this place." He picked up his clothes and stomped off toward the front of the cave. I looked at Tim, who just shook his head. I let it go.

At dinner, Bud made a big show of giving Charlie an extra bit of his food. It was a lame attempt at an apology, but Tim accepted it, "for the good of the group" he told me later. I didn't accept it, though. I knew Bud would never voluntarily do anything for the good of the group.

⁂

We killed a few more rats over the next couple weeks. Wish more would have found their way down here, though. Where's the Pied Piper when you really need him?

We made sure all the food was safe from them, but they weren't safe from us. Nothing with four legs was. Except Charlie. Yeah, I saw the way a few of the others looked at him when they thought I wasn't paying attention, like they were imagining how he'd taste slow-roasted and peppercorned, but none of them had the balls to actually do anything. Bud, on the other hand . . . That asshole would've barbequed Charlie that first week if Tim weren't here to stop him. He probably would've thrown me on a spit, too, if he thought he could get away with it. After he showed me what a "real man" was, of course. Bud would be right at home in the militia.

⁂

We heard some people in the woods above us this morning. It was the first we've heard in a couple months. It sounded like eight or nine people in their group total, but it was hard to tell. We took positions around the bottom of the ladder and waited. After a few minutes, the voices grew fainter, and then disappeared.

Bud wanted to go after them. Said he'd just hang back, then sneak into their camp at night and see if they had anything worth taking.

"What if they're militia?" Tim asked.

"I ain't worried," Bud said.

"And if you get caught?" Tim asked. "Should we be worried?"

"They ain't gonna catch me," said Bud. "If they try, I'll go full Rambo and take 'em out."

"By 'take 'em out' you mean kill them?" I asked, incredulous.

"Hell yeah! You don't think they'd kill us to get what

we have?"

"Over the little bit of rice and beans we have left? No, I don't."

"Then you're even dumber than that dog of yours we ate," Bud sneered. "We started out with a lot, and now we're almost out. Look at us. Livin' in the dirt, eatin' rats and worse. And I guarantee this place looks like a fucking Hilton compared to what those people up there have. They got nothing to lose coming after the little bit we got. Don't believe me? Ask the others, see what they think."

I looked at the people I'd spent the last six months with buried in this damn hole in the ground. They looked like shit. Pale, hollow-eyed, and thin, sharp angles. I'm sure I didn't look any better. None of them met my gaze. And none of them spoke up. Was I the only sane one left? Why was no one else arguing with him? Not even Tim was taking my side this time.

"You really think you could do it?" Tim asked.

"I think so," Bud said. "The snow would definitely help cover the noise. And it would help me follow their tracks. Probably too late now, though."

"Not if I go with you it isn't."

I turned and faced Tim. "I'm sorry, what did you say?"

"I said I'm going with him. It'll be faster and safer with the two of us."

"What about the two of *us*? How is it faster and safer for the two of us if you go out there with that asshole?"

"It's not just about us, Lisa. It can't be."

"Bullshit."

"It isn't bullshit, and you know it."

I wouldn't answer.

"Hey, why don't we put it to a vote?" Bud asked, smiling.

"Shut up, Bud," Tim said, then he looked back at me. "Well, do you want to?"

"What, vote? Why bother. We already know how it'll turn out. You'll do whatever the group says, just like always. You don't give a shit about what I want. About what we want. You never did."

I turned and headed down to the lake, leaving a trail of silent tears.

※ ※ ※

The raid didn't go so well. Big surprise. Bud and Tim were seen, and Tim's left leg got sprayed with buckshot. They made it back to the cave without being caught, but Tim's leg looked like hamburger. I think he got a concussion when he slipped and fell off the ladder, too.

We tried peroxide on his wounds, but it didn't help. Over the next week his calf swelled up twice its normal size, and he was in and out of consciousness from the pain. The skin turned black and cracked, and a viscous green pus oozed out, leaving shiny slime trails where it dribbled down his calf. The stench made it almost impossible to keep down the little bit of rations we got every other night.

Almost.

When Tim was lucid he demanded the others take a vote. Not whether to let him die, but whether to amputate his leg to keep the infection from spreading. He wouldn't let me vote, of course; said I was too emotional. Not that it would have mattered. Tim would do whatever the group decided, no matter what it meant to us.

Without my vote, it was unanimous. Bud sawed Tim's leg off above the knee, doused the cut with the last of our peroxide, then cauterized the stump.

It worked.

Five days later, all signs of infection gone, they fed Tim to the group.

※ ※ ※

I was wrong. Turns out Tim did give a shit about us. That's why he sacrificed himself. The group thinks he did it for them. But I know the truth now. I was wrong about myself, too. That's why his sacrifice didn't matter.

I wouldn't eat Charlie, although Tim tried to make me,

reminding me what was at stake for the two of us. But I just couldn't. Not poor little Charlie.

I wouldn't eat Tim either, although Bud tried to make me. "Gotta keep your strength up," he said, laughing as he shoved a few strands of shredded meat into my mouth. I spit it back in his face. Pissed him off and got me slapped hard enough to loosen a tooth, but what do you expect. Bud's an asshole.

Still, I get by. The space where they're holding me is pretty tight, but Bud said they had to tie me up to keep me from hurting myself. From hurting the group. He has the women bring me back a bowl of rice or beans once every other day. Plus the occasional spider or beetle when they find one. I even got half a rat leg once. It's not much, but it's enough to keep the two of us alive. And that's enough to keep the group's hopes alive.

The others took a vote, you see. Bud wouldn't let me vote, of course; said I was too emotional. Not that it would have mattered. Without my vote, it was unanimous. In three weeks, when my baby is born, they'll finally have fresh, tender meat again.

THE PASSING OF A SURVIVALIST

ERIC BLAIR

The survivalist knew he was being followed. It was his second day on the outskirts of this city. He had spent it foraging for what was left in those suburban neighborhoods, the knowledge of the other near him growing as he moved through the city. This city was like him. Once it had a name, a name he knew, but no more. Now, there were no more names, only vestiges. Now, there was only what remained. It may persist another day, or it may fall as so much had before. The weapons he had were meager, but he had fire. It had served him well, and would again. But still he felt the urge to destroy. To light a pyre of the house in which he now sat, and then the next, and the next. He would light them all until they surrounded him, until there was nothing left in his sight but burning remains, and then, he would join them.

He felt that urge, and he knew that some day would be his day, when this still surviving vestige would cease. A day when he, himself, would cease. But it would not be this day, so he lowered himself into the shadows near a broken window and took stock of the world around him. There was another nearby. Where there was another, there was danger. Keeping his head carefully out of the dim light entering the window, he looked and saw nothing. He listened, even smelled at the air for the heady scent of another unwashed human being. Still there was nothing. Always feeling safer exiting from the rear, he moved out from the back of the house. He hopped a fence, hoping it would hold. It did, as did the next.

He left the complex of houses, moving quickly across an open road into the shadow of an abandoned gas station. He did not come to search. Commercial locations were always the first to be raided, particularly anything that catered to the addictions of the dead world. If it had once contained gasoline, nicotine, or alcohol, there would be nothing left. But the windows were intact, and he had good fields of view from which to lay a trap.

He entered through the smashed open door and hid behind the one shelf that remained standing. The place was in shambles, old food rotting on the floors, broken glass. But it would do. Enough of it remained. Hunkering down, he waited, he watched, and he listened. His crossbow was loaded, a cocktail and lighter removed from his satchel. Soon enough a sound alerted him, the soft reports of footfalls on the gravel that covered the rear of the parking lot.

His evaluation was quick and deadly. The man who sought him was alone, he was trying to sneak up on him, and he was a fool. The gravel was an instant giveaway. Smiling to himself, he watched his exits, eyeing the rear entrance. A shadow fell on the doorway, another easy giveaway. He was in motion before the shadow could give way to a human form.

The survivalist raked his thumb over the wheel of his lighter and threw the cocktail. It landed perfectly, lighting the ground outside the station. His prey reacted, and reacted poorly. More footfalls, sloppy and misplaced, followed. They led to the road, open ground rather than the easy escape of the houses on the other side. Moving quickly and with purpose, the survivalist ran out the front door to the edge of the building. Just as his opponent was about to bound a fence and disappear from view, he fired the crossbow around the corner. The man's next step fell short, and he collapsed to the ground. He could hear the quick suck of wind, could barely see the soft, red spray leaving the dying man's mouth.

It was a lung shot. The man was done, but the pack falling about his shoulders was large. Instead of beating a quick retreat, he reloaded and drew down on the vestige of what had once been a very foolish man. The bolt licked quickly through the air and struck true, and the body moved no more. Neither did the survivalist. He crouched. Looking briefly at the body, he listened, scanning around himself for any sign of movement. Nostrils flaring, he searched the air for any new scent. He could make nothing out, but out of sheer instinct, he quickly duck-walked backward, staying hunched close to the ground. Soon he was out the back door, beating his way through the rapidly diminishing flames that, as he intended, had failed to set the structure alight. The pack on the dead man's back was forgotten. The two bolts would be missed, but the lone man ran as fast as he could, certain he had just narrowly escaped death.

The scent of decay remained in the air. It often did. He could smell it, the sweet scent of rot muted by the passage of some short period of time. He had come to an apartment complex, moving through the night and into the next day. The smell had stopped him. He ached, having run far in hot weather with his heavy pack. Knowing the strength of the scent of sweat and filth he now trailed in his wake, the dead would make the perfect cover.

He entered through an already broken window and

moved through an apartment into the hall, following the stench. He found a door broken open, a shattered frame next to an extended deadbolt. Pushing it forward, the smell of putrescence multiplied upon itself. He found them together. The ceiling had been torn open, a wooden post located above. The adults hung from it, hands by their sides, heads angled downward. The child was dead beneath them, tucked gently into the dirty comforter of a king-sized bed. He looked tiny, emaciated under the huge blanket.

The survivalist surveyed the scene before him. The child had probably died of natural causes, some passing infection or virus taking brutal advantage of his frail form. He cut the parents down and stacked them atop the dead child. Just between the two of them, he could barely see the cracked and rotten flesh of the child's forehead. He hesitated, staring at that small bit of exposed skin. A second's hesitation was far too much. A single wasted second, in this world, could kill. He swung the knife from his belt, horrified at his own weakness, and struck. Three quick stabs to a weak man's chest, three tearing motions to remove the knife following each. The sound of breaking bones, the soft rasp of the last remaining air driven from his chest, and the weakness was expelled. He held his arm high, feeling strong, feeling focused. Calmly, carefully, he lowered the blade. Quickly, he wiped it clean across the end of the bedspread.

It took only a few moments to prepare the place. The windows he covered from a spool of barbed wire. Broken glass would alert him. Opening the windows would result in injury, and an almost certain cry of pain. The door was more complicated, though the small device was simple enough. The weight of the door triggered a spring, the blades rose at shin height. Neither wire nor sharpened steel were meant to kill. They were meant to injure and alert. If he was lucky, they could even delay a potential opponent long enough for him to strike. This done, he did a quick check of the apartment, then checked the suicides' supply. It was meager, as evidenced by the thinness of their child. But it was something, some small bit more than he had possessed only minutes before.

In only a few more moments, he was sleeping lightly. He remained on edge, even asleep, always alert and waiting for what might come.

The survivalist awoke to darkness. Eyes opening with a start, his hands immediately searched for his weapon. No light penetrated, and the knife was gone from his belt. Both hands clawed the empty sheath as a heavy blow fell upon his head out of the darkness. Lifting his arms to his face, he tried to find the light, tried desperately to pull away whatever was blocking his vision. But another blow followed, and then strong hands tightening down on his wrists.

He exploded upward, trying to roll away and free himself. For a moment one hand was loose, but only one. The darkness remained impenetrable, the sack over his head wrenching his neck as he bucked and rolled. For a second he thought his vertebrae might give, that the struggle would be over. For just a second he thought that it all might end in that instant. But then another blow fell upon his bound face, and the darkness was complete.

He awoke to more darkness. His face was still covered, hands bound tightly behind his back. His wrists were lashed to his legs, hog tying him. He was in motion, he could tell that much. A distant, metallic squeak rose from beneath him. The sound seemed far away, though some distant portion of his mind attempted to assign great significance to it. For a few distracted moments he tried to struggle, but the blackness returned. He felt unconsciousness coming on, felt a disgustingly heavy sleep falling over him. He had not felt the stab in the leg after the blows to the face. The tiny instrument, a vestige that had once brought sleep when needed, had been slipped in just after he passed out. That vestige now returned him to the deeper darkness of sleep, and he did not awaken again for some time.

Consciousness returned slowly. The survivalist had been aware for some time of brightness above him. A harsh, naked bulb forced the light underneath his eyelids, slowing working its way into his reality. Blinking rapidly, he realized over the course of several muddled seconds that it was an electric light. It stood on the other side of a network of bars, a shadowy figure looming over him and blocking out some of the light. His hand rose, instinctively shielding him from what stood above. Into that hand was thrust a jug of water. The man's bruised hand hung menacingly after it, still extended toward him.

He had no reason to trust the man, or the gifts he presented. But the jug was cool against his hand, and his thirst quickly won out over his suspicions. The refreshing liquid washed over his parched lips, down his dry throat. This set some small precedent, and when food was offered, he accepted it as well. Warm meat met his lips. He chewed at it hungrily, soon consuming the entire morsel.

The man above him smiled—a wide, knowing grin. For a second he thought he had been poisoned. But he dismissed the idea quickly. Why waste the poison? Why awaken him at all, only to waste clean water and good food upon a man they meant to murder? But that smile was hideous, so full of mirth and contrived hatred. He thought the man might speak, but instead he only turned away, slamming the cage shut behind him. In the seconds before the figure disappeared and the light vanished after him, the survivalist could make out a whole gathering of forms on the other side of the bars. They were nude, horribly thin. They stayed tightly together, huddled in fear. None of them wanted to be any closer to the front than necessary, as if they each may have been selected for some horrific torture simply for being the most convenient person to grab. Then the light was gone, and there was only the muted sound of soft voices, and the heady scent of the unwashed mixed with the smell of rotten food.

None spoke loud enough to be heard. Their hushed whispers only added to the horrible feeling something terrible was being hidden from him. He pondered it in the darkness, that last bit of light burned into his retinas. Just enough light remained in them to illuminate the memory of that terrible smile, the one that seemed to speak so clearly and still hide some infinitely important point.

Time passed. Indefinable, it moved through the solid pitch surrounding him. A few bare facts remained to him. They were thin, naked, poorly fed. Cordoned off from him, there was clearly a palpable difference between the two classes of prisoner. They were not being fed good meat and clean water. He could smell the filth they were brought, even though they had certainly consumed it to the last. It was a surprise any of them still lived. He did not think that they would do so for much longer.

After some long period of poorly metered time passed, the light returned. The captors came with it. Three of them walked down a narrow flight of stairs into the space that seemed to be an earth-floored cellar. The large man was with them, carrying a heavy bludgeon. Behind him came a smaller man, though still threatening in appearance. He carried a large steaming pot, and a too few high stack of bowls to accompany it. Another man, unassuming but well composed, followed.

The two went about the business of feeding the naked men, the bruiser standing between the poor souls and the bowls being filled with some form of gruel. Observing them, the survivalist could see the maggots sitting high in the off-white, pasty mush.

The third man slowly made his way to the front of the cage, silently taking the survivalist's stock. After a moment's silence, he spoke. "We've been watching you," he said. "But you knew that already." The words came out calmly, almost cordially. His dark eyes, shown clearly on the other side of the unvarnished light, were deep and almost sanguine. It was as if this were a propitious meeting, to garner great reward for both sides. "You knew we were there. At first we hunted the other, the weak one that followed you. We were very impressed with the ease with which you dispatched him. I do not think he meant you harm." His words rose warmly in pitch at the end of the last sentence, as if to indicate approval.

"The traps were very impressive as well. We almost sent a man through the window, before we realized it was wired. Very smart of you, alarming both the doors and the windows."

He was silent for a moment, his gaze wandering to the emaciated figures to the side. He nodded, and the giant removed himself, allowing them to feed. They rushed forward, the biggest and the strongest grabbing at the bowls. What food fell to the ground was left to the others, a brief contest of intimidation determining who would eat little and who would have none.

"What is your name?"

The survivalist said nothing, choosing simply to look deeply into those calm, brown eyes. A scoff came in reply, though it seemed lighthearted enough.

"Did you like the food?" He smiled again as he spoke, that same knowing, devious smile that the giant had given him. "How long has it been since you had fresh meat?" He let the question hang in the air. A wave of nausea rose in the silent captive, bending him double in disgust. When the smile opposite him broadened, he knew that his estimation of the situation was correct. They had fed him human meat. The calm man stood opposite him, watching this knowledge move across the captive man's face. He seemed to await some response, but after a moment he turned his back, and the three of them exited.

Just before he was returned to darkness, he looked

back at the living skeletons across from him. He caught the eye of one of them. He was one of the alphas, one who had garnered an entire bowl of gruel and maggots to himself. The gaze was cold and condescending, as if the thin, nude figure was staring at some foul breed of vermin. Hardened though he was, even though he had killed and knew he might kill again, that look chilled the survivalist down to his bones. Then, he was mercifully returned to the endless black, left alone in the dark with his new and hideous knowledge.

* * *

The light returned, as he knew it would. Time, still impossible to accurately measure, had passed. A guess placed it at a day and a half. He still had not slept. He had only sat in the darkness, staring at nothing and waiting to see what would happen next.

Four of them came this time. The giant walked straight up to the cage holding a pair of handcuffs. "Turn around," he grunted bluntly. The survivalist only stared coolly. "Look," he said, "if you ever wanna see the outside of that cage again, you're gonna turn around and stick your hands through the cage. Otherwise, you can fucking rot in here." The survivalist continued to stare. But the calm stare turned quickly to a hateful glare, and he knew he was going to let the man cuff him.

The other three were moving toward the human stock across the room. They had again backed against the wall, huddling together. The guards pushed their way into the thick of them, grabbing for one of the larger ones near the back. They offered no resistance, despite their greater numbers. When one was finally selected, the others slunk away from him as if he had just been possessed of some virulent contagion. They wanted no part of the man they now considered dead.

When he looked back to the giant, the grim smile had returned to his face. "Come on, man. You don't want to be one of them, do you?" That threat was enough. The survivalist stood and turned his back. He stuck his hands, one above the other, through the bars of the cage. The cuffs shut with a dry clack. He stepped forward, knowing the cage door would soon swing open. The others moved silently behind him. Still, there was no struggle. The man selected went quietly, seemingly willing.

The cage opened. He knew now why he was here, why he had been kept separate. They had selected him. He was to be one of them. The idea of cannibalism disgusted him. He had committed that sin once already, and rage pulsed through his veins, the overpowering desire to stamp out every life involved in manipulating him toward it. But still he let them lead him forward, up and out of the cellar. The outer doors led into a large, unfenced yard. In the center stood a large podium. They had the other man bound on top of it, and were tying him into a complex group of restraints across a large wooden board. His feet and knees were bound to the platform. Pulling his arms forward, his head was forced into his armpits by the harsh angle of the rope, in turn tied to a stake yards away. His neck was clearly exposed over the edge, at the height of a standing man's upstretched arms.

That podium could burn. The thought drove the survivalist's mind away from that dark place. Suddenly he was back in the neighborhood he had stalked through a few days before. As if in a fever dream, the flames rose around him. They surrounded him, moving ever closer. That thought had come to him so many times, on so many occasions when the world and surviving in it seemed impossible to bear, the thought of those flames, brutally, mercifully, closing in.

But he was not in that neighborhood. He was here, now, and his footsteps led him to the podium without coercion. The leader was approaching him, breaking from a group of only a few others. They looked like hard, tough-minded people. They were survivors, not entirely unlike him. The small man approached him. His cupped hand carried a small knife. It looked extremely sharp.

"We never ask anyone to join us. We never have to ask. The choice is simple. Your decision will speak more than words ever could."

The cuffs were quickly unlocked. An instant before the smallest man in the crowd handed him that instrument of death, a shotgun racked behind him. With a look of assured confidence, an expression on a face that seemed never to have known fear, he pressed the knife into the survivalist's hands. With a forward sweep of the arm, he stepped out of the way.

Time seemed again to slip away from him. He stepped forward without realizing it, thumb softly caressing the thin hardness of the back of the blade of the knife. He looked to the rope binding the hands of the prisoner. He thought he could reach it, thought that if he stood tall enough, up upon his toes, he could cut it. He flicked his thumb across the blade. It was razor sharp. It would go through that rope very, very quickly. He did not turn to see the man with the shotgun behind him. He knew he was there, and knowing without seeing was enough.

His eyes followed the rope, back to the hands. Gazing over his arms, he was there, but he was not. Those houses burned bright in his mind. They burned and he could almost feel their warmth. He felt it caressing the blade. He felt it eyeing the rope, felt that heat as he listened for the breath of the man holding the shotgun.

He finally found himself gazing into the man's eyes. The heat disappeared. The thin and weak, emaciated man begged him silently without words. They had gagged him at some point, mouth bound with thick tape. His mouth worked nonetheless, and whether his mumbles begged or prayed it did not matter. A new coldness had emerged, wiping the flames away in a swift, calming stroke. This survivalist no longer burned.

He had always thought of himself that way. Even before the fall, this man was one who knew how to survive. Had they been the horrors of the world before or the horrors of the world now, it did not matter. He would overcome, he would persevere. He would survive. And now, he knew that was no longer true. He had ceased to be a survivor.

That man bound before him, he was not another survivor. Nor was he a simple impediment to his own continued survival. This man, tied down, naked, too pathetic even to fight back in the face of certain death, was prey.

And he was a predator. He was and he had been for a very long time. Knowing this, he coolly raised the knife above his head. This was no moment of deliberation. That was over. It had been replaced, in an instant, by the overwhelming power of realization. And with that realization, he calmly dragged the blade of the knife across his throat. As the blood sprayed downward, covering his upturned face, the coldness left him. It was quickly replaced by the palpable and much more powerful feeling of hunger. He was hungry, and more than even feeling that, he felt relief at knowing that there was now more to life than simply survival.

Now, covered in blood and holding an instrument of death, there was power, real power felt for the first time in a new world. He thought of the man he had killed earlier, shot dead with his crossbow. He thought of the two men he had killed before, thought of how he had twisted their deaths to seem necessary. They may have been necessary, but they were not only necessary. They were empowering, ensuring his proper place in this new world. That power warmed him as he waited to feed.

WHAT THEY CALL DISBELIEF

SHAUN AVERY

They'll find his body laid out on the grounds of his huge mansion.

They'll find what's left of the head one hell of a distance away.

Wherever it landed when I kicked it.

The bastard.

The plague swept across the land like a lover's hand, infecting all it came into contact with.

Millions panicked.

But I knew just what to do.

I was watching the TV when my wife Laura came into the room.

"It's coming," I told her. "This is it."

I had my back to her, so I couldn't see her.

But I could feel the frown coming from her face, sense the rolling of her eyes.

"I mean it, Laura," I said. "Put your suit on before you go anywhere." I thought about it. "Suit the twins up, too."

She just shook her head.

Looking back, perhaps I should have tried harder.

But I guess it was doubt that stopped me really getting into an argument with her.

Still, when she slammed on the door of the house a short while later, bits of her dropping off, begging to be let in, it was kind of hard not to feel a certain sense of satisfaction. I mean, this just proved it. I'd been right. *We'd* been right.

I was in my own protective suit now. It had been sitting down in the basement for years, just waiting to be used. I'd had it on a few times before. Luckily, I hadn't grown too fat to fit into it these past few years.

Safe in my suit, I shook my head sadly at my wife.

At my kids.

I felt bad about them. *Of course* I did. But she'd brought it on herself, and in doing so had ended both her life and theirs. She should have listened to me.

But now they were gone.

And I'd be making the coming journey alone.

The rest of my town was dying in the street as I drove past.

They'd always laughed at me. Called me names, sniggered behind the back of their hand when I walked past. The twins, though, and Laura, they'd felt kind of sorry for. "Those poor children," I'd always hear them mutter, frowns upon their faces. "Walking around in hand-me-down clothes, while he gives all his cash to . . ."

But they didn't know.

They hadn't seen the same light that I had.

I'd been drinking pretty much nonstop for ten years when I came to with my cheek stuck to the floor of a room that I didn't recognize by my own sick, cigar butts floating all around me in a sea of the same bile.

For all of my other vices—and they were legion when the drink took hold, from sleeping with strippers out back of the club where I'd just watched them dance to picking increasingly aggressive fights with the door staff of all the local bars—I knew I didn't smoke cigars.

So God only knew *whose* house I'd ended up in, or what I'd done—or had done to me—when I got there.

Well, not *just* God.

The booze would know, too.

See, that was how I thought of it. A living thing. A walking, breathing foe that I couldn't pummel down no matter how hard or how many times I tried.

But I was lucky that day.

For there was a TV switched on in that room.

And my bloodshot, weary eyes looked straight up into it. Into *him*.

He was so beautiful.

And I'm not saying that in any kind of queer way. No, sir. I'm completely, one hundred percent heterosexual, thank you for asking. But I know good design when I see it, and the Reverend Mitchell Hollis was right up there with the best of them.

He was preaching about the Apocalypse.

And as the alcohol began to leave my system, I suddenly saw why I'd been on this destructive path for so long.

See, I had clearly always known that the End of Days was coming.

The way the Reverend explained it that day, there were those of us who could see and sense what others could not. Who understood where this world was going, and soon. Watching him, I now saw that *I* had always been one of those people. And I had been trying to blot out the horrors of the coming future by climbing throat-first into a bottle.

But now I understood that there was another way.

I stopped drinking that very day.

I ran out of that room and away from my old life, and I never did find out whose house I'd ended up in.

And the money I saved by not drinking?

I sent it straight to the Reverend.

Mrs. Higgins from down the block was hammering on the window when I woke up, begging me to help her.

She was in a pretty poor state, one eye dangling down from her face, swinging on its optical cord as she banged against the car.

"Sorry, darling," I said, voice muffled slightly by my protective suit. "But who's laughing now?"

Then I drove onwards.

There's not much you can say about driving through the end of the world. From stopping to fill up at gas stations littered with the rotting dead to drifting along lost highways that had been lonely and desolate *before* the Apocalypse and were now almost unbearably so, it was all pretty depressing.

But I kept on going.

With just one destination in mind.

The first time the Reverend declared that the end of the world was officially coming, he said it would be via a global computer systems crash.

"Come join me, brothers and sisters," he told us all, via the TV. "You know where to go!"

I did.

But this was back in the days when I was single.

Plus newly sober.

I didn't trust myself to drive all of that way alone.

It was easier to stay off the drink when I was around people, when I had someone I could talk to—at work, in a shop, whatever. No matter how meaningless and full of small talk the conversation was.

It was a tense night that time, watching the hands of the clock crawl around to midnight, knowing that when that moment came the planes would fall from the sky and missiles would launch from underground silos. I spent it in my house, the TV switched on and playing loud, with the Reverend and my fellow believers in spirit form only.

Midnight came.

The world did not end.

The Reverend looked slightly embarrassed when he next appeared on his channel, but he never explained the reason behind his mistake.

A few years later, he told us all that some kind of avian flu was about to wipe out mankind.

The twins had just been born, and Laura, in no fit state to travel anywhere yet, put her foot down.

"Fine," I told her. "We'll all die here at home. Together."

But we didn't.

This time, it seemed that Reverend Hollis felt obligated to provide some kind of explanation.

"I got the dates slightly wrong," he said, and grinned that grin he'd worn the first time I saw him.

It was hard to stay mad with a man who could smile like that.

That said, after two announcements of global Armageddon that had gone nowhere, it was easy to start doubting the man a little.

But then came the plague.

It started off in densely packed city areas, where people lived one atop the other like a pile of stacked cards.

"This is it," the Reverend said, appearing on TV. "Can't you *feel* it?"

Actually, I could. Or, rather, *see* it. Disease had now found its way to our leafy suburb, and with my wife and children dead I decided it was time to be moving on.

And I knew where to.

"To the Compound," Reverend Hollis said. "All those who have contributed will know the location. Now go!"

I went.

But when I got there . . .

The Compound wasn't actually a compound—it was actually just a flat and barren piece of land with a cliff overlooking it. I'd always figured the Reverend had picked that name because it sounded kind of cool—sort of Biblical, but modern, too.

It didn't look very holy now, though.

I stood and looked upon it, gasping inside of my mask.

Now, with that mask on, I know that I couldn't possibly have smelled anything.

But it *seemed* like I could.

All those bodies that lay before me . . .

All that rotten flesh . . .

And spread all around the place, discarded protective suits. Just like the one that I was still wearing.

I walked over to one of the bodies. It had been a man. Or a woman. It was kind of hard to tell, with the bits all running together like this.

"Why did you take your suit off?" I asked.

"He said we could," the person said.

"Who?" I said.

But I had a dark feeling that I already knew the answer.

I was right.

"The Reverend," he said.

"No," I replied, shaking my head. "He wouldn't do that."

The person pointed.

I followed the trail of his finger.

Saw a mobile phone lying a few footsteps away.

I picked it up.

"Watch the video," he said.

Then his face slid off.

Shivering but grim-faced, I went into his recent media files.

Found the newest video and pressed play.

And saw the Reverend, standing up atop that cliff, looking down toward his thousands of followers.

"You must show your faith in me," he called. "You must take off your protective suits!"

A hush fell over the crowd.

"Why don't you take off yours?" cried one doubting

Thomas.

"This is a test," he replied. "You have to prove your devotion to me. I am the one who predicted that the plague was coming, and only I have the power to drive it from your bodies. But first, you must present your bodies to me!"

Well, he put up a pretty good argument, you had to say.

If I had been there in time, I probably would have joined the masses, shed my clothes.

But I wasn't.

And from the looks of this video, it was just as well I hadn't been.

Because the results weren't pretty.

As soon as they were exposed to the open air, the bodies of the believers began to sprout sores—sores that were soon open and weeping, leaking pus and infection out into the open air.

And then their bodies began to fall apart.

It takes a while for the final stage to kick in for some, depending on the strength of their immune system, the healthiness of their general lifestyle before the plague took them. So some managed to run away, head out of shot, before dying. Some of them may have even lasted a few weeks—I'd done my research on all of this stuff, before leaving the house. But make no mistake: it kills everyone in the end.

There is no cure.

Clearly one of the unlucky ones who don't last very long, the impromptu cameraperson collapsed and dropped the phone a few seconds later. So I was spared some of the gorier details of what followed. But the phone caught a shot of the Reverend just before it fell from their fingers.

It could have just been my imagination, and the mask made it kind of hard to tell besides, but . . .

I'm sure it caught him smiling.

But still I didn't want to believe.

The Reverend's guidance, delivered through a TV

screen, had helped me beat my alcoholic demons.

I just couldn't accept that he would ever be anything other than blissfully benevolent.

And despite what the camera phone had shown me, I had to see him with my own eyes.

So I got back in the car and drove.

Lucky I still remembered his address from all the checks I'd sent.

But I was surprised to discover, as I pulled the car to a stop, that the address in question did not belong to a church or an office.

No.

It belonged to a giant mansion.

It had once been a guarded mansion.

But now the guards were dead and rotting, sprawled out on the huge front garden.

I don't know what made me bend down and pluck a gun from one of the corpses.

I guess I just wanted to feel a little safer about what was to come.

I heard voices coming from the side of the house, and I walked toward them, gun in hand.

And saw the Reverend.

He was playing tennis with a blonde-haired young woman, both of them in suits.

But when he saw me, he shouted, "Shit!" and dove for a pistol that was lying next to one of the poles that supported the tennis net.

I had a weapon of my own, of course.

But I didn't really want to use it.

Instead I said, "Wait!"

He paused, one hand on the weapon.

"It's me, Reverend," I said.

"Who?"

I took a step back, shocked.

His voice had come out like a sneer.

Not at all like the smooth one he used on the TV.

The doubt hit me again.

"Michael," I said. "Michael Robinson. I'm one of your faithful."

That was when he did the scariest thing of all: he laughed.

"Shit," he then said. It was disturbing to hear a man of faith use bad language twice in quick succession, reminding me uncomfortably of my own uncouth drinking past. "I thought we got rid of all you loonies up at that cliff."

"Loonies?" I said.

My doubt took a step closer to anger.

And I, in turn, took a step toward him.

"It was just a scam," he said. "Mike—I can call you that, right?—that's all it was." He looked to the woman, who was standing there giggling. "And when I heard a bunch of you losers had shown up, well . . . I thought I'd use 'em to have a little fun."

Behind the mask, there was that grin again.

But it no longer seemed charming and handsome.

It seemed to me something much darker.

"It's hard to have fun," added the woman, twirling his tennis racket around in her hand, "since the plague came." She squinted at me, smiled a gap-toothed smile. "You know how hard it is to *fuck* wearing these things?"

"That's right, honey," said the man—I could no longer think of him as the Reverend—as he looked back toward the woman. Then he glanced back at me. "Still—third time lucky, huh?" he said, laughing. "There really *was* an Apocalypse coming."

But I'd heard enough now.

And I leapt at him.

Yes, I know I had the gun.

But what I wanted to do to him, I wanted to do it with my bare hands.

Sadly, he made no such distinction.

He grabbed his own weapon and fired.

The bullet hit me a split second before I landed on him.

But it did worse than that, too.

It punctured my protective suit.

Let in all of the plague germs that had infected the air.

But I didn't care.

I had just one thing on my mind, and it was punishing this monster.

My hands found his throat and I squeezed and then banged his head against the ground, squeezed and I banged, banged and I squeezed, smashing him down into the hard gravel of the tennis court again and again until there was little more than a bloody stain left above his shoulders.

The woman tried to run back to the house.

I had no trouble shooting *her.*

Then I stepped over her body and headed into the house.

Started looking for the knives.

So now my tale is done.

I'm holed up in good old Mitchell's house, which seems pretty fair to me—I mean, I helped pay for it, right?

My suit is now off and it's a race to see what kills me first: the plague or the bullet in my stomach.

But, you know, when I gave up drinking I started taking care of myself: went for runs, joined the gym. My health was good. It might take me a while to die. And if the pain ever gets too much . . .

Well.

That's why I kept the guns after taking care of Mitchell and his female friend.

And as I drift into delirium I find that my last thoughts are not of Laura and my children but of the Reverend who gave and then took away my faith.

So if anybody reading this goes a-wandering around the grounds of this house in which they've found my body, I ask that they do me just one little favor:

Give the bastard's head a few more kicks from me.

A PERFECT WORLD

CLINT JEWSON

I live in a sunken city, what's left of the glittering Gold Coast. My three-story walk-up floats among a string of abandoned high rises that rise from the water, stretching north to south along the old coastline. To my east the thick crumbling face of the nearest building protects me from the brunt of incoming ocean swells. Beyond it lays open ocean. More three-story walk-ups litter the space between high rises, and to my west lay the sunken suburbs, a scattered pattern of rooftops that rest just above water level. The water stretches west several kilometers to the new shoreline, where it laps against the mountains' foothills.

I don't know how or why the world ended, the world as it was anyway. To be honest I kind of missed the whole thing. Ironically, it was my imperfections that kept me safe. Before the waters came I'd never really fit into the world; social anxieties prevented relationships, agoraphobia kept me inside. I lived alone, read a lot, smoked a lot. I was a squatter of sorts, and already largely self-sufficient.

While people tore each other apart out there, I read Cormac McCarthy by candlelight. Any hint of the troubles beyond my isolated little world was silenced by the boards nailed over my windows. I didn't even realize anything had changed until I ran out of noodles, waited up late one night to slink down deserted streets to the general store, and found my stairwell flooded with water. What the fuck? Flashbacks I thought, so climbed up to the roof, and found I was on a concrete island. Global warming, maybe? How long did it take me to read that book for fuck's sake?

My building, like the rest of the city, was abandoned as people moved inland, and for the past year or so I've lived quite well; the fleeing tenants left plenty behind. Life for me is much as it was before. I fish a lot now, and there's still plenty of books I haven't read. If the tide keeps rising I'm gonna have to move to a higher building, but I'll deal with that when the time comes. Time slides past, and apart from the occasional run-in with main-landers, I enjoy my own company more and more. To be honest I kinda prefer it this way.

The rising sun finds me checking my crab pots from the roof, and faint voices drifting over the water draw my eyes to the west. They've been trying to get to me again lately, the other survivors. Fuck 'em. I've been through this before.

I lean over the balcony and lower a bucket of offal into my dingy, which I'd snagged drifting past a few weeks ago. I can see them paddling out from shore, five men in a small boat, the sides barely above the water. My guard dogs, which I fish to feed daily, will have no trouble with this lot.

I climb awkwardly down a rope ladder to my boat. It rocks with my weight and the bull sharks, which swarmed out of the canals when the waters rose to form the city's newest gangs, swim up and around, brushing against the sides, ready to be fed. I wait until one gives a particularly hard nudge then trickle the fish offal over the side, a tiny bit at a time, offering more food the harder they push, the more aggressive they become.

The party from onshore paddles closer, weaving their way through buildings that jut from the water, their weapons glinting in the harsh summer sun. A particularly eager five-footer hurls itself into the air and smashes into the side, almost making it over the rail. Good lad. Well trained these dogs of mine.

I dump the rest of the blood and guts over the side and the water boils, the sharks in a frenzy. Grinning, I climb the rope ladder to the building's rooftop, pick up the compound bow I've pilfered from another apartment, and crouch behind the balcony, leaving the ladder hanging as bait. Their war cries draw closer, echoing between buildings, and as they approach I start lobbing rotten fish heads down around their low-lying boat.

"Is that all ya got for us, boy?" They laugh up at me.

Banging blades and bats against the boat's sides, rocking and screaming and laughing, it's more than my babies can bide. Ten meters off they get their first nudge, five meters and they're surrounded by a mass of moving gray. They stop paddling, and as the sharks press in more and more, they panic.

That's it, boys, rock that boat. Frustrated at not being fed for their good behavior, my guard dogs get pushier, more aggressive, until a little three-footer thrusts itself up onto the gunwale, and over she goes.

Amongst the splashing, through the spreading, seething stain of blood, only one, a kid of maybe nineteen, makes it to the rope ladder.

I whistle down, and when he looks up with terror-filled eyes, pleading, I smile him a warm hello and he starts to climb. I struggle for a moment with his welcoming present, take careful aim, then drop a cinder block on his head.

I haul up the rope ladder, and I laugh and laugh and laugh. In a world gone to fuck, you gotta take pleasure in the small things. I really do prefer it this way.

PART VII

ZOMBIE LOVE

CHURCH OF THE NEWLY RISEN

STEPHEN D. ROGERS

As I reached the mouth of the alley, a zombie stepped in front of me.

I moved to the right, and the zombie countered.

I moved to the left, and again the zombie countered.

That was that, then. I could wait or go around. "I don't suppose you want to hire me? Maybe I could track down your loved ones."

The zombie didn't answer. Behind him, a car sped past, doing at least double the speed limit. What did that make now, three? Three times that I would have died had it not been for the zombies.

"When heaven is full, the dead will walk the earth, doing everything in their power to keep us alive." That's the popular explanation for what had happened, and nobody had yet succeeded in debunking the theory.

For six hundred and thirty-three days, zombies had blocked paths, had woken the deeply asleep, had placed rotted hands on supposedly diseased flesh, keeping the living from dying.

My zombie wobbled out of sight, probably off to save someone else, and I crossed the road.

The living dead, they weren't angels in white. They didn't possess wings or wear halos or play harps.

Instead, they looked and acted like the zombies you saw in the horror movies, with one important distinction: instead of craving human flesh, they protected it.

I entered the building that contained my office and set off up the stairs. I'd once been stopped from going into the elevator, and since then had been haunted by the image of the zombie arriving a tad too late, leading to dozens of zombies diving into the muck at the bottom of the shaft, piling in on top of each other until they created enough of a cushion that the elevator car bounced twice before settling.

I unlocked my door, noted the darkened answering machine, and turned on the television.

War had broken out in the Middle East again. So far, four hundred and twelve zombies had been destroyed, fifty of those by throwing themselves in the path of a helicopter that would have otherwise crashed with loss of life.

As neither country had yet suffered any casualties, both were claiming victory.

Turning away from the nonsense, I started my computer and returned to the report I'd been writing yesterday.

"September 17. Followed the subject to his place of business. He left the building at noon, and I followed him to the Westerly Motel."

Here I paused. Everybody had responded differently to the arrival of the zombies. For whatever reason, infidelity was up, and the mix of my investigative assignments had shifted accordingly.

I'd never liked divorce work, and I didn't like it any better now.

Sure, your spouse is cheating on you. The year before the zombies began to walk the Earth, fifty-seven million people died, which meant that since then almost a hundred million people have been kept alive who were now consuming a greater share of the resources on which you depend.

Let's just put things in perspective.

I should have stopped for coffee this morning. I should have stopped somewhere and ordered a full breakfast and then sat there until they started serving lunch.

When I felt like being maudlin, I wondered about the timing of the zombies. Who was the last person allowed into heaven? Who was the first person to be turned away?

What about Suzy? Had she made it through the pearly gates?

Even if she'd been no angel, she certainly deserved better than what we had now.

I'd buried Suzy in the cemetery located between our apartment and this office. Would I someday see her lurch in front of me in order to save my life, a life not worth living since she died?

If your spouse is cheating on you, they're still alive. Be grateful for what you have.

If I were honest with myself, this is why I hated divorce work. I'd been given no choice. My wife had simply been taken from me, no questions asked.

I crossed to the window.

If I'd been able to open it, I probably would have looked down to see a group of zombies forming a firefighter net to catch me when I jumped.

Instead, I watched them wandering the streets, waiting to be sent on their lifesaving missions, however that worked.

In the distance, a building burned. The riots occurred more frequently lately. The "Right to Die" coalition. The Survivalists. The Church of the Newly Risen. We couldn't kill each other, but that didn't stop us from hating.

I glanced at my computer. My client had hired me to do a job, and that included writing a final report.

All the pain in the world wouldn't change that.

* * *

A new client, however, could.

There she was, climbing out of her car, which she'd parked on the far side of the parking lot as usual. She gathered herself before starting for the hospital.

And there he was, leaving his car and moving toward her.

The makeup was good, as was the stance and the movement. Too bad that driving a car destroyed the illusion.

I reached through my window and tapped my horn.

My client returned to her vehicle.

Her stalker tottered to a standstill.

Moving at faster-than-zombie speeds, I knew I could keep him from escaping if he maintained the charade, especially as I was coming at him from the rear.

"Hey, mister zombie wannabee."

He lurched around in a slow circle, his jerky motions giving me time to get between him and his car.

"Yeah, I'm talking to you. The hospital, they don't want any more bad press. Me? I don't care."

He blinked. I couldn't really blame him for that mistake.

"My client wants you to find a new hobby." While I kept her stalker busy, my client parked elsewhere so she could report to work on time. "I don't want her to see you ever again."

His shoulders went back. "I'm saving her."

"From what?"

"From all the evil in the world."

"Wow. You must really be busy. To cut down on the workload, you might want to start by leaving her alone."

He took a step back. "I'm not afraid of you."

"That's good. Because I want us to talk as equals. Only then will our deal mean anything."

"What deal?"

"You leave my client alone, and I'll leave you alone."

He stiffened. "You don't scare me. If you ever try

anything, my brothers and sisters will surround me with a wall of protection."

I shook my head. "Only if I intend to kill you, and I don't think I'll have to go quite that far to make my point."

"You don't understand. I love her."

Maybe it was all the zombie movies I'd watched when I was younger, but I suddenly wanted to take a baseball bat to his head. Bam! My client would never have to worry about him bothering her again.

Unfortunately, I needed to be subtler than that.

For one thing, a real zombie would interfere if I tried to kill him, and for another thing, the fact that one wasn't lurching in this direction to separate us proved my fantasy was nothing more than that.

"Listen. Dying is not the worst thing that can happen to someone." I lowered my voice as if sharing a confidence. "You've got quite the fake limp going."

"Thanks." He blinked, confused, unsure.

"If I hear that she ever catches sight of you again, I'm going to make it permanent. And that will just be the beginning."

🖤 🖤 🖤

Back in my office, I returned to the report—anything to take my mind off Suzy.

"The subject checked into room 110 and emerged from the motel some forty-two minutes later. Photographs of everybody who left within ten minutes of the subject are enclosed."

Service with a smile. That was something the zombies couldn't promise. The most you could hope for from them was that lips had rotted in such a way that it appeared the zombie grinned.

The stalker's makeup had been good, but he couldn't begin to approach the horror of the real thing. And yet they almost went unnoticed.

Unnoticed unless they were aimed at you.

That's how it felt the first time it happened to me, that the zombie was more of a threat than what it was supposedly saving me from.

While the zombie was real, the alleged death had to be taken on faith.

Thus the rise of conspiracy nuts who claimed that the whole "savior" thing was a crock, and that the zombies were in league with the government. The nature of the conspiracy varied with the day and the particular twisted imagination of the theorist.

I didn't care so much what people believed so long as their belief system included paying their private investigator in full and on time.

※ ※ ※

I noted the motion before I noticed they were zombies. Eight of them formed a loose circle around me.

As I walked toward my car, the cordon moved with me. Should I feel honored or horrified?

As we reached the parking lot, the circle opened to swallow my car. They stared at me through the windows.

The drive home proceeded at a snail's pace, but they stayed with me the entire time.

Historically, the zombies disappeared as soon as the risk ended. The fact that these stayed with me meant I was still in danger, still a target, which didn't sound like I might die in an accident. That sounded like somebody with a rifle was serious about seeing me dead.

Given the slow speed of my commute, I had plenty of time to review my recent cases.

The last couple weeks had consisted of due diligence jobs, and my efforts hadn't harmed anyone. Before that, I had the zombie stalker and the infidelity investigation. Before that, behind-the-scenes corporate work.

That left me with the stalker and the adulterer as the most likely suspects. Less likely, the two clients.

But zombies came between the threat and the victim. I couldn't quite buy that eight people were hunting me, stalking me with rifles as I made my way home, which made the cordon a puzzle.

Four of the zombies preceded me up the stairway, and four followed me.

Maybe it was just possible that eight sharpshooters had managed to stalk me home. That four of them were now behind me on the stairs and four of them were in front was unlikely at best.

The zombies created the protective cordon as soon as we entered the hallway, adjusted to squeeze through the door, and then shuffled back into position.

In my office, I slowly spun in a circle, examining the eight zombies huddled around me. Protecting me from what?

Only two of them could be said to be blocking shots through windows. And the other six were, what, supervising?

"I bet you're all wondering why I asked you here today."

Actually, I don't think they did.

They formed a semicircle around me as I scrambled two eggs with onions, red peppers, and cheese.

They formed a circle around me as I ate at the kitchen table.

They formed an audience as I went to the bathroom.

Unless someone intended to unload an elephant gun at me as I sat on the toilet, packing the zombies three-deep seemed overkill.

So why didn't they disperse?

Their job, as conventional wisdom held, consisted of stopping people from getting killed. These zombies didn't seem to be doing that.

Washing my hands, I studied the zombies in the mirror. Perhaps their job description had been modified. After never being late for six hundred and thirty-three days and never calling in sick, perhaps they'd been promoted.

They backed as I left the bathroom and then formed a

circle around me as soon as space allowed.

If they stayed with me much longer, I was going to give them nicknames. Individualize them. Bond.

"I have no plans for the evening, just in case that changes anything."

They didn't respond. Didn't react. While zombies didn't interrupt, they couldn't really be considered great listeners, and bodyguards were no exception.

Desiring distraction, I turned on the television.

My zombies stood around me, the light from the television screen flickering across what was left of their faces.

I'd never really seen one up close long enough to study the features and state of decay. These had been in the ground for a while. In the beginning, only the most recently buried were raised.

Those who hadn't been killed in car accidents usually didn't look all that bad. But, as they were destroyed trying to save human lives, others were raised. Eventually, I assumed, we'd be seeing near-skeletons.

Maybe piles of dust and ash would fly into people's eyes to keep them from taking that next dangerous step.

When heaven is full . . . and what was being done at that end? Were expansions being planned? Were the not-really-all-that-good being told that they might be relocated to somewhere a lot warmer?

The zombies felt like a stopgap measure. The dead-but-not-completely-decomposed were a limited resource.

What happened when they ran out?

I glanced from one zombie to the next.

They stood so unnaturally still. They didn't breathe. They didn't blink. They didn't fidget.

They were more like wax figures than people. Wax figures of horror movie extras. Wax figures that stared at me as though I wasn't here.

I jumped to my feet and poked the nearest in the chest.

My finger did not encounter the usual amount of

resistance, and I declined the opportunity to think too much about that.

"What do you want? Why are you here?"

The circle had shifted as I moved, and that was the only response I saw.

"What are you saving me from? Myself? Am I that close to the edge that eight of you are required to make sure nothing can happen?"

Arguing with the dead was anything but satisfactory.

They were still in my bedroom the next morning. And while I got ready. Deciding I didn't want to hold up traffic again, I walked them to work.

The only way I could explain the lack of response by people who saw us was their assumption that these were wannabees. After all, zombies just didn't act this way. Or at least they hadn't, not that anybody knew.

Was I really that much in danger?

Was I really that much of a threat?

In my office, I caught my breath as I located the various numbers for the client who'd been stalked and I tried each of them until I reached her.

"So you've never been bothered by him again?"

"Isn't that why I paid you?" Her voice turned wary. "Why are you calling? Should I be concerned?"

"I'm just following up, making sure you're satisfied with my work. Service with a smile."

"Yeah, well, as long as you don't start stalking me, I'm smiling."

Next I called the client with the adulterous spouse. They'd split up, but were thinking of getting together again.

As I disconnected, I asked the nearest zombie for suggestions.

None were forthcoming.

Eight zombies had been assigned to me, had been beholden to me for almost eighteen hours. Were they suddenly overstaffed? To what did I owe the honor?

Why me?

I searched the news for any signs that the stalker might have become unhinged.

I searched the news for any signs that I wasn't the only person graced with a zombie harem.

I searched the news for any signs of financial irregularities that might indicate somebody knew something major was brewing.

Finally, I searched for my horoscope, which was no more enlightening.

Which left me where? Where I was. Sitting at my desk, surrounded by the living dead.

Which is not where I should be. Too many people had seen the entourage I'd brought to my home and my office. I didn't want any interference until I knew what was what.

I packed my computer and grabbed what files I might need, and then I and my zombies headed to the one place where nobody saw anything and asked even less: the Westerly.

The gloomy-eyed clerk behind the counter didn't even blink.

🐾 🐾 🐾

As soon as I sat on the edge of the bed, someone knocked.

"Hello?" Seeing as the zombies weren't reacting to the visitor, I brought them over to the door and peered through the eyepiece.

Suzy.

The air emptied out of my lungs.

I took a moment to refill them and invited her in.

Suzy.

Compared to my zombies, she didn't look dead.

Of course the tears that coated my eyes probably helped.

"Suzy. I've missed you."

Then she spoke, making me reach behind for the bed as my legs went weak. "I have been sent to hire you."

"Hire me."

"You are a private investigator."

Her lips moved a fraction of a second too late to make the sounds that emerged from her mouth. Still, the illusion swelled my heart. "Hire me to do what? Yes, anything."

"The Church of the Newly Risen. Find out what they want." Suzy shambled to the bureau and placed a handful of large gold coins next to my computer.

"I'll do my best."

She lurched toward the door. "Your protection will not follow you onto church property. There will be more when you complete your task."

"More?" I glanced at the bureau. "Oh."

Suzy let herself out.

As soon as I thought my legs would support me, I walked over and closed the door. Suzy. Why send Suzy?

Of course the question was ridiculous. By sending Suzy, my cooperation was guaranteed. Only when I finished the job would she return. She knew I despised clients who didn't pay the final bill.

I touched the coins she'd held in her hands. They were cold.

� � �

The Church of the Newly Risen had appeared as mysteriously as the zombies that they worshipped.

Nobody seemed to know for certain who started the churches, or in which cities they began, but grassroots congregations quickly gathered in all heavily populated areas.

They taught that we had sinned, and that's why the zombies had been sent to . . . well, I wasn't exactly able to determine why the Newly Risen thought the zombies had been sent, only that it was important for true believers to emulate the zombies and thus prove their faith.

I didn't see how anybody profited, unless the leadership grew fat on donations, but I saw no evidence of that.

Pacing had always helped me think, and now I stood to wear the carpet thinner.

If I was chosen to investigate the Newly Risen by a

being powerful enough to raise the dead, I had to assume I wasn't chosen randomly. That meant I was the right person in the right place at the right time.

Which meant the answer was here. Now.

All I needed to do was find it.

※ ※ ※

As Suzy had warned, the zombies didn't follow me onto church property.

Which might have been a clue, but I didn't know what it meant.

The parking lot was empty except for one car.

The church itself was silent.

A lone figure sat in the first pew.

He turned and stood as I approached. "Welcome to the Church of the Newly Risen. I don't recall looking out from the pulpit and seeing you in the congregation."

"No." I shook his hand, relieved he wasn't decked out in full zombiewear. "But I was in the neighborhood and thought I'd check the place out."

"This is a weekday, or you'd see I do a better job of packing them in." His eyes carried the smile started by his mouth.

"I was just killing time on the Internet when I realized that I couldn't find any documentation on the origins of the church. There doesn't seem to be any central governing body."

He nodded. "That's true. We just sprouted like mushrooms after a warm rain." He stepped closer, lowering his voice. "In fact, you're standing in the very first church. This is where it all began."

"You're kidding."

"I kid you not."

The church was simple, a box with a roof, crossed by pews, a raised pulpit at the front. I was reminded of a show I'd seen about a group of farmers raising a barn. "Are you the founder?"

"I've always led the congregation, but someone else is

responsible for the church, the man who caused the dead to live again." He paused as if waiting for me to say something.

"So what is it the church wants?"

"For it to end."

"For what to end?"

"The obsession."

"I'm sorry, but I'm not following you."

"That's because you refuse to see what you are, one of the newly risen. The first newly risen."

I chuckled, almost enjoying the game of words. "I'm no zombie."

"You became one when you rejected life. When you refused to move past the death of your wife, Suzy."

A chill went down my spine. "Hold it right there. How do you know about my wife? How do you even know who I am?"

He placed a hand on my shoulder. "It's time to let her go."

⚶ ⚶ ⚶

The line of zombies encircled me as I left church property and escorted me back to the Westerly Motel.

Only after I was inside my room did I seriously consider what I'd heard.

I'd always thought of myself as apart from the world. As a private investigator, I remained aloof and unaffected, gathering information and generating reports because that was my job. I was as impartial as an eyeball that recorded everything it saw.

Except when I was with Suzy. Then I was one with the world, because Suzy was the world to me.

Had I kept her a prisoner by refusing to experience my grief? Had my actions refashioned the meaning of life and death? Had I been responsible for all that had transpired?

The thought of my impact humbled me. I would have expected the opposite, but then I could appreciate how much I'd affected people, even strangers. Mostly strangers.

A knock at the door interrupted my musings.

Suzy. I just knew it was Suzy, because no one else knew I was here. No one else cared.

I let her in.

My dead wife stepped far enough into the room for me to close the door, and then turned to face me. "Do you understand now?"

Again, the words and the lips didn't synchronize correctly, and I wondered who spoke through her.

"I don't think so, Suzy. But then I never understood our love, but that didn't stop me from thriving under its spell."

She raised her hand.

Instead of gold coins, this time she held a red tulip. Our flower. The flower I'd presented her on our first date. The flower we'd picked to celebrate our wedding. The flower I'd placed on her grave.

I took the red tulip, symbol of undying love. "You know it's true."

"Then let me go."

Mister Uninvolved. How many hundreds of millions of lives had I touched?

"Because I'll always love you, I let go of the chains with which I've held you back." I choked on the lump in my throat. "I'm sorry."

Suzy shambled out of my hotel room then, and my circle of zombies left with her.

Feeling strangely alone after being surrounded by the living dead for so long, I turned on the television for the companionship and watched live footage of zombies returning to the ground, the commentators as baffled as when the zombies first appeared.

I knew what the reporters didn't: the dead could die now that the living consented to live.

I snapped off the television and rejoined the world, converted.

ZOMBi 6: SALVATiON

JAMES PARK

March 23, 2064

Dear Nobody,

I've struggled endlessly over the most appropriate way to address this letter. The truth is, I could have addressed it any number of ways—To Whom It May Concern; To Whom It Doesn't Concern; To Whom It Will Never Concern—and it wouldn't have made one severed-hand's worth of difference.

Given that our population has dwindled to meager proportions, Dear Nobody carries the charm—or better yet, *the genuineness*—that I'm after. I pity the imbecile that's chosen to carry on in this world of shit, just as I laugh at the nincompoop who truly believes that the world has reached its end. Our own insignificance never occurred to us, *now did it?* We're nothing more than a supercilious species that refuses to acknowledge the fallibility of our own instincts. We ignore our own shortcomings, marching through life like a schizophrenic Third Reich, adamant that our own demise will inevitably equate to the end of all existence. Well, I spit in the eye of those who refuse to acknowledge the footprints of those who've marched before us. Look at all the psychopaths we've lived with, and ask yourself this: *How is it that the human species never managed to completely destroy the world?*

I credit our own incompetence, for I know we tried. We bit the hand that feeds us, many times, but we never managed to bite off any fingers. Sure, we left our share of scratches, some scars along the palm, but the damage wasn't anything that couldn't be ignored. We carried on, and we shouldn't forget that we're still carrying on. Our history hasn't completely ended. I'm still writing the written word, and that makes it true, that there's still a chance that we'll finally do ourselves in. Maybe we'll pull off the big one before the plague wipes the rest of us out. Maybe we'll bring back the bomb, and obliterate the ground that nourishes our tired feet.

Go ahead. Push the button. I dare you. It's the only thing left of value, so we might as well take it too. All other ideologies are lost. Nothing matters anymore, not one bloody torso, for my immortality is dying the same slow and agonizing death as the greater human species. I'm a published author, you have to understand, and I've lived the better part of my life under the misconception that my words will live forever. That's what we writers want, you know. We seek immortality. We want future generations to collect our works and preserve our thoughts. And even more so, we want coming of age geniuses to acknowledge the trail of inspiration that we leave behind. Let them read what we've written. Let them rise to fruition on the influence of our words. The path we're paving only matters so long as our followers continue to pave a path of their own.

My organs have always been destined to die, to slowly rot their way into the soil. *But the words I've written?* I used to fancy them living on in perpetuity. *And why not?* I've frightened thousands of people with my ghost stories, so much so that even the most devoted horror aficionado dare not read my work after dark. I'm brilliant, I tell you, I'm fucking brilliant. That's why it pains me to admit that the rate of conception is dwindling; there'll be no future generations to embrace my stories for the twisted right of passage that they are. I've dedicated my life and my blood to giving the world nightmares, and now that we're living in a nightmare, there's no more interest in my work. We're a peculiar species, you have to understand, for we're easily captivated by stories that introduce the unfamiliar, yet we bore much too quickly with the perplexities of our own surroundings. The world used to embrace my nightmares, now we shun the horror of our own survival.

Everyone says that the end is upon us. I've seen it written across the countryside, painted on barns and rooftops, graffitied beneath the underbelly of metropolitan wastelands: *The End Is Here.* And when you come across a living, breathing human being (you know, the kind that has yet to die and then reanimate into a walking corpse), they'll tell you the same thing: "This is the end of the world."

I suppose we shouldn't blame them for thinking such simplistic thoughts. Without schools, education has become a burden of the past. Just ask the Jack Kerouac reincarnate, if you can find him. And if you can't, then I encourage you to lament the fact that we no longer have a media to warp our thoughts. There's no more television, and radio broadcasts are the luxury of a long forgotten era. I can't even get a landline to work, let alone my cell phone. *And the Internet?* It's dead and buried, just like Dan Quayle. We have no military, no coast guard, and no Interpol. They quit making cars in Detroit well over a decade ago. Smoke no longer gushes from factories into smog-infested skies. It's true, I tell you, it's true. You can walk down the street without a gas mask, though you'd be foolish to embark on such adventures without a samurai sword. I'll be the first to admit that I'm no Sonny Chiba, but I carry my weapon with pride, and I've slayed my share of reanimated dead.

Ugh. I quiver at the thought. It makes my stomach churn, like I've swallowed a strip of dirty blotter paper. The walking corpses are such a vile and disgusting continuation of our species. They carry no shame. *None.* It sickens me, but I'm not going to waste Nobody's time discussing the obvious, for when you've lost the ability to think, or even rationalize, *then what's the point in accepting shame?* All they know is hunger, but it's not a breed of hunger that shows in their eyes; all you see in their eyes is the blank nothingness of a drug addict. They crave our brains and our blood like a junkie craves a great big dose of nothingness simmering atop a burnt spoon. The similarities are countless, but there's one small difference, and this difference matters more than those reanimated slabs of death will ever understand. You see, the earth provides the junkie an endless supply of medicine; it's simply a matter of cultivation and distribution, which eventually works its way into a matter of preservation. The addict's stash may run low, and the occasional bout of junk sickness may take hold, but it's only a matter of time until the junkie finds warmth in a new supply. Zombies are different. Those piles of walking bones, wrapped in dead flesh that hangs from their shoulders and clings to their ribs, are not feeding on an endless supply of brains. It's a bitter truth, though they'll never understand the economics of their own demise. The sad thing is, the human species doesn't much get it either. We don't have television to inform us, just as we don't have journalists to mislead us. I can't even remember the last time I received a piece of mail, had one of my ghost stories published, or read any halfway intelligent commentary on the current development of our own depravity.

Call it a big step backwards if you will, but this is not the end of the world; I don't care what anyone else has to say about it. Darwin figured out evolution on his own, and he didn't have the benefit of social media to help spread the word. It's true. But the man did have access to a printing press, and this seems to have made all the difference. I have no such luxury. When your resources include nothing more than a pen and a piece of paper, then you might as well stuff your letter in a bottle and hurl it out to sea. Or maybe tie the wretched thing to a birdie before he heads south for the winter. That's all the hope I have. Some of us will carry on, and my work might find its way into the hands of a survivor. But it will never be preserved in a library, or garner the type of cult following that's previously been reserved for literature that rises from the catacombs of our own bizarre sickness.

The human species is doomed, I tell you. But the truth is, I don't see the reanimated dead surviving this thing either. Sure, the fewer in number we become, the larger their population grows. I've watched them, and I understand their needs . . . but still, it's not what you think. This hunger that drives them, it can only be satisfied with human flesh. I've tried feeding them rabbits, even thrown a few rodents their way. They won't have it. I left the carcass of a freshly slaughtered boar on the roadside, and they hobbled right past it, arms outstretched as they wandered aimlessly in hopes of human flesh . . . you should see what happens when they go too long without. If you've ever taken the kind of drugs that you really shouldn't have taken, then you know what it's like to need. You've had every organ in your body working against you, collaborating in an effort to pump sickness through your blood, to the point that you want to crawl out of your own skin. Watch what happens when the reanimated dead go without human flesh. They actually do it . . . the damn things will crawl out of their own skin. Oh, it all starts with a little shaking, and you can see the agitation palpitate on the surface of their rotting bodies. Their fingers will rattle, and if they've still got toes, they'll curl them inwards while the rest of their body convulses. Some of them will try to form fists, but they never quite succeed. What they do succeed at is ripping the skin from their skeletons. It's an intriguing yet disgusting spectacle. Their blood, for whatever reason, is black, tar-like. And their veins seep the depraved nectar of death. But even as their skin is separated from their frame, they're still undead, and they'll quiver on the ground, flapping like a fish that's been culled from the ocean and discarded along the shore. They'll gasp for air and they'll clutch at the open wound of their dismembered torso, but the hunger is never quenched, and a permanent death inevitably follows.

It's a most unnerving sight. And you, my nonexistent reader, you might be wondering why I share such vulgar insight. Fact is, I shouldn't have to. The most rudimentary concept of economics is supply and demand. They're eating us faster than we can possibly reproduce . . . much faster. We grow small in number as they grow dense in population. And now they're dying of starvation. That's why every survivor I encounter claims it's the end of the world. *This is the end, my friend, the end.* I've heard it everywhere I wander, and I laugh in the face of this ridiculousness.

I can breathe metropolitan air. I can walk down the street without the protection of a gas mask, though it's still not an overly enjoyable experience. *But do you know what has become an enjoyable experience?* Let me tell you. I've been living in the Maymont Mansion of Richmond for a spell longer than a year, and every week I catch some fish from a nearby pond. Mother Nature still holds employment, for seasons come and seasons go. It rains and it pours. The sun rises and the sun sets. I've watched this happen, Dear Nobody, just as I've watched the Earth make an entire lap around the sun, and I swear, the water in this pond looks cleaner than it did a year ago. It's simply astonishing.

Plants grow naturally the whole world over, yet it's been more than a decade since humans have smothered them with growth chemicals and pesticides. Things have changed. We don't drink from plastic bottles anymore, and we can't pilfer meat from the grocery stores. We kill what we need, and what we don't need keeps on living. *Quite amazing, wouldn't you agree?* Animals used to die needlessly, only to have their meat spoil on a shelf, all in the interest of providing the suburbanites with whatever variety might suit their whim on any given day.

They call the zombie apocalypse the end of the world, and I spit in the face of this absurdity. The humans will suffer their extinction, and the zombies will follow. But the world, if anything, needs this to survive. Our planet will continue to make laps around the sun, and the animal populations will grow larger and larger. All we're experiencing is the end of the human species. And I assure you of one thing: the other creatures have yet to express even the tiniest morsel of disappointment.

But let's not grow overzealous with the promise of a rejuvenated world, for we're embracing the reality of our own extinction. In a Henry David Thoreau sort of way, it's really not that bad. Oh, the bloody hypocrite hated humanity, but still, he thrived on the notion that a literate population existed, for without one, only Dear Nobody would have read his work. I have no such luxury, yet here I sit, pen in hand, leaving my thoughts behind. You have to trust me when I emphasize that it's not nearly as bad as you think. Ted Kaczynski survived just fine inside his little hut. Nature provided for him, and in return he did his part to control the population problem. Oh, the things society did to him, they certainly weren't kind. *But what more can we expect?* It's just like the masses to lock up a murderer, label him a madman, then give the media free reign to exploit the innocence of his beliefs. Maybe the lies are true. Maybe he deserved incarceration, for he was a tyrant to civilization, but to the world he was a bit of a savior.

We have a history of environmentalists being cast aside as crazies, and this history is a bloody one indeed. Charles Manson used to complain of factories being built where his trees once grew. His water was so bad that the fish couldn't live. It's no lie. The polar icecaps have melted away; they were murdered by the hands of manmade machines. We never took the time to notice, and we're going to get what we deserve. But deep down inside, I know things could have been different.

When the holy wars moved upon the planet, Mr. Charlie Manson saw the blood splattered on the wall, and he warned us. He told the people to follow him, that they'd get free LSD and girls if they'd just quit cutting down trees and polluting the water. Call the man a lunatic all you want, but these days the offer doesn't sound half bad, *now does it?* I'll take that deal. Really. Just give me a chance, and I'll ride dune buggies into the desert. I'll wait there until the race wars are over. Hell, I'll even buy your music, Charlie Manson, and I'll listen carefully for your subliminal retort to the Beatles prophecy of that notion known as Helter Skelter. But in the end, no one cares to listen to the world's most outspoken malcontent, just as nobody places the good of the earth in front of their own need for survival.

Charlie took the world for what it was: just a great big prison. He understood that confinement doesn't begin and end at the gate, but that prison is in the mind, locked to one world that is dead and dying, and unlocked to another that's free and alive. It's all about atwa, get it; it's about the air, the trees, and the water. Charlie grasped the true workings of the world. He's walking through forever, man. And look at us. We're clinging tenaciously to an immediate impulse called survival. It's because we refused to listen. We locked him up over a few measly murders, you know, just a couple of grocery store owners and a pack of celebrities that the world wouldn't have missed. And look at us now.

What's happened in the past is a shame, and what's happening right now is no small concern. Sometimes I don't even acknowledge the predecessors of my own surroundings. I've seen cities overrun with the reanimated dead; it's like a great big fucking infestation of malformed vermin. But I've also seen cities that harbor nothing more than the stillness and finality of death. In the wake of our dwindling population, I've explored ghost town after ghost town, searching for answers from the dead. We have such a breadth of history to learn from, yet hardly a soul remains to inherit this knowledge. It's only a matter of time until we're down to none. But still, I take refuge in the abandoned cities, even if the reanimated dead insist on scouring them for morsels of human brains.

No city has fascinated me more than Richmond, Virginia. The history here is so rich, yet so dated. I've been through the Museum of the Confederacy more times than I can count, and I never grow tired of the exhibits. When I wrote professionally, nothing tickled my interests more than a well-crafted ghost story. But sadly, I no longer find solace in a world constructed of fiction; I'm left with no choice but to embrace the marvels of our own reality, and this museum satisfies my ravenous thirst. Brother used to fight brother, right here, in our own country. Now brother fights the reanimated death of his brother, right here, in our own country . . . and the whole world over. Man has killed man. Ape has killed ape. Though I've never seen a zombie kill another zombie. It's not a moral decision, I tell you. They have no understanding of shame, just as they have no use for cannibalism. It's human flesh and brains that keep them alive, and their supply keeps dwindling. Some might see this as a changing of the times, but my solitary school of thought argues that the times haven't changed much at all. It was about survival then, and it's about survival now. It's evident that we're losing, but I'll go against the grain and argue that we didn't have a foot in this thing to begin with.

I miss the old days, when we lived under the guise that our actions were right, that they were just. We may not have been winning the war against our own stupidity, but our private sanctuaries were cozy, and we only forced ourselves to justify the wars that we raged against others; only the crazies cared to acknowledge the war that we unleashed upon ourselves. Locking them up was much too easy. *Problem solved!*

Now we're left with nothing more than the records of our own insanity, and I'm still alive to read them. I'll take whatever leftovers I can get, for I've always been a sucker for nostalgia. That's why I slay the reanimated dead with my trusted samurai sword. It's also why I've helped myself to a selection of muskets from the museum. They're not for protection, I assure you. They take too long to load, and cleaning the wretched things is a chore I care not to endure. You see, I've selected one of these muskets for a far more important purpose. And because I'm a sucker for nostalgia, I've also helped myself to an assortment of lead marbles. It's quite marveling what the bullets of yesterday looked like. They got the job done then, and they'll get the job done now. It's true. I've tried out all the muskets, taken my target practice, and like anything else, I've found some that work better than others. The musket that shoots best is named Charlene, and I know what you must be thinking . . . this is my rifle, there are many like it, but this one is mine. Well, Dear Nobody, this is my musket, and to my knowledge, there aren't any others like it . . . that's why it was in a museum. *And so what if I named her Charlene?* I speak to her daily. So go ahead, lock me up with the crazies. I expect nothing better from the masses. And I'll stand resolute, for talking to Charlene is a rather healthy practice. Given the bloodshed that I've witnessed, and the solitude that I've worked so hard to protect, I have to speak to something. Charlene rarely talks back, but I have trust in her, and I know that when the time is right, she'll perform the task that I've sequestered her to perform.

There are people out there, I'm certain, who wouldn't take the step that I'm going to take. Those people will live the remainder of their lives behind an illusionary veil of self-inflicted deception. Like I said before, this is not the end of the world, but a much needed turn of events. This, Dear Nobody, is necessary to secure the continuation of the world. Mother Nature is seeing to it.

I've selected a lead musket ball that's certain to get the job done, and I've named the bullet Salvation. It will be sometime next week, I suppose, before I venture out into the historic heart of Richmond, but the journey will be well worth my trouble. I'm going to have myself a seat beneath the statue of Oderus Urungus. I'm going to load Salvation into Charlene, and then I'm going to blow my brains all over the graffiti-covered monument. That's all there is to it. I am in a world of shit, and I see no reason to continue.

Go ahead, call me names, ridicule my decision, for if you're the Dear Nobody who reads this, then you're living among the foolish. You're struggling to survive in a world that brought back the dead for no other purpose than to purge itself of human waste. The cleansing is almost over. When it's done, the seasons will come and the seasons will go. Birds will migrate south for the winter, and flowers will blossom in the spring. The oceans will be blue again, same as the sky. And most importantly, we won't be here to ruin it. The death machine known as mankind is nearly extinct, and the world is already beginning to heal.

I wish you adieu, Dear Nobody, and I pity your struggle against the inevitable. You should follow my example while you still have the chance.

Regards,

Carlton Matthew Avery II (aka the William S. Burroughs reincarnate)

Made in the USA
Monee, IL
08 July 2026